Cowboy for Hire

NEW YORK TIMES BESTSELLING AUTHOR

VICTORIA JAMES

Entangled Publishing, LLC
10940 S Parker Road
Suite 327
Parker, CO 80134
rights@entangledpublishing.com

Amara is an imprint of Entangled Publishing, LLC.

Edited by Liz Pelletier and Heather Howland
Cover design by Hang Le
Cover art by Milan_Jovic/iStock, thekopmylife/iStock,
Winston/Depositphotos, miflippo/Depositphotos
Interior design by Heather Howland

MMP ISBN 978-1-64063-821-1
ebook ISBN 978-1-64063-822-8

Manufactured in the United States of America

First Edition April 2020

AMARA

Cowboy for Hire

ALSO BY VICTORIA JAMES

*To Andrew…thank you for
the most beautiful twenty years.*

There is a little bit of you in every hero I write.

CHAPTER ONE

"Stop! You can't go out there!"

Sarah Turner jolted back from the door, sending her coffee swishing over the rim of the mug as her housekeeper, Edna Casey, burst into the office. The older woman was panting, clutching a folded newspaper to her small frame, her eyes as wide as the antique wagon wheels leaning against the barn.

Sarah glanced around, half expecting a herd of angry cattle to be barreling their way, but the area was clear of immediate danger. "What's wrong?"

Mrs. Casey shoved the newspaper at her. "There's been a horrible mistake."

Frowning, Sarah took the paper. "Is there a problem with the ad I placed?"

Mrs. Casey made a strangled noise and nodded, her eyes still wide.

Dread pooled in Sarah's stomach. She'd checked the online version of the ad, and it had been perfect. So perfect, she'd already received quite a few calls about the new ranch foreman position. It wasn't even eight o'clock in the morning, and she had a dozen interviews ahead of her. This time tomorrow, she'd be able to hire a new foreman and get the family ranch up and running again.

She inhaled sharply as she read the only ad that boasted the ranch's phone number. The ad that Edna must be referring to. The ad she never, ever, in a million years would have placed.

A bead of sweat trickled between her shoulder blades, and she put her coffee mug down with a *thud* on the desk. Squeezing her eyes shut, she said a quick prayer that maybe when she opened them again, the ad would be correct. She opened one eye, and a wave of nausea hit. Nope. The "horrible mistake" was still there.

> *Cowboy for Her: Experienced and skilled cowboy companion for lonely young woman. Duties include social engagements, long walks, and romantic evenings. Excellent compensation, full benefits, and paid time off. Call for interview.*

"No. No, no, no. It was supposed to say 'foreman for hire,' not...what even is this?" She clutched the newspaper. "Experienced and skilled...social engagements...romantic evenings... It sounds like I'm hiring an escort!"

It was so bad, it was almost laughable. Except it wasn't.

Mrs. Casey was standing so straight, she could have been a sergeant. Her thin lips were pursed, hands on her narrow hips. "Your parents would be mortified!"

Her parents were the least of her problems right now, especially since neither was alive. Sarah rubbed her temples, deciding not to respond. This was her first act as owner of the family ranch, and while Edna was like family, this was all on Sarah.

She looked at the paper again and groaned as she read the ad for a foreman—*her* ad—below the disaster in question, noting that it listed the wrong number. "They must have mixed up my ad with someone else's. Of all the stupid errors…"

She marched across the room to her computer, brought up the page, and breathed a sigh of relief when she saw the correct version was still in place.

> *Ranch Manager/Foreman: The ranch manager is responsible for all aspects of operating the ranch. Experience necessary, full benefits, immediate start date.*

Wait. So were the calls she'd been getting in response to the online ad or the print version? She glanced out the windows and swallowed hard. All those men out there had to be applying for the foreman position. *Right?*

Sarah put her elbows on the desk and rubbed her temples. This was so bad. "How could they have printed this? I don't even understand who would *write* an ad like this."

"They should be fired. All of them at that two-bit paper," Mrs. Casey said, her outrage clinging to her words like honey on a spoon as her loyalty shifted back to Sarah. "Are you getting a migraine? You keep rubbing your temples." She squared her shoulders and nodded once. "I'll take over. This is too much stress for you."

Sarah stopped the temple rubbing. "No. I'm fine, and I know what I can handle. This is my ranch, and I'm going to find a way to run it."

"There is a reason your father never wanted you in the ranching business—it's no way of life for a woman. Alongside all those men out there day in and day out…" Edna shook her head.

If they kept this conversation going, Sarah *would* end up with a migraine. It wasn't a new topic, but it was one that always ended in an argument. "You know that's not true. There are plenty of women ranchers, despite this myth you and my parents kept clinging to. This is the twenty-first century, and even if it wasn't, that kind of thinking is and has always been backward."

"It's prudent, it's wise, and it's realistic."

"It's a bunch of lies that even my father didn't believe. Before Josh—" She rolled her shoulders and forced back the immediate pang of grief. "Before Josh died, Dad knew that we'd be the ones to take over this ranch when he was gone, and he had no objections. The whole 'women shouldn't be in the ranching business' was a front. A cover-up for his fear that something might happen to me. I'm not living that way any longer."

Mrs. Casey pursed her lips, coming at it from a different direction. "You know you could sell this place; it's what your mother wanted. You could sell and afford to buy a house without all this land and live a comfortable life." Her eyes ignited with hope.

"No."

Mrs. Casey made a *harrumph* noise and squared her shoulders. "This is an argument for another day. For now, we must come up with a solution for the hooligans outside."

Sarah almost laughed at the hooligan remark, but it also reminded her of just how out of touch Mrs. Casey was with the modern-day world. The poor woman had been with Sarah's family for more than two decades and was the epitome of straitlaced, black-and-white-movie era, sheltered, small-town elderly lady. This ranch had almost become a compound in the last decade, keeping them away from the neighbors and friends—and progress. While Sarah wasn't exactly living a wild life out here in rural Montana, she considered herself worldlier than Edna Casey.

By the end of this year, all that would change.

"Okay, let me think. Those men out there…they must have read the online ad, right? I mean, who reads the paper these days anyway? And who in their right mind would even think that ad was real?"

Mrs. Casey adjusted the blinds and peered outside. "No proper man would respond to an ad for an escort. I will address the men out there and whoever so dares to admit to being here for an escort position shall receive a blistering lecture from me."

Sarah resisted the urge to rub her temples again. "*I* will deal with the men outside. This is my ranch. I'm the one doing the interviews. I'm more than capable of handling a few cowboys, regardless of the position they're here for."

Sarah joined Mrs. Casey at the window and took in the appearance of the men outside. There was nothing odd about them; they all looked like the typical cowboys she'd grown up around on the ranch with their well-worn cowboy hats and jeans, fit and strong bodies.

"I'll be fine," she told Mrs. Casey. "You go back to the house. I'm optimistic that most of them are here to apply for the foreman position. They all *look* like real cowboys." She slanted the blinds and peered out the window again, trying to convince herself as well as Edna.

"Well, if not, they should all be ashamed of themselves, and I don't mind telling them on my way back to the house."

Sarah placed her arm around Mrs. Casey's thin shoulders and gently nudged her in the direction of the door. "I've got this. You go on about your day. I'll be in for dinner."

Mrs. Casey gave Sarah one last look, as though she wondered if she'd ever see her again, before opening the door and walking out.

"Everything will be just fine," Sarah called after her, feeling like the biggest liar ever.

Hours later, Sarah slowly lowered her head to the desk, her hand on a bottle of Tylenol, ready to be done with the ranching business after one day. This was a disaster.

She was a disaster.

It appeared the small town of Wishing River had an exorbitant amount of cowboys who were ready to trade in their chaps for roses and wine. It also appeared the cowboys here did, in fact, still read the paper.

This couldn't be happening. Or happened. It was over. All of it. Her career as a rancher was done before it even had a chance to start, because there was no way word wouldn't get out about this. But hey, at least Sarah knew that there were six cowboys willing to take her around town and romance her—if she paid them.

She banged her head against the desk. So stupid. After her family's long-standing foreman, Mike Ballinger, walked off the job last Friday without any notice, she'd been left hanging. Thankfully, the other cowboys knew their jobs and were capable of continuing, but the role of ranch manager was essential to an operation this size.

She needed someone immediately.

The knock on the door was the final straw. How many men were available for escort services in this town? She stomped across her late father's office and whipped open the door to find...one of the most breathtaking men she'd ever seen in her entire twenty-six years.

The sun was setting in the distance behind him. Typically the sight of it disappearing over the mountains would make her pause and take it in, except tonight it was him she was noticing. If she were part of the Montana tourism board, she'd be hiring him to stand there, just like that, with the mountains in the backdrop, the sun casting a glow over his perfect...everything.

He must be an escort. Was that bad of her to assume? The bizarre thought that maybe she should rethink her whole position on hiring an escort crossed her mind for the briefest of moments.

She forced herself to focus. He was in his late twenties or early thirties. His worn cowboy hat dipped low, but not low enough that she couldn't admire the aqua-blue eyes that stood out against his tanned skin. Light stubble highlighted a strong jaw and lean features. His dark-blue-and-white-checked shirt was rolled up midway to his elbows and revealed strong, tanned forearms. His jeans were worn and clung to his lean but powerful-looking body. He was a man who could make her nervous just by standing there.

He was probably very good at his escort position.

"Good afternoon, Miss. I'm here for the advertised job. I'm sorry I'm late—I had an emergency situation I needed to deal with at my current position."

She had no idea escorts had emergency situations. Whatever. That was none of her business. She clutched the doorknob, prepared to close it on him and the rest of the terrible day. "That's okay. There was a bit of a mix-up in the ad, so I'm afraid you came all the way out here for nothing. This is for a ranch manager position."

He gave her a nod. "Right. That's what I'm here for. I saw the ad online last night."

Relief swept through her. *Online*. He'd seen the online version. She smiled and held out her hand. "Oh. Well, in that case, I'm Sarah Turner."

He grasped her hand firmly, and she tried to maintain eye contact, but this man had an entirely different effect on her than anyone had before. His large hand was warm, slightly rough…a working man's hand, and his gaze was that of—

"Cade Walker."

She pulled her hand back and opened the door wider. "Nice to meet you. Come on in and have a seat," she said, gesturing to the chair on the other side of the worn oak desk. Since she'd had no use for her notes, they were all still neatly lined up on the wooden surface.

Swallowing down the sudden slew of nerves

and emotions, she settled into the large leather chair that somehow seemed too big for her, as though she were still the little girl playing in her daddy's swivel chair when visiting him at lunchtime.

She blinked a few times. The days where she and her brother would race across the office, trying to beat the other one to get first dibs on the chair… those days were over. She avoided the framed family photos, because that family hadn't existed in well over a decade. It was all up to her now.

"Here's my résumé," he said, handing her two pieces of paper. She scanned them, quickly taking in the relevant points, relieved that he seemed to have so much experience.

"So you've been ranching a long time," she started, trying to act as though she held interviews all the time.

He crossed one leg over the other. "Yes, since I was sixteen. The last six years, I've been the ranch manager at the Donnelly ranch here in Wishing River."

She nodded. "That's great. I see you've also listed your references."

"Yes, feel free to call them. Martin Donnelly is my current employer."

She furrowed her brows, trying to rack her brain, but she'd been so out of the loop that she couldn't place it. "Donnelly… That sounds very familiar."

He smiled. "Not far down the road at all."

She wasn't surprised she didn't know any of the local ranchers by name. Little details like who their neighbors were hadn't been important enough for her father to share. She cleared her throat and gathered up her notes. "So as I'm sure you already know, the ranch manager is responsible for all aspects of operating the ranch, including: the preparation of our annual operating budget and our long-term rolling business plan, a grass-fed beef operations strategy, a pasture maintenance plan, care of livestock and feeding, pasture in summer, adverse weather conditions planning, hay in winter, health checks, calving, irrigation, ranch staff, leadership…"

He raised his eyebrows. "I'm very comfortable and familiar with all of that. It's very similar to what I've already been doing."

She took a deep breath and forced herself to get to the last part, the one that kept her up last night and, well, every night since she decided to step up and take over the ranch. "The ranch manager also must be able to train me."

If he was surprised, he did a good job of keeping his features neutral. "Train you?"

She placed her forearms on the desk, folding her hands together, trying to look as though it were perfectly normal that a rancher's child wouldn't know a thing about how to run a ranch. "Yes. I'd like to be able to share certain aspects of the ranch manager's job by the one-year mark."

A flash of surprise flickered across those eyes. "That would be fine."

She nodded, her shoulders relaxing slightly. She spent the next fifteen minutes giving him a rundown of their ranch. His questions demonstrated how knowledgeable he was, and his genuine interest in her vision was promising.

"I guess the last thing to tell you is that our ranch manager left abruptly last week, so this position needs to be filled as soon as possible."

He ran a hand over his jaw, drawing her attention again to his perfectly sculpted features. "Okay. If I were hired, I would have to make arrangements. I know the Donnelly ranch is in good hands and they'll be fine without me, but I don't want to leave them in a bind. I would like to ask them how soon I could leave."

She nodded, trying not to look as desperate as she felt. Calling his references was definitely a must, but other than that, he had a dream résumé for this position.

They continued talking for the next half hour, and she found herself drawn to his voice, the way he spoke. He had a way of making his confidence known, and he handled himself as someone of authority, which was perfect for this position, but he also didn't patronize her. She stood slowly, wiping her palms on the front of her jeans before she shook his hand again. "Thanks for coming out.

I will make my decision by tomorrow."

He gave her a nod before turning and walking to the door. Somehow he managed to make the small office seem even smaller, like his presence sucked out all her oxygen. "It was nice to meet you, Miss Turner."

"Sarah."

"Right." He pulled open the door and stepped outside. She held the door, ready to close it, when he turned back around, his cowboy hat shadowing his eyes slightly. "I forgot to mention, if you need any help with that escort service, I'd be glad to oblige."

Fire stormed through her body, but before she had a chance to sputter out a response, he gave her an utterly charming half smile, perfectly timed with a small tip of his hat, before turning around and walking away.

Sarah slowly shut the door, torn between laughing and dying of humiliation.

All the weirdness of the afternoon aside, this was the first step in taking over the ranch. The next step was going to be in Cade Walker's very capable hands.

CHAPTER TWO

"I still don't get why you're leaving. I hope like hell it's not because of me," Tyler Donnelly said as Cade placed his folded clothes—mostly comprised of jeans and shirts—into his suitcase.

Cade glanced up at his best friend, who was leaning against the doorjamb of Cade's bedroom as he packed. Their other friend, Dean Stanton, was sitting on the chair in the corner of the room with a scotch in his hand.

"Don't flatter yourself," Cade said before he continued his packing. It wasn't exactly because of Tyler per se, but maybe in a roundabout way, his friend was part of the reason.

The three of them went way back. They were the first friends he'd made in Wishing River, partners in crime all through high school, and they'd come along at a point in his life when he'd basically given up the idea that there were any decent people in the world—or that he was even worthy of decent people.

Tyler's family had taken him in and had shown him a new way—one of hard, grueling work—that filled him with pride at the end of the day. That had been a new beginning for Cade. He wasn't one for emotional, sappy exchanges of feelings, but if he were ever in a life-and-death position, he'd probably tell them they were like brothers to him.

"Seriously," he said when Tyler continued to stare at him like he was ready to call bullshit when he saw it.

"There's more than enough work for the two of us to share here. I know I said some harsh stuff when I came back, and I regret all of it, but you're family, and family stays together."

Cade shoved his hands in his back pockets and looked across the room at his friend. Last year had been rough. He'd thought they'd never be close to Tyler again, but the three of them had managed to work out their problems. "Just because you're married now doesn't mean you get to say sappy crap like that. While it may be appreciated, it's not necessary to vocalize."

Dean snickered and put his feet up on the corner of Cade's bed. Cade shoved them off. "Yeah, please spare us," Dean agreed.

He could tell Tyler wasn't buying it. Sure, when Tyler had come back after eight years of being gone and not reaching out to any of them, things had been rough. He and Dean hadn't welcomed him home, and they had all said things they regretted. Cade just couldn't get past the way Tyler had just…taken off, without warning, without explanation. Logically, he knew his own issues with abandonment had played into his anger toward his best friend, but he hadn't been feeling particularly logical when Tyler came back around.

When the truth behind Tyler's taking off came out, forgiveness had come fast. The three of them had picked up like no time had gone, but now his best friend had a wife. And wasn't that just something?

"Yeah, well, Lainey does have that effect on people. Look at my dad and me. A year ago, I never would have guessed I'd be working alongside him again."

"Martin's looking like a new man," Dean said.

Tyler's father had suffered a debilitating stroke, which had prompted Tyler to come and run the ranch and try to make amends. The first few weeks after the stroke, Martin hadn't been able to speak or move. Thankfully, the man was stubborn and had pulled through with Dean's help.

"When's Lainey coming home?" Cade asked, hoping to keep the conversation clear of him leaving for a while.

Tyler got a stupid grin on his face. "Two weeks. I was actually going to talk to you guys about planning a party."

Dean shot Cade a look. "I'm not a party planner."

Tyler held up his hands. "Relax. Betty at the diner and Mrs. Busby had no confidence in any of us anyway, so they volunteered to help."

Cade let out a sigh of relief. "Good. Just tell us what time and when and we'll be there."

"When I figure it out, I'll let you know. I thought I wouldn't be able to survive a year and now here we are, ready to get our life together going."

After they'd gotten married, Lainey had started an art program abroad. They'd seen each other only once during Christmas, when Tyler had flown to Italy to be with her.

"Hell, I'm counting down the days till Lainey gets back so we don't have to listen to you whine anymore," Dean said.

Tyler snorted. "Listen, kid, when you get older and *you* get married, you'll understand what I've been going through."

Cade smiled to himself as he zipped up his full suitcase. Truth was, he did kind of feel nostalgic about leaving this place. He wasn't one to dwell on the shit that had happened in his life, just like he wasn't one to dwell on sentimentality, so this was new for him. Even though it wasn't his, this was the first place that had ever felt like a home to him, the first place that he got an inkling of what having a home even meant.

Lately, though, Cade had started feeling…restless. Like this wasn't enough anymore. They were all moving on with their lives. Dean had his career as a doctor and was still running his family ranch; Tyler and Lainey were just starting out and had all their own things to sort through.

So yeah, Cade had started feeling like he needed to find his own way, build his own life…maybe even one day settle down. He didn't fear love or marriage or settling down the way Tyler had. There had even been a time he'd been interested in Lainey, before she and Tyler had gotten serious. He realized now it was what Lainey represented—she'd come from a family almost as messed-up as his, and yet she'd managed to hold on to her ideals and make something of herself. But there had been no denying the connection she'd had with Tyler, and when Cade had seen it, he'd backed off right away. And hell if she hadn't made his friend a better man. He was genuinely happy for the both of them.

"So when are you starting?" Dean asked, ignoring Tyler's obnoxious comment.

"Monday. I'll go over there tomorrow to get settled in the house."

"Perfect. So we can take you out for a couple of drinks at River's tonight," Tyler said.

Some things didn't change. The three of them going into River's had been a Saturday-night tradition for years. The local saloon was classic Wishing River, dating back to the eighteen hundreds and owned by the Rivers family since the beginning. Live music, good food, and better drinks made it the best place to spend your hard-earned money.

Cade nodded. "Definitely."

"So what's the name of the new gig?" Dean asked.

"Joshua Ranch," he said as he zipped up the suitcase.

Dean and Tyler shared a look. "Why is that

name familiar?" Tyler asked.

Dean rubbed the back of his neck. "I'm trying to place it. It'll come to me."

Both his friends were born and raised in Wishing River, and they knew everything about everyone. Since Cade had come here alone as a teenager, he'd never really cared about the local gossip circle.

Tyler frowned. "Hmm. Who was the foreman before you?"

"I don't know, but apparently he quit without notice, leaving them scrambling."

"I swear I know that family. What's the last name?"

"Turner."

"Shit," Dean said under his breath. "I remember who they are."

Cade's shoulders stiffened. "That doesn't sound good."

"They're on the border of Cedar Crossing, so they weren't as well-known in Wishing River, but hell, I remember...the couple had a son as well."

Tyler made a noise and grimaced. "I remember."

"The boy was maybe ten or so," Dean said. "He went out into the river, being your typical stupid kid at that age, and thought he'd go for a swim. The water levels were high and the rapids were strong. He got pulled under. There was a search party. His little sister was with him and they thought she'd drowned, too. Apparently they found her miles downstream, holding on to her brother. He was dead."

A chill rode through Cade, and his throat was clogged with emotion. What a brutal story. The image of Sarah played across his mind, and sympathy for her flooded him. He cleared his throat. "That's horrible," he managed to choke out in the silence of the room.

Tyler nodded. "Yeah. The community banded together, trying to reach out to the family, but they withdrew. From everything. If I recall correctly, I think they even pulled the daughter out of school."

Even though Wishing River was a small town, the big ranches out here were literally thousands of acres, so unless you needed to deal with your neighbors for something, it was conceivable that you didn't really get to know everyone, especially if they kept to themselves. "I think the father died five years ago and her mother last year. So she's on her own."

"Well, you're the man who can help her."

"Said no one ever." Dean laughed.

Cade flipped him the finger and pulled his suitcase to the door. He was glad for the information; it would make him more aware of the dynamic over at the ranch. "Well, I guess we'll see how it goes."

"Good luck," Dean said.

He would need it. Starting over wasn't new

to him, and there was a time it would have been scary, but he'd learned to get along with people, to anticipate their needs and moods. It was a skill he'd picked up as a kid when he was in self-preservation mode, but it had served him well as an adult, too. There were so many different personalities on a ranch, and he could tell from just a few hours which of the ranch hands were going to be trouble and which would be lifelong friends. Joshua Ranch and what Sarah wanted him to do was an entirely different kind of trouble, but he hoped that he'd be able to take over effectively while giving her what she needed.

He took in the family room one last time, and that odd pang hit him in the chest again. This was it. He was pretty much packed up, since most of this belonged to the cabin. It was the first real home he'd had. The first home that had felt like his. Even though the furniture and everything came with it, it had been the closest to owning something he'd ever gotten. That was all because of Ty's family.

"Have you had a tour of the place?"

"Briefly. But I'll be working with Sarah. She needs me to show her the ropes because she plans on running it as well." She'd made it very clear that part of his job was to teach her, and he'd do his job, but he wasn't a fan of working closely with anyone, and part of the reason he loved this job was the solitude. It was also kind of unsettling to think that he was essentially teaching her how to replace him. He'd tried to shrug that part off because she had never hinted that his job was only temporary, just that she'd be sharing responsibilities. Either way, he'd make sure he was too valuable to be let go.

Tyler raised an eyebrow, and Cade knew a dumb-ass comment was imminent. "How's that going to go?"

He shrugged. Sharing responsibility hadn't been his strong suit in the past. "I have no idea, but you and I managed this year."

"Not at first." Tyler chuckled. "What's she like?"

Beautiful. Cade wanted to kick himself for that being the first thought that popped into his head. If she'd been a man, he wouldn't have even noticed what he looked like, but it was pretty hard not to notice Sarah. Or think about her. She was curvy yet petite, and beautiful with her honey-colored hair pulled back in a ponytail, her full mouth and pale skin, and those striking green eyes. The woman would have stood out in a crowd—hell, she'd have stood out at River's on its busiest night—but he was pretty sure he'd never seen her there.

When she'd first opened the door, Cade thought she looked ready to kill someone. It had taken everything in him not to smile and say something to put her more at ease right out the gate—professionalism and first impressions and all that—but he was betting she'd had quite the morning with that other ad running in the local paper.

He'd had a laugh over his morning coffee with that one. He just bet she'd had her share of applicants for that position, especially when word got out about who was doing the hiring. A beautiful woman like her would be no hardship to escort around town, no pay required.

He smiled to himself. Sarah might've been way younger than he expected, but she carried herself with an air of sophistication and confidence. The woman would kowtow to no one, and he respected the hell out of that. He'd have his work cut out for him until they found their rhythm, but he was looking forward to showing her the ropes.

When she spoke about her family, though, she seemed quite guarded. Now that he knew what she'd gone through, he wanted to offer his support, let her know he'd be in her corner if she needed it, but that wasn't his place. He'd be the ranch manager, nothing more.

Fortunately, he had no problem compartmentalizing. Nothing had ever come between him and a job. He'd learned long ago that the most important thing was to earn a living and never be dependent on anyone else because people couldn't really be trusted—except the guys in this room and Ty's dad. Before them, he'd had to find his own way in the world, without a family to fall back on for support. That would stayed rooted in his belief system forever. He'd always had to prove himself, to prove that he could work hard, that he could be a valuable asset, and when he did, he'd get a roof over his head and a hot meal. If he couldn't be of use, then there was no point in his being around.

He turned his attention back to his friends. "She's nice. Young. Determined to get to know how to run her family ranch. Gotta respect that."

"For sure. Well, I hope it works out for you, and you always have a place here if things don't go the way you want them to."

Cade held his gaze for a moment. "Thank you. I appreciate that." He did. He would never forget what Tyler and his family did for him. Even though he worked hard for it, they had shown him the way. The way to earn a living, to be proud, to live by rules, and to have goals. If it weren't for the Donnelly family, he didn't know where he'd be.

"I want to get an early start tomorrow, so if we're going to River's, we have to hurry up."

"Don't worry, we'll make sure you don't make a bad impression on your first day."

Good, because tomorrow was the first day of his new life.

CHAPTER THREE

Cade sat down in his newly unpacked foreman's house and took it all in. He placed his feet on the dark-wood coffee table, linked his fingers behind his head, leaned back, and breathed a deep sigh of satisfaction. So this was his new home. Not that he was one to become overly attached to a place—he'd learned early on in life that a home was just a roof over your head and nothing more—but this was a place he could get used to.

He glanced out the large picture window in the family room with its view of the mountains in the distance and couldn't deny that it was probably the nicest home he'd ever had. Sure, the place he'd had at Tyler's ranch was nice, but it had been more like a bachelor pad, and an extension of his friend's family home. Not…his. Just another reminder that he'd always been at the mercy of someone else's pity.

Sure, it hadn't been like that with Tyler's family because they had treated him better than his own biological family, but he knew that in the beginning, they had felt sorry for him. *Especially Tyler's mother*, he thought with a slight smile. She had been the real deal. The first time he'd seen what a real mother was like, she'd taken him in like a wounded animal, mothering and doting and making him envy the love his friend had grown up with. But he'd never had time to dwell on his lot in life—work and earning his keep had been priority one.

He took a deep breath, pride seeping its way into his body, shutting out all those old voices of how worthless he was. This wasn't the home of a worthless man. This was the home of a hard-working man. He just needed to prove that he was a worthwhile investment for the Joshua Ranch. He could and would outwork anyone.

This was a true family home with three bedrooms and a large-enough kitchen that there was a place to put a table. The furnishings were modest but clean and neutral. The front porch was welcoming, and in the future, he might even put a pot of some kind of flowers out there.

Or not. But if he were so inclined, it *would* be on that kind of a porch.

Dusk was settling in, and it was his favorite time of day. If he didn't already know that his best friends were busy, he would have invited them over. He sat up a little straighter as he spotted a woman walking quickly up the driveway.

Already standing by the time she knocked on his door, he opened it a moment later. A tall, thin, gray-haired woman stood there with a pie in her hand. Her smile was so tight that Cade thought it looked like someone was holding it up with puppet strings. "Cade Walker?"

"Yes, ma'am."

She held out a thin hand and then gripped his with the force of a much younger person, her steely gaze holding him. "Edna Casey. Housekeeper for the Turners."

He held the door open and gestured for her to enter. "Nice to meet you, Mrs. Casey."

She gave him a quick nod of semi-approval and walked in, holding out the pie in his direction. "This is a welcome pie. Strawberry rhubarb."

Despite the claim that it was a "welcome" pie, "welcomed" was not exactly how he was feeling. He didn't know if she was suspicious of all newcomers or if it was him specifically. Knowing they'd be crossing paths repeatedly, he thought it best to try and get on as good terms as possible. Part of being successful at a new ranch was having a great camaraderie with all the employees—especially the ones who baked pies. "Thank you, that's very kind of you. Can I offer you a slice?"

She folded her hands in front of her and kept her chin high, no signs of warming in those steely eyes. "No, thank you. I have another one at the house. I thought I would come out here and get to know you, since you'll be spending time with Sarah."

Ah, so she was protective of Sarah. He walked across the room and placed the pie on the counter. "Sure. Would you like a cup of coffee?"

"I drink tea."

He grimaced. He loathed tea. He'd rather drink water from the horse stalls. "I'm afraid I don't have any of that."

She nudged her chin in the direction of the whiskey bottle on his counter. "I wouldn't mind a small glass of that. It's the end of my workday."

He hid his surprise while he poured her a glass. "Would you like to sit down?"

"That would be nice, thank you," she said, taking the glass from his hand and sitting on the edge of the couch, as though she had no intention of getting comfortable. He crossed the room and sat opposite her. She adjusted her skirt and then drank her scotch in one fluid motion, then placed the empty glass on the coffee table with barely a sound. "I thought I would give you a little insight into the Turner family before the workweek starts tomorrow."

He leaned back on the sofa, placing one ankle over the other as he stretched out, trying to look casual and not at all like he was on high alert. He wasn't about to let on what he already knew. He cleared his throat. "I appreciate that. It's always a bit of a process starting a new job."

She raised a neatly formed brow. "You've had a lot, then?"

"Jobs?"

She nodded, her hard gaze not leaving his.

He sat up a little straighter, realizing she was looking for his flaws. He'd already completed his interview, already been hired, but she was obviously close to Sarah and would report back anything she saw that was alarming. Knowing he had to keep his cool, he played along and answered her question. "Well, I've been at the same ranch for more than seven years. But then, Sarah knows all that information."

"Yes, of course. Sarah mentioned something about that. We are very close. I should tell you that I have worked for the Turner family for more than twenty-five years. I knew Sarah when she was just a baby."

He raised his eyebrows, waiting for her to continue. When she didn't, he was forced to come up with something. "She must be like family, then."

"Like a daughter. They are a very special family, and I treat them as though they are my own. Her parents died much too young, leaving her with a great burden to deal with. Her father died a few years ago, followed by her mother last year. The ranch was running itself until that hoodlum, Mike, just up and ran off, leaving her to scramble to find new help. I would like to assume that you know better than to do something like that."

He leaned forward, not feeling very casual anymore. "I've never abandoned anyone, and I'm not the type to take off in the middle of the night."

She gave him a nod. "That is good to hear. I worry about her. Sarah has had too much to deal

with in her young life, and I take it upon myself
to ensure that nothing else happens to her. I'm not
sure this is something you need to know, but I feel
that if you fully understand the type of woman
you are dealing with, your job and my job will be
much easier."

He was careful to keep his expression neutral.
Hell, he wasn't even sure how accurate any of
what Dean and Tyler had said was, and it wasn't
his business, either. "Okay."

"Sarah has spent the last three years nursing
her mother through an illness that ended in death.
She's been surrounded by tragedy her entire life,
and I need someone to watch out for her."

Alarm bells rang loud and clear in his head as
he processed this. He wasn't in the habit of babysitting or getting involved in people's problems.
"Can I ask what kind of tragedy?"

She pursed her lips and sat a little straighter,
even though he had no idea how that was even
possible without a steel rod in her back. "I am not
at liberty to discuss the family's history. Do you
have any family?"

He blinked at the sudden change of subject. "I
don't."

"I'm sorry to hear that."

Yeah, well, so was he. He didn't want to be
rude, but he didn't talk about his family life, his
past, or any of that kind of stuff to anyone. Even
his best friends. Especially not another employee

at the ranch where he was working. "Thank you."

"It is my understanding that Sarah's goal is to learn how to run this ranch herself by the end of the year. Sarah is a wonderful young woman, but she is not cut out for the ranching life."

He shifted in his seat. "What makes you say that?"

"It is not realistic for her."

He didn't want to be in the middle of family problems. He hated drama. He also wasn't going to do anything that might jeopardize his relationship with his new employer. He'd found it odd that Sarah needed the help of an outsider to learn about her own family ranch, but he'd assumed there was a reason. "I would think that as an adult, she would know what is realistic for herself."

Edna smoothed a hand down the front of her skirt and then gave him a pointed stare. "She doesn't know her limits. She has a medical condition that can get triggered by stress, among other things."

He didn't say anything for a moment while he processed what she was saying. He got that Edna was trying to protect Sarah, but he found the entire conversation odd. Why would Sarah put herself at risk? Why wouldn't she just let a foreman run the place? "What health condition?"

Her eyes shifted to the window, almost like she was feeling guilty. "I'm not at liberty to say."

He stood up. "Then I'm afraid I can't help you.

This is Sarah's ranch, and as foreman, I answer to her. She seems like an intelligent young woman. I'm confident that she knows what she wants and what she's capable of."

Edna pursed her lips and stood. "Just keep in mind what I've told you. Watch out for her. Her parents trusted her with me. Right up until the end, I looked out for her. Now that they're gone, Sarah seems to be going through this phase where she feels like she needs independence, even if it puts her at risk."

He rolled back on his heels. This had felt like a dream-job scenario. Now things were getting complicated. When Edna didn't budge, he realized he was going to have to give her some kind of reassurance. "Well, don't. No one has ever died on any ranch that I've worked at."

She pursed her lips even tighter and spun on her heel, marching to the door. Clearly she'd hoped for more from him. He followed her to the door, his eyes landing on the pie she'd baked him. Even though he knew it was meant to disarm him and make him feel indebted to her. "Edna," he said when she opened the door in an angry, jerky motion.

She turned around and raised a thin brow.

He swallowed hard. Despite his feelings about the conversation, she was the only person who'd brought him a pie, ever. And she was trying to help Sarah, to protect her from...he had no idea what. "I'll watch out for Sarah."

Her harsh features relaxed slightly. "See that you do."

He stood there silently, the warm night breeze washing over him, watching as dusk rolled in over the pasture, the image of Edna disappearing, the distinct tightening in his gut warning him that he was getting a lot more than he bargained for.

$\mathcal{S}$arah took another sip of piping hot coffee and tried not to let her nerves take over. While she knew she was doing the right thing, finally stepping up and taking over the ranch like she and Josh had always planned, she still worried that maybe Mrs. Casey was right, maybe she wasn't cut out for any of this. She was nervous as hell, not that she'd ever let on. She had no idea what she was doing. She was about to go against every single rule she'd had growing up...or really, since she was ten.

The family pictures that lined the green-and-white-floral-wallpapered hallway were so familiar to her that she knew the exact order they were in, and she knew the last picture before she came to the mudroom would be her favorite—the one of Josh and her by the horse barn. Most of his pictures had been removed, but she'd begged her parents to keep that one up. That picture symbolized the life she yearned for every day, the one she still visited in her dreams at night, the one that was filled with promise and the love of a family who she thought she would have by her side forever.

She never stopped at any of the pictures, but today she stopped in front of the last one and glanced down the hall to make sure Mrs. Casey wasn't watching. Satisfied the coast was clear, she allowed herself to look deep into Josh's eyes, not caring how silly she looked. She stared at him until the picture became blurry and the only voice she had was a whisper.

She knew she wouldn't cry; she never did. Learning that tears wouldn't change anything, wouldn't bring anyone back, made her decide long ago not to bother with them.

"I can still outride you any day, Josh." Her throat tightened as she held his gaze, wishing it were real, wishing he were here. "If you're around and you're watching me today, can you make sure I don't make a fool of myself? It was supposed to be the both of us running this place. You would have handled the guys, not me. You would probably have been friends with Cade, but don't worry—I can handle this. I'll…see you later." She kissed her index finger and then pressed it on the glass over his face before hurrying to the mudroom.

Nerves were settling deep in her gut, but

what she was doing felt right. Once her fleece sweater was zipped, she stepped out into the early morning and took a deep breath. Wishing River, Montana, had been home forever, and this was the first time in a long time that she'd been out here before the crack of dawn.

The damp, clean air filled her lungs as she headed to her father's office, where she'd be meeting her new foreman. She was always slightly in awe of her surroundings on the ranch. The morning dew sparkled, and the mountains in the distance reminded her just how small they all were in this place. The vast skyline was tinged with a cool pink, promising a sun-drenched day ahead.

Gravel crunched under her feet in a comforting rhythm, and the unfamiliar tingle of anticipation at seeing him again caught her by surprise. When she'd set out to find a new foreman, she had assumed he'd be a middle-aged, fatherly type of man. She hadn't expected someone like Cade.

Her eyes caught the tall figure leaning against the office wall. Cade. He was early. "Morning," he called out, his deep voice holding a note of friend-liness.

"Good morning," she said, taking the last steps before reaching him. "All settled in?"

He nodded. "I am. And I'm looking forward to getting started today. I've met all the men this weekend and have familiarized myself with the buildings and operation. Still lots to learn, but I feel I've got a pretty good handle on things."

"That's great," she said, unlocking the door and turning on the light. It felt strange to be in here, the musty old office a smell she always associated with her father. Sometimes it was overwhelming to think how quickly life could change, how fleeting all of this was, how little control any of them had over their own lives. But thinking like that didn't get her anywhere. Today, she was the owner of Joshua Ranch, and she needed to act like it.

She pushed aside her embarrassment and decided to get the whole Mrs. Casey thing out of the way. The older woman had mentioned her... visit, and Sarah didn't want there to be any awkwardness between them. "I'm really sorry about Mrs. Casey. She just told me that she'd stopped by your house. I hope she wasn't interrogating you?"

He smiled, not looking bothered at all. "It's okay. Her loyalty and protectiveness of you are admirable."

She let out a sigh of relief. "She can get a little dramatic when it comes to my safety."

"No hard feelings."

"Great. Did you mention anything to any of the men that I'd be joining you guys and learning the ropes?"

He followed her into the old office. He stood in the doorway and seemed to fill up the small place with his presence. He had the ability to be nonthreatening and yet exude power in a way that was very unique among the men she'd worked with.

A flicker of something passed across his features before he spoke. "I did. I think they were a little surprised, but it won't be an issue. Seems like you've got a good group of men out here."

"So you think by the end of our year together, I'll be able to run this ranch?"

He gave her a slight smile that made her stomach do an odd flip. "I don't see why not."

CHAPTER FOUR

"Hi. I was hoping I could shadow you today."

Cade paused, bent over the blue tote he was filling with the supplies he'd need for the fence repair he'd planned on tackling today, when Sarah interrupted. She was standing there, dressed for a day of ranch work, the optimism of a novice shining in her eyes.

"Nothing too exciting planned," he told her. "There's a lot of fence work to be done, especially before we move the cattle, but that's part of the job."

She nodded, a faint smile touching one corner of her mouth. "I remember my dad used to say that sometimes he felt like the more fence he fixed, the more needed to be fixed."

He gave her a nod. "Very true. Maintaining fence is a never-ending job."

"What are you putting in there?" she asked, crouching down beside him.

He pointed to the compartments he'd filled. "Those are wire tighteners. Seem like just another little tool, but they save a hell of a lot of time. I can show you when we're out there. Those are T-post clips used to attach barbed wire to metal posts. That's smooth wire for patching staples to attach to wooden posts. Then there's a hammer, of course, fencing pliers, and a flat-head screwdriver for twisting the T-post clips," he said, standing and picking up the tote.

"Okay, uh, I guess I'll figure it all out as we go along," she said, crossing her arms over her chest, that optimism diminishing slightly.

"You can saddle up, and we'll get going. Don't forget to pick up a pair of gloves," he said, pointing to the extra ones under the table.

"Sure," she said.

He was curious to see her riding skills but not curious enough to make him happy she was coming along. Especially now that he'd really dug in and seen the level of work needed. Not that the ranch was falling into disrepair, but there was usually more work than people on a ranch and since their foreman had ditched them, there was more than usual. He wouldn't be able to work quickly if he was showing her how things ran, and there wouldn't be a lot of time to familiarize himself with the business end of things until they'd caught up.

Within a half hour, they were well on their way, and he was relieved to see that Sarah knew how to handle herself on a horse, even though they weren't doing any challenging riding. The day was gorgeous and the air crisp and cool, which was his favorite for ranching work.

"So what exactly are we looking for," she asked, "or will it be super obvious?"

"Different things," he said, slowing down a bit to point. "Sometimes it's a fence with a strand coming loose or a fence post that might be pulling out of the ground. Damage to the bottom strand is pretty common, like over there," he said, pointing to a patch he just noticed. He dismounted and she followed him over. "So it's a matter of replacing with another T-post clip because calves could lie down next to the fence and easily roll underneath and find themselves separated from their moms and the rest of the herd. And that'll cause the mom to be pissed and cause even more damage," he said, taking the necessary tools out of the tote as he spoke.

Sarah listened attentively and nodded, watching as he went about repairing the wire. "Can I try?"

He finished what he was doing. "Well, I've already done this one. Maybe watch me do a couple more and then give it a try?"

She stood along with him. "Sure," she said. The disappointment that tinged her voice made him feel slightly guilty, but it wasn't a job a novice could just rush into.

They rode side by side like that for the next two hours, on and off their horses, fixing fence, him giving Sarah a play-by-play as he repaired various patches of fence.

"Are you going to let me fix this next one?" she asked as they dismounted.

He handed her the tote. "It's all yours. See if you can identify what's wrong with it and how to fix it. Just be careful with the wire," he said, unable to help himself from issuing a little caution.

"No problem," she said, lifting the tote and walking over to the fence.

He shoved his hands in his pockets to resist picking up the tote for her or pointing out the best way to go about repairing the broken strand. Not for the first time today, he noticed the way the sun caught the lighter shades of brown in her shiny hair…and that was just plain stupid. Who cared about the way her hair looked, pulled back in that ponytail? Or the way she filled out her jeans and sweater? None of his business. Not professional.

"Shit," she said and quickly grabbed her hand to her chest.

"What?" he said, walking over to her and crouching down.

She was holding her hand to her chest, and her eyes were watering. His gaze went from her eyes to her hand, and he cursed under his breath as a trickle of blood ran down her wrist. "Let me see," he said, holding out his hand.

She shook her head. "It's fine. I'm fine. I can finish this."

"Did the wire snag your skin?" he asked, wincing when his words came out harsher than he intended.

She shrugged, then nodded.

Damn. He should have been paying more attention. But he'd been too busy thinking about stupid things like shiny hair. "Why did you take your glove off?"

She frowned. "They're too big. It was hard to work like that. I thought I could be careful."

He bit back his remark. "When was your last tetanus shot?"

Her eyes widened. "Um, like, when I was a kid?"

He clenched his jaw and started packing up the tools. "We have to get that looked after," he said, standing. When she didn't move, he extended his hand, trying to look less angry.

"I don't want to go back yet. I can finish this and then get my shot," she said, her green eyes spitting fire.

"Let's see it," he said, crossing his arms.

She jutted her chin out and held his gaze, and for a long few moments, he didn't think she would. Finally, she thrust her hand out, and he couldn't help the curse that flew from his mouth. It was a nasty-looking gash. "See, not so bad," she said as blood oozed from it.

"Nice try. Let's go now before it gets infected," he said, picking up the tools and walking back to the horses, not giving her an opportunity to argue with him.

"I appreciate your concern, but I can make my own decisions. This is my ranch," she said, standing in front of him now, tilting her head back so she could stare him in the eyes.

"You're right. But I'm the foreman, and I'm training you on how to be a proper rancher. A real rancher wouldn't let that go. So you can either put on a brave face and continue fixing that fence for the next hour or so that it'd take a novice and end up with a nasty infection because that wound would get dirty, or you can deal with it and be back out here this afternoon," he said, mounting his horse to show her that obviously there was only one right answer.

After a few seconds, she made some kind of sound and stomped back over to her horse. "Do you need help?" he asked, wondering if it would put pressure on the wound to mount her horse.

"No. Thank you," she said, her politeness a complete contrast to the anger in her voice. So, day one wasn't exactly a roaring success.

As she turned the horse in the direction of the ranch, a pang of pity hit him unexpectedly. She was trying hard. She wanted this. She was trying to be a contributing member of her own ranch, and he really did admire that.

"Hey, Sarah," he said as they approached the ranch.

She turned to glance at him, her full lips pulled into a thin line, her eyes filled with a pain that he wasn't sure was completely physical. He felt compelled to make her feel better, and he didn't know why. If that had been Tyler, he would have laughed at him and probably called him an ass. But she wasn't Tyler. "It wouldn't be a first day without some kind of mishap. Happens to everyone," he said, trying to be positive.

He was rewarded with an almost smile. "Did it happen to you, too?"

He hesitated. "Well, it happens to most people."

She made a sound and stared straight ahead.

"Do you need a ride into town?" he asked.

"No thank you."

"Are you sure?"

"Yes."

"Okay, then I'll probably just get back out there and continue fixing fence for the rest of the day. No time to waste," he said, slowing as they approached the barn. He was being practical and also trying not to make her feel like a bigger fool by driving her to a doctor.

"Thanks," she said over her shoulder.

He paused there for a minute and then turned his mare around and headed back out. He'd hoped the tension would leave now that Sarah wasn't accompanying him, but somehow it didn't. It trailed him around for the miles of fence he rode next to that day.

Sometimes, when he was at the Donnelly Ranch, the odd post here and there would stand out to him. On some of those days, when Ty's father would be with him, the older man would point those out and explain that some of them were more than a hundred years old, some from tree branches set in the ground before milling. That kind of history was astounding. Even more so to know that some of these ranches went back that many generations.

Today, it made him think of the Turner family and this sad ranch they had been running this last decade.

He shared no one's history. His family lineage… went nowhere.

Nothing like the Turners. Nothing like Sarah. And that was just fine, because a woman like Sarah could never be for him, especially not if she was his employer. His livelihood depended on her. So all thoughts of curves and shiny hair would have to be shut out. His top priority would be proving to her that he was indispensable and that at the end of the year, even if she could run this ranch, she'd still need him.

$\mathcal{C}$ade was standing in the well-equipped tack room at Joshua Ranch a couple of days later, trying to not get involved in the conversation he was eavesdropping on. He'd never been one for listening in on other people's conversations, but since this had to do with Sarah, he stayed where he was and was careful not to make a sound.

"I worked with her dad for years," Sully, one of the younger wranglers, said. "If he'd wanted his daughter to join the business, it would've happened. She was never the same after she saw her brother die. If the stories are right, she didn't talk to no one for three years afterward."

"I heard the same. Don't know how long she'll last, doesn't look too tough to me," Jesse, another young ranch hand, chimed in. "Apparently she hurt herself the first day on the job. I saw her in here holding her arm, her hand all bloody. She's not exactly a natural at this."

Cade's muscles tightened. She'd worked hard alongside them all week. Sure enough, the day after her mess up with the fence, she'd been waiting for him outside the barn. They had worked on fences together, and by the end of that day, she'd known what she was doing. She'd been impressive. A quick learner.

And here they were, disrespecting not only a good woman but their boss. He hadn't expected to have to deal with these kinds of issues, but he knew he had to speak up because rumors spread faster than wildfire, and it was his job to quash this kind of talk.

With an inward groan, he walked out to join the chatty young cowboys. They stopped talking the minute he emerged from the tack room. At least they had that much common sense. "I think you boys have better things to do than gossiping about the woman who signs your paychecks."

He was pleased to see both their faces blanch

before turning red.

"Sorry, Cade. We didn't mean any disrespect," Jesse said, nudging his hat up and meeting Cade's stern gaze.

After another second of staring them down, just for good measure, he gave them a nod. "Fine. We've all had our fair share of accidents on a ranch and we don't sit around gossiping about it and questioning a guy's competence."

"Of course," they mumbled.

He gave them a long, hard look. "Just see that it doesn't happen again and this line of conversation ends now."

They both nodded and scrambled down the corridor and out the barn. He'd keep an eye on them and his ears open to any of that kind of meddling.

As he did his nightly ritual of one last check on the horses, a quick pop-in to make sure there was hay in every feeder and that the waterers were clean in the stalls, his mind wandered back to the woman at the center of the gossip.

The end of week one left him with the conclusion that there had been some verbal memo passed around that stated that Sarah was incapable of performing like the other ranch hands, just as Mrs. Casey said. No one let Sarah do anything. They stepped in every time.

He'd have a talk with the men tomorrow morning over breakfast when Sarah wasn't around.

She was working hard. She had gotten in there and tried to do what they were doing. He could read the frustration on her face, and hearing the men grouse about their idea of her failures wasn't the way he wanted to end the week. He was exhausted, physically and mentally, and for the next month he'd be playing double duty because after dinner he'd have to get accustomed to the business end of the ranch.

He headed for his house, his gaze lingering on the sun dipping behind those mountains he loved, painting the sky pink, and an odd feeling of gratitude mingled with weariness. Never in a million damn years would anyone back home picture him here. Joshua Ranch was a fine Montana operation, and the fact that he was foreman at his age was something that made him proud. He wouldn't screw this up, which was why he had no problem grabbing dinner from the canteen and taking a quick shower, then heading back to the ranch office to get in a few hours of work.

Three hours later, Cade was still knee-deep in spreadsheets and accounting, settled behind the desk of Sarah's father's office. While his favorite part of the ranch manager job was being outside, the business side of things was essential. He'd had to learn this part of the business fast at the Donnellys' ranch, and he had gotten good at it.

He glanced at the display on the computer and was surprised it was almost nine o'clock. He scrubbed a hand through his hair, resting his elbows on the paper-filled desktop, and willed himself to wake up a little. He should have brought in a cup of coffee after dinner. His gaze roamed the room, taking a break from the screen, and it settled on the bookshelf filled with family pictures. They were the typical photos, like the ones he saw in other people's houses, except the one with Sarah and a boy who looked almost exactly like her. He must have been the brother who died.

The knock at the door prevented him from wondering about it. He stood, rolling his shoulders as he crossed the room to answer the door. Sarah was on the other side, holding two mugs and smiling. Her grin wobbled slightly when she saw him, and something flickered across her eyes. "Um, I saw the lights on in here and thought that, since you were burning the midnight oil, maybe I could help out or at least bring you a mug of hot chocolate."

He was touched by the gesture, even though he wasn't really a fan of hot chocolate, and opened the door wider. "Thanks, that's very nice of you. Not necessary, but I was just thinking I wished I brought a cup of coffee with me tonight."

She handed him a mug. "Great. It's not a problem. If you have time, I'd love to watch what you're doing. I know you've had to go slower than normal while teaching me everything, and I don't want to slow you down with this, too…"

Her voice trailed off, and he realized that she sounded uncomfortable. Maybe he wasn't that welcoming. When working at Ty's ranch, he never had to think about how he came across or what vibe he gave off. Working with Sarah was proving to be different. There was also the added complication that he found her attractive. Too attractive. Her hair was still damp around the ends, and she smelled as though she'd just showered, which led him to imagine her *in* the shower, which was completely inappropriate.

Sarah was wearing a navy hoodie with jeans and sneakers. Her face was scrubbed clean, giving her this mix of girl-next-door prettiness and gorgeous, soft woman. That was a dangerous combination for him, a combination he never had. She was unlike anyone he'd ever been with…not that he'd ever taken the time to really know a woman.

"So what are you working on?" she asked, raising her eyebrows as she took a sip of her hot chocolate and entering the small office.

He pulled one of the chairs around so that she could sit beside him and see the computer screen. When they both sat down, Cade was very aware of how close they were sitting, how intimate a setting this was. He took a sip of the hot chocolate, surprised by how smooth the chocolate was and without a flooding of sugar. "I think this might be the best hot chocolate I've ever had."

She crossed one leg over the other. "Thanks.

Secret recipe. It has no sugar in it and is made with organic cocoa. Compliments of Mrs. Casey."

"Ah. I guess that's a good sign," he said with a low chuckle.

"I think it might be a sort of peace offering," she said, her eyes dancing.

He leaned back in his chair as he took another sip. "I thought that was what the strawberry-rhubarb pie was."

Sarah scrunched up her nose in a gesture he found inexplicably adorable. It was probably the hot chocolate and long nights making him think like this. "I'm still sorry about that. She's kind of like a second mother, and she's been with our family since I was little."

He didn't say anything for a moment, deciding what he should reveal and shouldn't. Despite the fact that there would never be anything more between them other than colleagues, they would get to know each other very well this year. Getting things out in the open would be essential if she was to become as involved as she claimed. "She mentioned some kind of health problems? If there's anything I should be aware of, especially in situations where we're out there moving cattle or really physical things, you can let me know. I would never tell anyone else."

Her mouth dropped open slightly, and she averted her gaze, but not before he caught a flash of anger in her eyes. "There's nothing other than

the typical stuff people have. I'm sure you have...
things," she said, motioning her hand in his direction.

He shook his head slowly. "I have nothing."

She frowned. "Everyone has some kind of
problem. Back, headaches, IBS, joint issues..."

He felt a grin coming on and fought it back for
her sake. "I'm not eighty; I eat everything and it
stays where it should."

"Oh. Well, I guess you're lucky."

"So you have IBS?"

He had the pleasure of watching her face go
red, but it also reminded him that he shouldn't
be having this much fun teasing her. She was his
employer.

"*No.* Basically I'm like you. Minor issues."

"I told you, I have no issues."

She placed her empty mug on the desk with
a *thud*. "Fine. I'm not exactly like you but pretty
close. I have no issues that should be of concern
to anyone but me, and I can control them. Which
reminds me, since I'm robust and filled with good
health, I'd like to go on the next cattle drive."

Hell. He kept his poker face on just long
enough to try and figure out how that would work.
Of course she could come—it was her own damn
ranch—but it was just that Sarah coming along
would be one other element he had to worry
about. It wasn't a full-out cattle drive; it would
only be one night out there. But it would have

been easier with just a bunch of cowboys. He cleared his throat. "Sure. Sounds good. Have you ever been on one before?"

Her mouth tightened slightly. "Uh, no. I always wanted to, though."

He ignored the pang of sympathy he felt for her. He couldn't imagine growing up in a place like this and being denied the ranching life. "What about Mrs. Casey? Will she have an issue with this?"

Sarah sat up a little straighter. "Edna may be like family, and she may believe otherwise, but she doesn't control me. I'm going on that cattle drive. I begged my father to let me join him, but it never happened. And then the last few years of his life, he didn't go on them, either. Health issues prevented him from having an active role on the ranch, so he kept himself busy with the business side of things."

Interesting. Everyone really had sheltered her from everything. From what he was seeing, the books were a mess. He was going to have to meet with their bookkeeper to get a clearer picture, but the day-to-day wasn't looking great. Cade was going to track down the previous foreman to see if he could get some insight, because this hadn't happened overnight. If the man was still in Wishing River, Cade would find him.

"Well, this is your ranch now, and you can do what you want," he told her. "I'm sorry to hear that about your dad, though."

"Thank you." She gestured at the papers on the desk. "How are...things? I'm embarrassed to admit that I know next to nothing about the ranch's finances. I meet with the bookkeeper and accountant but don't actually know the everyday side of things."

"It's not that complicated, actually. And while it's not good, it could be a lot worse." He nodded at the computer screen. "It's pretty much the same system they had over at the Donnelly ranch, just on a bigger scale. Last year, Ty and I switched it over to something newer that I'd like to try here. It'll be a lot of work initially but in the long run will save us time, and we'll even have better records."

She nodded, leaning forward.

He knew none of that would mean anything to her without an explanation. "Right now, we're tracking the essentials. With the new system, we'll easily be able to go way beyond grazing records, rainfall, and water testing and easily track things like calving times, breeding times, pasture usage, input costs, feed, medical costs, labor, and on and on," he said, clicking through the screens as he spoke.

"That's amazing," she said, leaning back and smiling at him.

He gave her a nod. He was proud of the system he'd introduced over at the Donnellys', and it made him feel like he was bringing something few other ranchers could.

She tilted her head slightly, and those gorgeous eyes of hers seemed to look right through him, searching for something he was pretty damn sure he didn't have. "I know you've worked on a ranch out here in Wishing River—did you grow up on a ranch, too?"

He finished his hot chocolate and placed it on the desk, averting his gaze. "No. Far from it."

"Oh, well, you must really love it. It's a hard profession to just jump into."

He gave her a nod and fixed his gaze on the computer screen. "It's getting pretty late. I'll probably be here for a couple more hours. If you want to stay, I can go through this with you?"

Not wanting to be rude, he tried to keep the defensiveness from his tone. He needed to help her, to do his job, and nothing more. He didn't want to share his past, and he didn't want to risk knowing more about hers. He already found her attractive, but if he got to know her, it would be harder to keep his distance, which was vital with their current roles at the ranch. She needed to remain his boss and nothing more.

A tinge of pink appeared on her cheeks, and she stood abruptly. "Like I said, I don't want to slow you down. I know you have an early start tomorrow. We all do. Maybe when things settle down in a bit and you have some more free time, you can show me what you're going over?"

Guilt pricked his conscience. "I will. I promised I'd have you ready to run this ranch in a year, and I'll make sure you are."

She smiled. "Good night," she said before opening the door and leaving.

He let out a breath and forced himself to get back to work, but his gaze lingered on the family pictures in front of him, and he realized what was so strange about the photos—there were repeated ones of Sarah at different ages, her parents at different ages, but there was only one picture of that boy he was assuming to be her brother.

He glanced at his empty mug of hot chocolate and mentally chastised himself for caring about any of this. Cade was a worker, an employee—he always would be. People like Sarah were owners. He'd best keep his mind focused on who he was, not who he never could be.

Reminding himself that he was here as a foreman and not anything more, he settled in for a night of paperwork.

CHAPTER FIVE

After two weeks of working alongside Cade and all the other ranchers, Sarah was fairly certain she would never be invited into their club of manly cowboys. That was fine. She didn't need to be friends with anyone; she just needed to know what she was doing. Her plan was to continue proving she was just as competent so that when she stepped into a more active role in a year, there'd be some level of respect.

She walked out of the barn after another long day. Loneliness pooled inside her as she headed in the direction of the main house while cowboys headed toward the bunkhouse.

Despite their conversation, Cade was treating her like some kind of royalty instead of just one of the guys. Their night last week in her father's office had made her want to know more about him. It had felt very strange to be sitting there with him, isolated, just talking. Clearly part of the reason she found it strange was because she had no life and talked to no one under the age of seventy, let alone at night. She'd felt a mix of excitement and safety that she'd never experienced before.

But then something had shifted. When she'd asked him about himself, he'd just closed up. She had been embarrassed that she'd pushed too far, even though she hadn't intended on it. She was rusty with people her age and needed to get out way more. He probably thought she was weird for sure. And now he thought she had IBS on top of everything else.

"Cade," she called out, spotting him as he was heading into the canteen for dinner. He stopped and turned around, and her stomach did that fluttery thing she was now accustomed to when he gave her his full attention.

He fit in here better than she did. It was as though he'd always been here. He had a way of making people comfortable around him but still maintaining an air of authority that no one questioned. His greenish-blue eyes were striking against his tanned skin and were just visible under the brim of his cowboy hat as he approached. "Hi. Anything I can help you with?"

That was the other thing. He was over-the-top polite to her. It was always about him helping her with something or making something easier for her. "Yes, that cattle drive next week. Can I get some details? When we're going, what time, what I should bring with me. You know, that kind of thing."

He ran a hand over his jaw. It was unshaven, and when she had a few seconds to daydream, she found herself wondering whether or not she liked the clean-shaven Cade or the stubbly Cade.

It was obvious she'd had way too boring a life and was becoming fixated on a man who saw her as nothing more than an employer—and a helpless employer at that. "I've been meaning to talk to you about that. I'm not sure it's a good idea if you come along with us."

She inhaled sharply. "What? I told you I was coming and you agreed."

He winced. "Yes, but now that I've gotten to know the situation here, I'm thinking it might be too much too soon. That trail through the mountains is pretty damn treacherous."

She straightened her shoulders and took a step toward him. "I'm not a novice rider. I haven't ridden in years up until these last few weeks, but make no mistake—I can ride. I could probably outride you and half these men out here. I know those mountains. We had an agreement, and this is my ranch, so if I want to go on a cattle drive, I'm going."

He shoved his hands in his jeans, his steely gaze not leaving hers. "All right. You're the boss. It's a two-day cattle drive. We leave at four in the morning. I'll get you a list of things you'll need."

"I'm looking forward to it."

"I'll have to redo my cattle drive positions, since I've already picked my team and what position they'll be riding in," he said, more to himself than to her.

"Well then, I'll let you go and get to it."

"Those medical issues you don't want to talk about…it'd be wise to tell me about them before we leave."

It was like Edna sent him her entire lifetime chart from the doctor. She threw her hands in the air. "Mrs. Casey greatly exaggerates many things. Have you seen me sick or tired? I'm perfectly fine."

"Then why haven't you done this before? Why didn't you go out there on last spring's cattle drive?"

She lifted her chin, scrambling because he was asking a lot of questions that she didn't want to give answers to. "Because my mother had just died. I was in no *emotional* condition."

His jaw clenched. "I'm sorry. So what about the year before that?"

She crossed her arms over her chest. "My mother was very ill, and I was here taking care of her. I couldn't very well take off for a few days with no way to be reached."

"What about the year before that?"

"What is the point of this?"

"I'm just trying to ensure that there are no surprises out there—not just for my sake but for yours. You've got a bunch of cowboys going out into the mountains for two days with hundreds of heads of cattle. If you can't keep up or you need help, it's going to be pretty hard to slow down."

She balled her hands into fists. "I won't need

help."

He turned his head, staring out into the distance for a moment, his jaw clenched. "Okay," he said, turning back to her.

She smiled and resisted the urge to jump in the air with excitement. He had no idea what a victory this was. This was the beginning of her new life. "Have a good night," she said before all but running back to the main house.

Triumph washed through her. *Baby steps*, she said to herself as she climbed the back porch steps. Dinner would be waiting for her inside just like it always was at this time, but she didn't want it. She was hungry for something that wasn't food. She was hungry for that life she'd led when she was a child, when Josh was alive. The one that promised her the world could be hers for the taking, the one that had vanished along with her brother.

"Sarah, is that you? I have a wonderful new Paleo stew simmering along with some grain-free biscuits. Wash up and I'll have everything on the table for you," Mrs. Casey called out from the kitchen.

"Smells delicious," Sarah said as she tugged off her dirty boots. The aroma of tomatoes and beef and baking filled the home, and her stomach growled. She'd barely eaten today, and that would sometimes trigger a migraine. She was going to have to be more careful or Cade would second-guess his decision to let her come along. "I'll just take a quick shower and join you in the kitchen," she said as she walked down the hall. Instead of running up the stairs toward the bathroom, she paused outside the living room, her gaze resting on the piano.

She hadn't played in so long. But tonight, the music called to her, and she wondered if it was because of everything that was happening.

Back before Josh died, the piano was her voice, something she and Josh shared. Sometimes he'd sit beside her on the bench and purposefully press the wrong key to be silly. Other times, he'd be horsing around while she played. He'd call out the name of a song and see if she could play it.

Her favorite memory, though, from shortly before the accident, was him lying on the couch, casually tossing his football in the air. But in typical Josh fashion, he threw too hard and the football crashed into the chandelier above, sending crystals all over the floor. When their parents had rushed into the room, she had played a rousing rendition of Beethoven's "Symphony No. 5"—the *dum-dum-dum-duuuuum* one—and then they'd all broken out into laughter.

But that kind of joy died along with him. So she'd stopped playing.

Slowly crossing the large, shadowed living room, she approached the piano and opened the lid on the bench, taking out an old songbook and flipping open the cover. She stared at the picture of her brother she knew would be there and pulled it out.

She tucked the book back in the bench, closed the lid, and sat down. She stared at Josh's picture, into his eyes, and smiled. "You'd be proud of me. Part one of our plan to take over the ranch is happening. I wish you were coming on that cattle drive, though," she whispered.

Letting her fingertips trail over the keys without pressing any of them, she shut her eyes and silently played the song Josh had loved most. She didn't want to share this moment with anyone, and Mrs. Casey would come running if she heard the music.

She had decided not to tell Mrs. Casey about the cattle drive just yet. Cade's continued inquiries about her medical history made her wonder how much the woman had blown her migraines out of proportion this time. They could be bad, sure, but Sarah would just make sure she was prepared and avoided all triggers. She'd have her medication in her pocket at all times, she'd stay well hydrated and would avoid stress. If anything, the fresh air would be good for her.

She closed her eyes and continued playing silently, the memory of the music flooding her senses and drowning out all the doubts in her mind. Just as she'd played for the family, for guests, for audiences when Josh was still alive, she played tonight, without ever pressing a key.

She would never go back to the life her parents wanted for her.

*C*ade cursed out loud in his bedroom. He'd hoped to actually have one early night since moving to Joshua Ranch and had been counting on a solid eight hours. He glanced at the glowing numbers on his alarm clock and realized it was only eight o'clock, but still.

He groaned as he got out of bed and made his way to the door. Judging by the loud pounding, he suspected it was either Dean or Tyler. But he whipped the door open to find Mrs. Casey standing there in her pink velour night-robe, her gray hair in rollers and her face the same shade as her robe.

"Is everything all right?" he asked, holding the side of the door.

She shielded her eyes. "You should put clothes on, young man, before answering the door!"

He glanced down at himself, belatedly remembering he was only in his boxers. "All right. Come on in and I'll go get a shirt and jeans," he said, leaving the door open and walking into his laundry room. Mrs. Casey was a funny one to figure out; she barked orders like a drill sergeant, knocked back whiskey like the best of them, while being as prim and proper as a nun. He grabbed a neatly folded T-shirt and jeans from the laundry basket and made his way back to the front door.

Mrs. Casey was pacing his entrance. "There's been an emergency."

He tensed, even though something told him their ideas of emergencies were two very different things. "Well then, it probably wasn't a good idea to make me waste time getting dressed," he said, putting on his boots.

She pursed her lips. "Well, it wasn't proper to parade yourself."

"What's the emergency?" he asked, not wanting to engage that line of conversation any more.

"Sarah has taken off," she said with a swoop of her hand.

"Like, on vacation?"

She made a sound. "No, on a horse!"

He frowned, slightly concerned now. "Pretty late for a ride."

"Yes! And by herself. You need to go find her. It's dangerous. There are rules; she should know better than this."

Cade frowned. Rules? About when and where she could be outside? Mrs. Casey was probably overreacting, but the story Dean and Tyler told him about what had happened to Sarah's brother popped into his head.

"She'll be fine," he said, grabbing his hat and holding open the door. He attempted to pat her shoulder as she passed him, because he wasn't used to having to reassure elderly women. But she just swatted his hand away as though she were shooing a fly.

It wasn't dark out yet, and he knew Sarah was levelheaded, but the medical stuff Mrs. Casey kept hinting at did make him concerned as well. Sarah really needed to tell him what was going on beyond her vague "don't worry" type of answers. Still, riding alone once night fell wasn't the best idea in the world, and boss or not, he was going to tell her that when he caught up to her.

The thing was, he was sensing something in her changing. She'd made it clear from day one that she was going to take over the ranch, but there was something else happening below the surface. She was frustrated. He knew she was irritated with him and his cattle-drive warning. He'd been trying to just take the easiest route for everyone involved. It wasn't that the men would mind having her…it just complicated things. He was so damn overworked right now that complications only added to his list of problems.

"Well, I can tell you she took the trails that lead toward the mountains. It's ridiculous. Foolish of her to do this. She knows what could happen," Edna muttered as she walked with him.

"I'll catch up to her," he said, heading to the barn. Once he was saddled up, he took the trails Mrs. Casey had mentioned and picked up speed. Sarah must have had a good head start and was riding pretty fast, because it took him a good few minutes at breakneck speed to finally spot her. There was no mistaking, though—Sarah knew how to ride. Her form in the saddle was that of an experienced rider. He'd noticed that on their first day. He wondered if this ride into the mountains had anything to do with her trying to prove herself.

"Sarah! Wait up!" he yelled.

She glanced over her shoulder for a second and then kept going. He had no idea if she was going to listen to him. After another minute, she finally slowed down at a grassy clearing, above a pretty steep bank. There was enough grass for the horses to graze, and the narrower band of water from Wishing River meandered through. He tried not to look as irritated as he felt. "What are you doing?"

She frowned at him. "Going for a ride."

"By yourself?"

"Clearly not, since you're here now," she said, dismounting like a pro. Again, just seeing how comfortable she was around horses reminded him she was no novice, as much as Edna treated her as such.

He dismounted as well. "Edna wanted me to come find you."

She shrugged, walking toward the edge of the bank that overlooked the river. "Edna should know I can take care of myself. This isn't in your job description."

He ignored the jolt of sympathy he felt for her. There was something about her that seemed so lonely. Clearly they weren't really friends, because she thought of him as an employee looking out for his employer. That was the right way to view their relationship, of course—that was all it could ever be. He followed her, sitting down next to her. "Doesn't hurt to have company."

She zipped up the navy hoodie she was wearing and crossed her arms, staring out at the river. "'Company' and 'babysitting' are two different things. I wasn't running away from home like a troubled teen. I just wanted some solitude."

He could relate to that, but what was her reason? A part of him wanted to know more about her, and the other part—the one that cashed checks and made sure he had a roof over his head—told him that would be unwise. Getting tangled up with an employer on a personal level was never a good idea. Look what had happened when his boss was his best friend.

He spread his arms out behind him, leaning his weight on his palms. The grass was prickly and slightly wet to touch. "Probably wise to do it during the day, though."

She let out a sigh and faced him, her green eyes settling on his. "Why are you here?"

"Well, I was trying to get to bed early, and Mrs. Casey started banging down my door like there was a five-alarm fire. Except there's no fire, just you going for a ride by yourself."

She rolled her eyes. "Ugh. I'm so sorry. She's a little over-the-top."

"A little?" He chuckled and crossed one ankle over the other, staring ahead, catching the mingling of pink and purple ribbons across the skyline. "Or maybe she's actually protecting you from something. Have you told her you're going on the cattle drive next week?"

"There's no point in worrying her in advance. I'll tell her the night before. Apparently she's still having nightmares from the scratch on my arm."

He swallowed a laugh. "How is your arm?"

She held it out. "Fine. It was nothing. And now I'm up-to-date on all my vaccines, too."

"See? That's multitasking for you. So now that everything's good and you've seen enough of the sunset, let's go back."

She frowned but made no move to get up. "I'm not going back yet. I want to stay up here and watch the sunset."

He let out a rough sigh. "Fine. It's almost gone anyway."

"No, *I'm* staying here. Not you. I don't need a babysitter. Also, I need to sit with the fireflies a bit."

"Well then, just ignore me. I like a good sunset, too," he said, leaning back and getting comfortable.

She let out a choked sound. "This is slightly humiliating."

"What?"

"This pretend interest you have in the sunset. We both know you're here because of Edna."

"Fine. But just so you know, Edna's the scariest person on the ranch."

She turned to him and burst out laughing.

He didn't crack a smile. "I'm dead serious."

"I guess she is slightly scary. But she's family."

"Family is good."

She chuckled. "I guess. So how have your first few weeks here been? Do you like Joshua Ranch so far?"

The question caught him off guard. He mulled over his answer, listening to the rush of the river, the crickets, and the comforting sounds of the horses nearby. "I do. It's a fine ranch. I can see why you're so proud of it and determined to take over."

The smile she gave him sent a jolt to his gut. Those rich grass-green eyes sparkled, and her full lips parted to reveal a perfect smile. Hell. He forced his gaze back to the river.

"I'm so glad," she said. "I don't know what I would have done without you."

"Seems like those escorts would have helped with whatever you wanted," he said, unable to resist the tease.

She let out a strangled laugh. "Thanks for reminding me. At least you turned out to be the real deal, though I honestly thought you were there for the escort position, too, at first."

He stilled. "What?"

She bobbed her head. "Yep. I was ready to slam the door on you."

"I'll try not to be insulted."

A strange expression flashed across her eyes, and hell if a tinge of pink didn't streak across those high cheekbones. "Well…I mean, you are obviously a good-looking man, and…"

He didn't say anything for a long moment, just let the sound of the water distract him. He didn't want Sarah attracted to him, even though she technically hadn't said that. It would make things more difficult. Hearing her say that she found him good-looking was…not what he wanted. Attraction that was mutual was a hell of a lot harder to control.

Time to change the subject.

He cleared his throat, looking out toward the sunset, the streaks of pink chasing away daylight. "Why don't you tell me why you're really out here?"

She leaned her head back, letting it hang as she stared up at the almost dark sky. "I like to come out here. Sometimes, I wish I didn't have to go back."

His stomach dropped at the honesty of her confession. "Where would you go?"

"Anywhere but where there are memories," she said with a vulnerability that clung to her words and filled him with an ache that he didn't know what to do with.

His mind immediately went to her brother and her parents…and his own past. "In my experience, even if you leave the place, the memories trail behind you regardless of where you are."

She blinked a few times, still just giving him her profile. "They follow you around?" she asked, a slight hitch in her voice as she turned to him.

He wanted to lie to her, because she seemed so alone. He wanted to pretend that you could outrun memories, but he couldn't. He didn't want to be all those other people and give her a pat on the head and tell her everything would be okay. "I've never been able to outrun them—especially the worst ones. They are always there, simmering beneath the surface. On your worst days, they find you; on your best days, they stay hidden. But they're always there. Maybe some people find solace in companionship, being able to share the burden. For me, hard work helps keep everything quiet."

"What kind of memories are you trying to outrun?"

He sat up, uncomfortable with the direction of this conversation. "I'm not outrunning anything, remember? That's you. What are you running from?"

The green of her eyes was shadowed. "Nothing I'm used to talking about."

He swallowed. He shouldn't have asked her that. "Fair enough."

She stared at him for a long moment. He knew better, but it didn't stop the longing to know more about someone, to share in their feelings, from hitting him. Cade didn't share.

"Have you ever felt like you've wasted half your life being someone you don't like?" she finally asked. "Or not the real you but the you others want you to be?"

He let her question hang in the air between them, trying to decide whether or not he should answer. But as much as he hated talking about himself, he couldn't just leave her opening up to him without giving anything back.

He thought for a moment before answering. "I was a person I didn't like for years when I was younger, so I get that. But as far as the person others wanted me to be? No. I had no expectations placed on me." He knew that he was almost making it sound like his parents had encouraged him to be whoever he wanted to be, but the reality was that no one gave a shit enough to even have any expectations. Who cared what he did? Not them. Not then or now. No one knew where he was, if he was even alive. The same went for them, though, because he had no idea where his parents were.

"That's amazing. You're out here living your life, free, just the way you want it," she said wistfully.

He stood, brushing his hands against his jeans. "You make it sound a helluva lot better than it is."

She stood as well, looking up at him. "Do

you know that I don't have a single friend in Wishing River? Or anywhere, actually. Not one. I'm twenty-six years old, and my only friend is a seventy-five-year-old housekeeper."

It was painful to look in her eyes, because the longing there was so real. "So what's stopping you now?"

"I don't know. I never thought about it. Like, what, am I just supposed to walk up to people my age and ask if they want to be friends?"

Sadness stained her eyes, and he was struck by an idea. Oh no. He shouldn't, because it would make things complicated, and his friends would be all over it, but it was wrong for someone her age not to have any friends, or any life, even. He let out a rough sigh. "So next weekend, a friend of mine is throwing his wife a party."

Her mouth dropped open. "You have friends who are married?"

He frowned. "Why is that surprising?"

Her cheeks went red. "Oh, nothing."

"No, I'd like to hear. Believe me."

"It's just…you seem like a single man with single-man friends."

He cracked a smile. "Oh, like escort friends?"

She waved a hand. "See? I'm totally awkward from not being around people my own age. You were saying?"

He smiled. "My friend Tyler's wife is coming home after being away from Wishing River for a year. He's throwing her a big welcome-back party. Her name is Lainey, and she owns Tilly's Diner in town. She's around your age and really nice. Her best friend, Hope, is also going to be there. You three would probably hit it off."

"I…don't want to impose. I can't just show up," she said, even though the excitement radiating from her was palpable.

"Why not? We're not going to be the only people there. Really. I think you'll have a great time. There will be other people from town there, too. You were just saying how you don't know anyone."

"I know, but…going to a welcome-home party for someone and not even knowing them is sad. I'm this lady you work for, tagging along with you."

He shouldn't be affected by the awkwardness in her tone or the sad eyes, but he was. He shouldn't be happy that he'd made her happy. He shouldn't be wanting to see her smile one more time before it was completely dark out.

He took a step closer to her. "I wasn't planning on introducing you as only my employer."

"Well, what were you going to say? Your friend? Are we even friends?"

He didn't know what they were, but it felt as though a line had been crossed. She wasn't just his boss; she was…more. He cleared his throat, coming up with the only possible explanation of what they could ever be.

"Friends. We're friends."

CHAPTER SIX

Friends. We're friends.

Sarah knew she had to stop repeating that in her head. But Cade's deep voice, the gruffness in it as he said those words, played in her head over and over again. Even as she was getting ready to go on her first cattle drive and had way more important things to be thinking about—like how she hoped she wasn't going to make a fool of herself in front of all the men—she was *still* thinking about him.

Cade was different than any man she'd met. He was very different from her father.

She glanced over at the brown cowboy hat on the top shelf in the closet. When her father had died, her mother had told Mrs. Casey to leave it there, that it would not be given away.

Sarah reached into the closet and slowly pulled down his hat. Lifting it to her nose, she breathed it in. Josh would often steal their father's hat when they were little and they'd make a tent in his room, pretending they were on a cattle drive. The worn leather didn't smell like that past, or her father, or any of them.

She ran her finger around the brim of the hat, remembering the man her father was before Josh died. Maybe it was wrong, but on most days, she remembered the man he was after Josh's death, the one who could never quite get it together, the one who was quick to anger, to never think twice about a harsh word or criticism.

That man had become an alcoholic, had become a gambler, and Sarah often wondered whether on his nights away, he'd even cheated on her mother. The arguments between them had been fierce and frequent, and Sarah would spend that time in Josh's room. She'd play with his toys, all the ones she hadn't been interested in before, just to be close to him.

Sometimes she'd sit at his window seat and stare out the window, imagining him outside, remembering what their family had been like when he was still alive. There were family dinners, vacations, lazy summers, and lemonade on the front porch. Their father had infinite patience for them, even for all the mischief Josh would get into. Their mother always had a kind, soft word for them, would kiss their foreheads and tuck them in at night. Sunday mornings would be church and then brunch, followed by an afternoon of riding.

It was far from the life they lived after Josh died. No one had tried to keep it together, even for her sake. As a child, she hadn't realized that, but now as an adult she could feel the stab of resentment sometimes, that they hadn't tried harder for her. Instead they'd left her with awful versions of themselves and, in the end, she was the one who'd cared for them. She would never regret that because despite her anger, she knew they were good people, but they had been broken. They hadn't had the strength to put themselves back together. Maybe they hadn't loved her enough to try.

They had both cried for Josh on their last days, had both wept with the certainty of seeing him again. They called out to him in their turbulent sleep, and Sarah just sat there holding their hands, saying goodbye, praying for them to find peace soon. But she refused to pray to go with them. Instead, she asked to have the strength to continue living without them. She prayed to God that she would one day find her purpose, a man to love, a family to raise. And then she wept with the fear that none of it would ever happen and that she'd truly be alone forever.

When her father died, her mother had turned in to herself even more. She was reclusive and despondent. Sarah tried to get her to go to church, something her mother had always looked forward to, but she refused. She wasn't mean to Sarah, but she was a hollow version of the woman she used to be. Maybe that was what happened when you lost a child, a part of yourself, and then your other half. Maybe you could never be whole again. Maybe the tear was too deep, becoming too cavernous, too wide to ever come back together, even for the people still here.

Sometimes, when her parents argued at night, they'd forget to say good night or that she was even there, and she'd fall asleep on top of Josh's bed. At some point, late at night, Mrs. Casey would come in and cover her with a blanket, and even though she never said it, and even in that first month when Sarah spoke to no one, Mrs. Casey's steady resolve, her unwavering strength, had been a beacon to Sarah.

Not all people changed. Some people could be counted on.

Mrs. Casey had been the only adult she could rely on, even on mornings like this, when she was frowning at Sarah as she strode toward her like a sergeant.

"Good morning. Great day for rounding up some cattle!" Sarah said in an extra-chipper voice, blinking away the beloved image of a younger, softer Mrs. Casey who would hold her when her own parents wouldn't. Like Cade had said, this Mrs. Casey was almost scary, and so hard to deal with, but it was those memories that kept Sarah from ever getting too mad at her.

She also wasn't planning on telling her about the party she'd be attending with Cade if she lived through the cattle drive. Baby steps. Go on cattle drive, kick ass, look tough, don't get a migraine, and then go to a party with your hot new foreman and all his friends.

To say she was nervous at the thought of being

Cade's date, be it real or just so she wouldn't feel like an intruder, was a huge understatement. Cade was…not someone she would have dated had her parents been alive. To meet their standards, he would have had to come from an affluent ranching family, belong to one of the churches in town, and be able to provide a very comfortable life for Sarah. They would never approve of him letting her run the ranch alongside him.

Ridiculous.

Mrs. Casey fussed over the supplies Sarah had packed. "I still don't agree with you risking your life today! It's bad enough you already hurt yourself once. Imagine what can happen out there!"

Sarah quickly picked up her brush and braided one low braid, her gaze on Mrs. Casey's reflection in the front mirror. "Please stop treating me like there's something wrong with me. I'm going to start believing it. In fact, I have kind of believed it for the last decade thanks to my parents. But I'm not going to keep living that way. I've never felt more alive than I have these last few weeks. *This* is the life I want to live—not the one inside this house. You should consider getting a life, too, Mrs. Casey."

She pursed her lips and crossed her arms. "Thank you very much, but I'm just fine here."

"Why? You need friends, too. We all do. Things have to change." She was almost going to suggest she come to the party at Tilly's Diner, but she wasn't *that* altruistic. Also, Cade. It wasn't every day a woman went from having no one to having… someone like him. She couldn't have Mrs. Casey coming along, watching their every move. Not that there would be any moves, because it wasn't a real date. It was a pity invitation from a man who worked for her. That was all.

She picked up the bottle of sunscreen and began generously applying it to her face. Even though it was cool and dark outside now, she knew by midday, the sun would be strong and hot. Her fleece sweater and vest overtop would do the trick for the morning.

Mrs. Casey stood in front of her, hands on her hips. "I have friends. We write letters to one another. More than that is too much effort. Make sure you use enough of that; you don't want to burn."

"It really doesn't matter whether or not I use enough, since I'll probably die before I come home, right?" Sarah asked, unable to resist teasing.

Mrs. Casey gasped. "Why would you say such a thing?"

"Because that's basically what *you've* been saying! Also, writing letters to friends and never seeing them is sad. You need to make some new friends in Wishing River. I'm going to find you some," she said, picking up her bag.

"You worry about yourself, never mind me," Edna said, uncrossing her arms only to wring her hands. "Do you have your medication with you? What's your plan if you get a migraine out there? Those men can't just stop and come back home!"

Sarah had already worried about this but decided the risk was minimal. She rarely had her migraines these days, and if one did strike, she'd take her medication and sit out. She didn't need someone to take care of her, and once her vision returned, she'd be able to make her way back home or she'd sleep it off. But that was worst-case scenario, and she had no intention of letting it get that far. "This is barely even a cattle drive. We won't be gone for days, miles and miles away. Think of it as a mini drive, just moving cattle—"

"You could be killed!"

A pang of sympathy hit her in the chest as she looked at the older woman. She was genuinely worried, not because she wanted to keep Sarah locked up but because Mrs. Casey had believed her parents all these years, and she was just trying to keep Sarah safe. She reached out and gave the older woman a hug. "I'm going to be fine," she said softly. "I'll be back tomorrow. You won't even know I'm gone."

She could do this. She trusted herself, and she trusted that Cade would have her back if she faltered. Time would fly.

*I*t was the longest day of Cade's life, and they were only one hour into the drive.

Trouble had started before Sarah had arrived at the barn. He'd explained the positions everyone would be riding, and he was obviously going to be the point man and lead the team. After a lot of deliberation, he'd decided he was going to have Sarah by his side instead of the next most qualified cowboy. It had been a tough call, but he needed to make sure she was safe. That hadn't gone over too well—he could tell when he was met with silence. But at the end of the day he answered to Sarah, not these guys. And all this land, all this cattle, was hers. They were just a bunch of cowboys.

They still had five miles to go, but the weather was already changing. Clouds were dancing in and around the mountains, and the wind had picked up. He knew the mountain areas because of his work on Ty's farm. It would be even more dangerous if the ground was slick with rain. He was also just getting to know these men, which wasn't ideal on a cattle drive. He'd have liked to be more familiar with all of them first, but he was going to have to make do.

Cows bellowed in the distance, and they slowed as they came to a clearing. Glancing around, he brought his horse closer to Sarah. "How are you doing?" he asked, keeping his voice low.

She turned to him, her cheeks pink and her eyes alive. "Fantastic!"

He couldn't help the slight smile he gave her, but he didn't want to show any coddling behavior, so he quickly schooled his features. "I'm going to try and avoid bodies of water once we have the cattle or they're going to want to stop and drink and not get moving again. Most of them will travel together, since they're herd animals, but there's always a troublemaker or two, and we can't afford to leave anyone behind." Losing a couple cattle meant a couple grand left on the table, and that just wasn't done. You didn't get to go home until all the cattle were home, and that was a fact, as tired as you were.

She nodded, listening attentively. "Okay, got it."

"I'm also hoping we can avoid the rain. Some of those trails in the mountains are brutal at best, and we'll have to go single file. If I think something's too dangerous…"

"Treat me the same as everyone else," she said.

Like hell he would. She wasn't like everyone else. She was inexperienced and far too important to risk. She owned this whole operation—was the sole owner, in fact—and besides, Mrs. Casey would string him up by his toes if he let her get hurt.

"Okay," he said, lying, before starting up again.

There had always been something so awe-inspiring about riding through the open-range country, and Joshua Ranch had almost thirty thousand acres of the nicest land in Montana. With nearly a thousand head of cattle, they had their work cut out for them. But he had never minded hard work. The biggest reward at the end of the day was sitting by the campfire, under the stars of big sky country.

He kind of loved that he was getting to show Sarah that part of this life.

By the time they'd made camp, everyone was dirty and tired. Tomorrow would be the real work, when they started the ride home, after they'd gathered a few of the cattle that were in the mountains. Normally he'd go and find them, but he didn't want Sarah up there on those trails. He was contemplating sending one of the more experienced men, as long as Sarah didn't figure out what he was doing.

He ran his hands through his hair and let his gaze roam their campsite. The rain had held off, so at least they didn't have to worry about that. For now.

After a hell of a day, all the men had scattered, some around the fire, some already lying down. Of course the hell part had been Sarah. Not that she'd done anything wrong—she'd been a trouper out there, and her skill as a rider was obvious. Having a woman out there with them added a different dynamic, though; no one could deny it. They all watched out for her, even though she'd held her own. And for Cade, there was constant worry in the back of his mind that she was going to get hurt and he'd feel responsible. Edna's stern expression kept popping into his mind, and he could practically hear the woman's scary voice warning him to watch over Sarah. He knew Sarah must be wiped tonight—he was, but at least he was used to this.

He glanced over at where Sarah was seated on her sleeping bag, using that bottle of foaming, strawberry-scented hand sanitizer that she kept offering to everyone. She caught his eye and dangled the bottle in his direction.

"No, thanks. I don't like smelling like strawberries."

"Oh. You prefer germs?"

He slowly pulled out his own bottle from his bag and with a slow smile used the lemon-scented cleanser. She laughed softly, and he noticed most of the other men smiled at the feminine sound.

"I guess lemons are manlier than strawberries?"

"Damn straight." He settled back on his sleeping bag. He didn't care how it looked—he'd set himself up beside Sarah. Everyone here seemed like good men, but he hadn't known them that long. He had never been the trusting kind, had never really given men the benefit of the doubt, mostly because the ones in his childhood hadn't left him with the best impression of adults. The only men he'd ever trusted in his life were Dean,

Tyler, and Tyler's father, Martin.

"Sarah, can I have some?" Jesse asked, suddenly appearing in front of them.

Sarah's face lit up. "Of course," she said, squirting his hands a few times. A couple of seconds later, there was an entire damn lineup, and the whole campfire smelled like a strawberry farm. With a self-satisfied smile, Sarah put her bottle beside her pillow.

She looked as though she'd just won the lottery, but he knew by tomorrow night, she was going to be in pain, and the pretty smile would be gone. It was one thing to be a good rider and entirely another to be in the saddle all day, roping, branding, trailing. They had enough men out here and they didn't really need her help, but this was important to her.

This was her ranch, her operation, her right. He admired her for taking ownership, and he had a feeling the other men did, too.

He glanced over at Sarah. She was staring up at the star-littered sky.

"Good night," he said softly.

She turned to him, her eyes glittering. "Thank you."

"For what?"

"For the best day of my life."

Her words hit him somewhere deep inside, catching him off guard, making him want to know so much more. How a woman who had grown up with money, with a ranch to her name, could call this the best day of her life. He wanted to know the loneliness inside her, the one that clung to her words, that glittered in her eyes, which he could understand. She turned abruptly, huddling under her sleeping bag, leaving him staring at the back of her head.

He linked his hands behind his head and rested on his back, Sarah's words echoing through him as he stared at the sky. He'd known the moment he'd met her that there was something different about her, something that spoke to him, or spoke to the man inside him, the one he'd always wanted to be.

This ranch had seemed like the opportunity of a lifetime, but he'd never counted on the people here becoming something more to him. He hadn't been searching for ties or heartache. But Sarah was a woman who had him thinking about all those things. He'd never seen such a mix of sheer will, strength, stamina, and vulnerability.

He'd also never met someone who he was attracted to like this. He'd barely touched her, and yet the moment she walked within his vicinity, something happened to him. He was aware of her on a different level. Having her lying beside him, especially here under the stars and wide-open Montana night sky he loved, made him…happy.

Having her lying beside him also had him thinking about all the reasons he shouldn't be thinking any of this.

He sat up after a half hour and scanned their campground area, noting most of the men were asleep. The fire crackled and sparked, and he lay back down, content that this was the world he'd created for himself. This was a far cry from the life he'd once led. This group of cowboys, the woman sleeping beside him, trusted him. Sometimes the thought of how far he'd come would humble him and other times would raise him up. This life was one that he wouldn't trade in for anything, and he would never jeopardize his accomplishments and his position.

Not for anyone.

*B*y noon, Sarah was wondering if she'd ever make it home. She'd die before asking anyone for help, but every part of her body was aching and she was covered in so much dust and dirt, she was pretty sure it would never wash off. Yesterday had been the best day of her life and today was…a more challenging day, but she wouldn't give this up for the world. It was necessary.

They were waiting for a few of the cows who'd wandered into a pond. No one was wanting to get into the muddy water to chase them out, so they were all trying to be patient.

She turned as Cade approached. How the heck did he manage to look so good and full of energy?

She sat a little straighter in the saddle and quickly tried to brush away some of the dust she felt settling onto her face. Sadly, she was pretty sure she might have unintentionally added mud to it. "How you doing?"

She forced a wide smile. "Great. *So great*."

He gave her a nod like he actually believed her. "We've got two cows up in the mountains and—"

"Let's go get them!"

He took off his hat and mussed up his hair for a moment before putting it back on. Good grief, he was attractive even when he wasn't trying to be. "It's narrow trails up there."

"Great. The narrower the better."

He bent his head and rubbed the back of his neck.

"Come on, Cade. You wouldn't think twice if I was your friend Tyler."

He clenched his jaw for a moment and then nodded. "Fine. But I call the shots, and you have to listen to me."

She placed her hand over her heart. "I promise. I won't cause you any problems."

Something flashed across his eyes. "Fine. We leave in five minutes."

She held on to her squeal of victory and sat silently and watched as he went over to a group of the cowboys. She assumed he was telling them his plans. Trying not to look obvious, she watched to see if anyone looked upset. But they all seemed nonplussed, and a few minutes later, Cade was signaling to follow him.

They took off in the direction of the mountains. Sarah drew a long, deep breath and allowed herself to acknowledge the magnitude of what she was accomplishing. The land that stretched around them wasn't for the weak or the faint of heart; this was land that could break a person. But she was here, she was riding with the toughest men, and she was keeping up. This was only the beginning for her—she would keep learning and trying until she was just as valuable a team member as any of the cowboys.

She loved it.

Cade paused at the foothills of the mountain, his profile to her, his back straight. He looked as though he belonged here. He was completely at home with his surroundings, his body as powerful as the rugged terrain that surrounded him.

She glanced up at the sky, squinting against the sun, and her breath caught as a feeling washed over her. Josh. This was supposed to be their dream, their job. But as Cade turned to her, his jaw set and his features hard, she knew that this was right where she should be. That Cade was supposed to be here. Somehow, she felt like Josh would approve.

"Let's go."

Sarah nodded and kept her eyes on the trail. Pretty soon, there was no time to be thinking of

Josh or anyone as Cade located the two cows. "We can take that trail back down, but we're going to have to split up so they don't get jammed on the narrow trail that follows the river. Let your horse take it easy and slow. I know you can ride, but this is different. We could slide down that slope into the river with just one misstep," he said, his voice grim.

Sarah nodded.

"I don't want to leave you behind me, but I have to be the one to lead," he said. A gust of chilly wind swirled around, and the cows bellowed. She knew they had to go.

"Don't worry," she said, not letting her nervousness show.

He looked worried. "Okay. Be careful. Call out if you need help."

She nodded, and in a few minutes, they began their descent. Her stomach was in knots, but she kept her eyes fixed on Cade's form ahead, the cows between them, and slowly followed along. Rocks tumbled down into the valley beside them in a disconcerting, erratic manner as they rode along. She did as Cade instructed and let her mare do the work, trusting that they would manage without slipping down that hill.

By the time they reached flat land, her muscles ached with pent-up tension. "We did it," she said.

He gave her a smile, and his eyes shone with... something. "We did. Now, let's see if we can catch up with everyone else," he said, tilting his head in the direction of the ranch.

"How many miles until we reach home pasture?"

He grimaced. "You don't want to know. We'd better get started."

She nodded, trying to look as though she wasn't worried at all.

Sarah was pretty sure that by the time she reached her house, she'd be crawling up the stairs. If she'd thought she was exhausted when she woke that morning, the rest of the second day tore her apart. Everything was on fire. Each step away from the barn and toward the main house took so much energy that she didn't think she could keep going.

As soon as she was out of eyesight of the men, Sarah let her shoulders fall and slowed her walk, trying not to curse out loud with each step. Her palms were blistered and close to bleeding, her legs felt like they were a mix of fire, and her joints were so stiff that just the thought of having to climb the stairs made her want to cry, because swearing in the house wasn't an option.

She stole a glance behind her, seeking out the figure of one man among all those cowboys. She spotted Cade immediately, not going in the direction of the bunkhouse or his house, instead striding toward her. His hat was pulled down low, but he moved with the same grace and strength as always. You would never think they'd just been on the same cattle drive. She tried not to hate him for it.

"Hi," he said as soon as he was within earshot.

"Hi," she said.

"I, uh, I just wanted to say that you did good out there; you should be proud of yourself. Get a good night's sleep. Tomorrow you're going to hurt like hell, but that satisfaction of what you accomplished will help you get through it—along with some ibuprofen. It's a pleasure to work alongside you."

That praise pierced her in the heart. This man she barely knew had offered her more praise in two weeks' time than her parents ever had. She had accomplished so little the last ten years and now, here she was, pursuing her dreams, not failing, not scared. "You too. Thank you for never patronizing me or holding me back. This was very personal for me," she said, holding his gaze.

"I get that. So…I'll pick you up tomorrow around seven?"

"Tomorrow?"

"The welcome-back party," he said.

Right. That was tomorrow. She wasn't sure she'd even be able to walk tomorrow, let alone go to a party. "Yes, uh, of course. Looking forward to it," she said, alarmed that her voice sounded breathy. It wasn't a date.

"Me too." He reached forward and gently grasped her wrists, and her breath caught in her throat as he slowly turned them over, looking at her hands. Her palms were blistered and dirty. He held her hands gently in his larger ones and winced. "Take a long, hot shower and clean these out, then put some kind of balm on them. Drink a lot of water, have dinner and ibuprofen. You'll wake up feeling like a new person."

Her breath was caught somewhere between here and the reality of how easy it would be to fall for this man. He didn't coddle her like everyone else. He hadn't dismissed her—he'd helped build her up into the beginnings of the person she wanted to be. He hadn't judged her, hadn't made her feel inferior—he'd encouraged her and he'd helped her. No, he'd given her everything she'd ever wanted since he'd come to work here, so many dreams come true.

With that, he gave a small tip of his hat, and her throat constricted painfully as she stared into his eyes, shadowed under the hat's brim. He turned and strode back toward his house, broad shoulders, lean form, walking as though there wasn't an ache in his entire body…and he became the star of every single fantasy she'd ever had about the kind of man she wanted. She placed her hand over her racing heart. Wow.

The screech from the house, followed by the

sound of the screen door bouncing against the frame and Mrs. Casey running toward her, lurched Sarah back into the reality of her actual situation and not her fantasies about Cade.

"What happened to you? Are you injured?"

"I'm fine," Sarah said, her hand dropping from her chest. She forced herself to keep walking because she was afraid if she stopped for much longer, she'd need a stretcher to get her into the house.

"You were clutching your heart as though you were having chest pains."

She wasn't even allowed to have a five-second fantasy? Not that she was admitting what she'd been thinking to Mrs. Casey. "I was on a cattle drive, not high tea—of course I'm going to look like a wreck."

Sarah walked up the back steps, her knees protesting the movement. She could barely even think straight at this point. She also wanted to keep replaying what Cade had said to her and what it had felt like when he'd stood so close and touched her. Or last night, when he'd slept beside her. She hadn't felt so…safe like that since she was a child.

"Your parents would fire me on the spot if they knew I let you go on this."

She whipped herself around, using up the last bit of strength she had to defend herself and her dreams. Mrs. Casey had to move down one step because she'd been following Sarah so closely. "My parents are gone. It's bad enough that I had to live my life according to their expectations when they were alive; I'm damn well not going to do it now that they're dead. From now on, I will be going on all cattle drives, and I will be involved with all aspects of this ranch, just as my father was."

She wasn't in the mood to sugarcoat things, and she was tired of having to explain and defend herself every single day. Marching—or attempting to march—into her bathroom, she shut the door behind her and let out a small gasp as she caught her reflection in the mirror. Part of her hair was matted down, and what was left of her braid hung limply from her head. Her face was dusty, her eyes rimmed with red, her lips chapped. She took a deep breath and started the shower, turning the knob until it reached a steaming hot temperature.

She stared at the beginnings of the calluses on her palms that Cade had noticed, wondering what else he'd seen. Cade was unlike any man she'd ever met before. He was unlike any person she'd ever met.

But it was more than that—it was the way he made her feel. He was undeniably, completely, and wholly masculine in a way that made her very aware of her femininity in the best possible way.

Pity invitation or not, she couldn't wait for tomorrow night.

CHAPTER SEVEN

$\mathcal{S}$arah walked into her parents' bedroom, a wave of familiarity and nostalgia overwhelming her. She rarely came in here. It was silly, maybe. She hadn't gotten rid of their things, so it looked as though time stood still.

Her mother had assumed that Sarah would one day take this room, but she didn't think she'd ever be able to. Memories clung to the air like moths to a flame, and it was hard to catch a breath. At one time, this had been a happy room. It had been the place she and Joshua would come tearing through when he was chasing her around the house, or on Saturday mornings, they'd all watch television on her parents' big king-size bed.

But after Josh died, that energy, that happiness had vanished so quickly, she wondered if she'd actually dreamed that part of her childhood. How could happiness disappear in seconds? How could life change in seconds? The entire course of their family had changed faster than a clap of thunder.

She walked farther into the large room, the plush carpeting soft under her feet, silent. The room was spotless, the large bed meticulously made, the soft-blue-toned quilt without a wrinkle. Opening her mother's wooden jewelry box, she took a deep breath and then shut it, looking at herself in the mirror over the dresser.

"What are you doing, Sarah?" she whispered to her reflection. She was going out with Cade, a man who made her remember that she was a woman. She had never wanted to be treated differently, and he didn't. Cade made her feel safe and alive and young. Why had she been feeling so old? Maybe because she'd basically been in confinement for more than a decade and had lost touch with the real world.

Tonight was some kind of sad attempt at her reintegrating with normal society, she supposed. Okay, so what did normal people her age wear? It wasn't like she didn't have an Instagram account or anything, but what did people her age wear to a party at a diner in rural Montana? Jeans. Check. But what about her hair? Makeup? She had a few things she'd ordered online after watching a makeup tutorial. She'd also ordered a wide-barrel curling iron, so she could attempt some beachy waves. She'd done that last week when Mrs. Casey had offered to lend Sarah her hair rollers she slept with at night.

It was clear at that point that Sarah needed major life changes, fast.

It was time to enter the real world. She opened the jewelry box again and carefully picked through the simpler items, looking for the locket. *There*. At the bottom of the box. She didn't open it to see the picture she knew was inside—just carefully clasped it around her neck. Another step closer to reclaiming her life on her own terms.

Thirty minutes later, she was actually smiling at herself because she'd accomplished the beachy waves without any significant mishap other than the slight burn on her thumb. Better the skin on her thumb than a hair emergency. Her navy and white, small-checked shirt was tucked into her new dark skinny jeans and the red lipstick she was wearing was bright enough without being totally *look at me*. Mascara done and a little blush and she was ready to go.

She spun around, ready to head downstairs, and gasped as Edna stood in the doorway, her brows drawn together tightly. "You scared me!" Sarah laughed.

"I'm sorry. I came to tell you that Cade is here."

Sarah's stomach jumped. "Oh, I didn't even hear the doorbell. Thank you."

"You told me you were going to a friend's party in Wishing River. I didn't realize it was with Cade."

Sarah stood a little straighter. "We both know I don't actually have any friends. These are Cade's friends."

"You don't know what kind of people they are."

Sarah rolled her eyes. "She owns Tilly's. Her husband is the son of the rancher Cade used to work for. I don't think it can get any safer or smaller-town than that," she said, walking forward but stopping when Mrs. Casey didn't move out of the doorway.

"Sarah, child…"

"I'm an adult."

"Yes, and before your mother died, she made me promise to look out for you, to guide you. That is all I'm doing. Cade is not a man I would consider a proper…boyfriend."

Sarah gasped. "He's not my boyfriend, and that's an incredibly rude thing to say about him. He's been the best thing to happen to us in years. I know what I want. I've lived in this house for too many years, abiding by rules made by people even more screwed up than I am."

Mrs. Casey inhaled sharply. "You should not speak of your parents that way."

Sarah took a deep breath and closed her eyes momentarily. "I know that my parents did the best they could. But doing their best wasn't the best, not for me or them or any of us. They were killing themselves with misery, and they were killing *me*. I will never live like that again. I will never be half alive again. It's a dishonor to Josh's life. This is my time—I'm not going to spend it cowering in a corner, knitting away the best years of my life every Saturday night."

Sarah slid past her, but Mrs. Casey followed close on her heels. "You don't know what kind of a man he is. Men have expectations, Sarah. They don't just take women out to be friends."

They weren't going to have this conversation, and especially not with Cade waiting downstairs. "We *are* friends. I'm his employer. This is a platonic relationship. There are no expectations, and I think it's pretty insulting that you would even suggest that."

Mrs. Casey worried her hands. "Sarah. Things are moving too fast. There are too many changes…"

A pang of guilt dampened Sarah's irritation. Mrs. Casey was a good woman who took her perceived guardian role very seriously. She reached for the woman's hands. "All of this only seems fast because everything around here moved too slowly for too long. I've put everyone's needs ahead of my own for too long. I know you mean well, but you need to let me go. Let me *live*."

Mrs. Casey's face crumpled. "You are like my own," she whispered, a softness to her voice that wasn't usually there.

Suddenly Sarah saw the woman as she once was—the much younger face, the one without lines of worry, without the sternness brought on by tragedy, as she spoke to Sarah after Josh died. She saw that worry in her eyes, the same as when Sarah couldn't speak for months.

She clutched Mrs. Casey's hands in hers. "You have always been family to me. I know we don't talk about it, but I remember everything you did. You were my only constant. When I didn't know what to expect even from my own parents, I always knew what I could expect from *you*. I will always be grateful."

She pulled the woman into a hug. Mrs. Casey stepped back a moment later, blinking away the rare display of emotion in her eyes.

"Then just…don't come home too late. And use the head God gave you."

Sarah smiled. "Well, it's the only one I have, now, isn't it?" She wanted to add that she had to leave because the hottest man she'd ever met was waiting for her downstairs, but she thought that might send Mrs. Casey to the ER with heart palpitations. Judging by the red on her cheeks, this was already too much rebellion and shared emotion for her to handle.

Mrs. Casey's worried gaze went from her eyes to the opening of her shirt. Sarah held her breath, knowing she hadn't done anything wrong but not wanting to be chastised for the locket. She didn't need any of this. Not tonight.

"Josh's locket," Mrs. Casey whispered, her eyes misting.

Sarah touched it. "I'm not going to keep him hidden away anymore," she said in a firm voice before walking out of the room. Beyond the door, she took a deep breath and let it out as a sigh, shaking off the weight of this house, of her family, of all the memories threatening to bury her. She could do this. With her head held high, she descended the stairs—

Only to come to a halt on the bottom one when she realized that Cade was there, watching her.

"Second thoughts?" he asked with a slow smile that made her stomach swirl and made her almost forget the conversation she'd just had with Mrs. Casey. She tried not to stare, but he looked even hotter than usual. He had cleaned up for the occasion. His jeans were dark and hugged his lean, athletic build in an altogether fantasy-inducing way, and his button-down shirt seemed to empha-size his broad shoulders and flat stomach. He had shaved, too, and his hair was neatly combed. He was…mouth-watering. And way beyond her current experience level.

"Never. I just appear to be the first twenty-six-year-old with a curfew."

He barked out a laugh, and she smiled at the sound as she slipped on her new shoes. The heels were a good choice beside Cade's height. While he'd still be a few inches taller, at least she wouldn't have to crane her neck just to look him in the eye all night. He held the door open for her, and she glanced over her shoulder as they left and saw Mrs. Casey walking down the stairs, an over-whelmed expression on her face.

Sarah could relate.

She took a deep breath once they were outside, letting the gentle warmth of the evening air fortify her.

"How are you feeling?"

"You were right about the ibuprofen. I've been medicating every eight hours," she said with a laugh.

He smiled warmly as they settled in his truck. "Good. Your hands better, too?"

She nodded, glancing down at them. "The cream helped. It'll take a bit for them to get back to normal, but all in all, I'd say my first cattle drive was a success," she said, leaning back on the headrest.

He glanced over at her, and her stomach fluttered. "You were great."

She let that sink in, let all of what was happening sink in. This man was changing everything for her, and he had no idea.

They drove toward town, and she let the excitement fill her, without guilt or worry. Tonight, she would have fun. She was going to enjoy being out with the only man who had treated her like an equal since her brother was alive.

Half an hour later, Cade held the door open to the packed Tilly's Diner, and when Sarah walked through, a group of men and women immediately flocked over to join them. She tried to shake off the unexpected anxiety that washed over her, but she was basically crashing an event that was meant for friends and family, and she was neither.

Despite what she'd said to Edna, she didn't know if she and Cade were friends. It had been easy enough to play this off as him introducing her as his friend when it was just the two of them, but this…this was another side of him. This was his real life, his real friends, and she didn't know how she fit into it. Had he mentioned her to them?

"Guys, this is Sarah Turner, a…friend, and also the owner of Joshua Ranch," he said.

Ignoring the pang of insecurity, she held her smile as he ran through the names of his friends. While their faces were familiar, she didn't know any of them, but they all greeted her with a friendliness that seemed genuine.

She had probably been to Tilly's once or twice when she was younger, so her memories of the place were vague. It had a vintage charm to it with old-school vinyl-backed chairs and a large bar with vinyl stools. She did notice a wonderful assortment of bright watercolor paintings of some local landmarks. That definitely seemed out of place for a rural diner but very charming.

The place was already packed with people, and there was an excited buzz to the air. A giant banner that read WELCOME HOME, LAINEY hung in the opening of the window that separated the front counter from the kitchen.

"Lainey, welcome back," Cade said, reaching forward to give the pretty young woman a hug.

She pulled back after a moment. "I'm happy to

be home," she said, smiling. Tyler, the handsome man beside her, put his arm around her shoulders and kissed her temple.

"The longest year of my life," Tyler said with a laugh and pulled her closer. They were a very cute couple.

"I hear you've left the ranch?" Lainey asked Cade.

Cade nodded and looked over at Sarah. "Yep. I'm working at Sarah's ranch now."

Sarah watched Cade's expression closely, but his handsome profile didn't reveal an ounce of irritation at the mention of her being his boss.

"How was Italy? School?" Cade asked Lainey.

The woman's face glowed. "It was amazing. I learned so much, I met so many great people, and you'll be pleased to know I have a lot more Italian dishes coming to the diner menu."

Cade broke into a wide grin, and Sarah made a mental note that Italian food was his favorite. Maybe she could request Mrs. Casey make some for him. "You know I'll be here," he said.

"Speaking of, you guys help yourselves to the food. It's all set up buffet-style, so feel free to dig in whenever," Tyler said.

"Well, I'm starving," Cade said. "Do you want to go grab some food?" he asked, turning to Sarah.

She nodded, relieved that he wasn't going to leave her here with his friends. She knew she should push herself to mingle, but the awkwardness was holding her back. "Definitely. Thanks," she said, shooting his friends a smile before walking with Cade to the buffet.

A large spread of different green salads, ribs, baked beans, roast beef, mac 'n' cheese, garlic bread, and lasagna was set up along the diner bar. Cade handed her a plate and then took one for himself. "There are some must-haves in this buffet," he said, stopping at the lasagna and picking up the spatula. "Starting with this."

He proceeded to slide the spatula through to two precut slabs of lasagna, perfectly place them on his plate, and smile triumphantly. There was a boyishness to his smile that she hadn't seen before and that she found adorable—and that was a word she'd never use to describe someone like him. She eyed the food, and while she normally adhered to a gluten-, sugar-, and dairy-free diet in an attempt to keep her migraines at bay, she didn't want to do that tonight. She wanted to be like everyone else. She wanted to be like the other women in this room, like Cade's friends.

"That's impressive," she said at the heaping plate. "I take it you're not a fan of low-carb eating?"

He grinned sheepishly. "I'd rather go on back-to-back cattle drives, in the pouring rain, without coffee, than give up carbs."

She laughed as she scooped up one of the salads with arugula and tomatoes and then a piece of the lasagna. "I like your logic."

They made their way back to Cade's friends, who were seated at a table by the window, next to some very loud, very excited older women.

"So, Sarah, Cade tells me you've taken over the ranch," Tyler said with a friendly smile.

"Well, trying to. It's a process." She shifted in her seat and took a sip of the Italian wine Tyler had poured for all of them. It was one thing for Cade to know that she had no idea how to run a ranch, but it felt pathetic to let others know.

"She's doing great. A natural. In no time, she'll be running circles around us," Cade said before shoveling a piece of lasagna into his mouth. She had no idea how he still managed to look attractive inhaling forkfuls of food that large.

"Did you go to high school here?" Lainey asked.

Sarah shook her head, holding her glass of wine tightly. "I was homeschooled."

"Oh, wow. Well, I guess you were spared from all the teen drama that comes with high school," Hope said with a warm laugh.

Sarah nodded, smiling. "That's one way of looking at it." The truth was that she always wished she went to high school. If her parents had allowed her to mingle with people her age, she might not have been so lonely. She might have met girls like Lainey and Hope. She might not have felt so awkward here tonight.

"So how do you like working with Cade?"

Tyler said, raising his eyebrows.

Sarah looked up at Cade, who was almost glaring at Tyler.

"Great. He's been great. I don't know how we would have gotten along without him."

"My father still cries over him leaving," Tyler said with a laugh.

Hope put down her phone and was scrambling to get out of the booth. "I'm so sorry, Lainey. Worst best friend ever," she said, standing up and holding her arms out to hug Lainey.

"As if. What's wrong? Is Sadie sick again?"

Hope shook her head, her eyes filling with a sadness that seemed like it went way beyond whatever was happening with this Sadie person. "No, my mother isn't feeling well. I should get back."

"Okay, go. Don't worry about me—I'm fine. We will have tons of time to catch up. I can drop by tomorrow and hang out with the two of you, okay?"

Hope nodded. Sarah watched the interchange with interest but tried not to look nosy.

"I can drive you back," Tyler said.

"No, no. I'll call a cab," Hope said.

"I wouldn't feel right about that. We drove you here," Tyler said, standing.

"We both know there's only one cab in town, and it'll take him an hour to get here. I can drive you home. I have to be at the hospital in a couple of hours anyway," Dean said, standing.

Hope's face turned red. "I don't want to inconvenience you."

"Not a problem," he said.

They stood side by side stiffly as they said their goodbyes to everyone.

"That should be a fun car ride," Cade said under his breath.

"Ten bucks says they don't say a word the entire ride to Hope's house," Tyler added.

"You guys are horrible," Lainey said with a laugh. "I'm pretty sure one day those two will see eye to eye."

Cade smiled at Sarah. "It's a long story, and I'd be happy to tell you when Lainey isn't sitting here and able to report back to Hope."

Lainey burst out laughing. An older man and lady approached their table. They were a charming couple. He walked with a cane and, despite his age, he still had retained the good looks of his youth. The woman was slightly plump and very cute in her fuchsia dress and matching shoes.

"I hope you're having fun, dear," the gentleman said, his voice slightly unclear but carefully articulated.

"I am. This is so wonderful, Martin. All of you did way too much," Lainey said.

"Sarah, this is Martin, my father, and Mrs. Busby, a close family friend," Tyler said, and they exchanged greetings.

"So you're the one Cade left us for," Martin said with a wink.

Sarah laughed. "Sorry about that."

They spent a few more minutes talking, and then Tyler and Lainey excused themselves to go mingle with the rest of the guests. An attractive young woman waved to Cade, and he stood. "I'm going to go catch up with an old friend. Are you okay on your own for a few minutes?" he asked.

She looked up at his handsome face and searched those aqua eyes for something…some hint that there might be something between them. Her smile dipped along with her stomach because there wasn't a flicker there. She picked up her wineglass and made a salute, forcing a smile again. "Of course I am. I'm going to check out that dessert buffet soon."

He gave her a wink. "Sounds good."

She watched him work through the crowd and ultimately end up with the woman, who threw her arms around him. He hugged her back, and the two of them spoke, looking completely at ease.

She sipped her wine, leaning back in her chair, letting her gaze slowly wander the room. Laughter and chatter floated around her, hovered, but never came back to her table. There were young people and older people and everyone was alive, happy. Resentment sliced through her, its unfamiliar sting immobilizing her. She resented her parents for not only ruining their own lives but for ruining hers. Staring at Cade and the woman, she knew she wanted to be her. She wanted to be that woman who was so comfortable throwing her arms around him. She wanted to be able to walk through a crowd and chitchat and know people. All these people were her neighbors in some way, and she barely could recognize a familiar face.

She toyed with the locket, willing some of that courage she had as a child to come out tonight. Taking over her family's ranch was step one in her mission to reclaim her life. Step two would be getting a social life.

CHAPTER EIGHT

"Ready to go?" Cade asked, finding Sarah after an old friend had talked his ear off. He'd felt bad to leave her, but he'd been confident that she'd be okay in this crowd.

"Yes," she said, standing from the booth. After saying goodbye to Lainey and Tyler, they made their way outside. The sound of rolling thunder in the distance and the flash of lightning made Sarah jump.

"Looks like we're in for a storm," she said, looking up at the sky.

"We could probably use some rain."

"I like your friends," Sarah said once they were settled in the truck and on the road again.

"Thanks." He glanced over at her before turning his eyes back to the road. There was something off with her. She'd been excited to come with him tonight, but something must have happened during the party. After his friends had left the table, she'd seemed to withdraw.

It was a new crowd for her, but everyone had been welcoming, and she laughed and joked with his friends and fit in fine. It had bothered him to see her by herself. She'd plastered a smile on her face and sat at their empty table and hadn't budged. "Lainey and Hope really liked you," he said. Hell, he didn't know how to tell someone to get out more, but she needed friends, women her age. It wasn't right for someone so young to be living the way she was.

"Really? How do you know?" She was staring at him expectantly, and he realized this actually meant a lot to her.

He racked his brain, trying to think of something that wasn't contrived. Truth was, Lainey and Hope were just nice people and so was Sarah. He didn't actually know that they really liked her, but he wanted to put her at ease. "They're not usually that chatty with just anyone."

She sat back in her seat with a smile on her face. "How did you guys all meet? Did you go to high school together?"

He clenched his teeth for a moment, that wave of embarrassment that he always felt for not having finished high school the regular way coming into his mind. "I didn't go to high school in Wishing River right away. By the time I came to town, I had dropped out. I decided to start working instead. I did end up going to high school with them for my last year."

He didn't *decide* to start working full-time. He had to. There were no other options for him when he left his grandfather's home. It was Martin who forced him back to school, to get his diploma.

He caught the flicker of surprise or maybe pity that swam through her eyes, and a part of him wished her eyes weren't so expressive. Pity was the last thing he wanted from Sarah. "Oh. I get not being in school. Sounds like we didn't miss much?"

He knew she was trying to be sweet and make him feel better, but instead it reminded him of how different they were, how different their backgrounds were. But it wasn't her problem that he didn't have parents around. He cleared his throat and kept his eyes on the road, turning the windshield wipers on as the rain started. "Did you like being homeschooled?"

She shrugged. "I missed hanging around other kids, but I didn't realize that until about a year later. I was in no condition to go to school…for a long time."

A jolt of sympathy for her twisted in his stomach. He knew she must be referring to when her brother died. He glanced over at her. "So you were out of school for a while?"

She tucked a few strands of hair behind her ear. "Some stuff happened in our family, and I left school for a few months. I wasn't ready to go back and I didn't want to. My parents were fine with it, and then my mother thought of homeschooling. It seemed like the right thing at the time. It wasn't until later that I realized just how lonely I was. Then there are times like tonight, when I see a group of people together, that I wish I'd had more of a social circle. Yours is great."

That hung there between them, and he wanted

to know more, but he also knew that would be opening a can of worms. Because when people started sharing secrets, they got closer, and he and Sarah couldn't get closer. "I met Dean and Tyler here, and we became fast friends. Lainey and Hope were best friends, but they were younger than us, so we didn't actually hang around together until Lainey and Tyler got together."

"Really? You seem to all know one another so well."

"It's a small town, so even though we didn't go to school together, we all knew of one another. Lainey, we knew because of the diner. Same with Hope—she was always *at* the diner visiting Lainey. She got married pretty young to a really good guy, they had a baby, and…he died a few years later."

She let out a small gasp. "That's so sad. Oh, I feel so bad for her. She's so young. That's why she had to leave tonight? It's just her and her little girl?"

He kept his eyes on the road. He'd always liked Lainey's friend Hope. He also liked how she spoke her mind and didn't take crap from anyone. Maybe she'd learned the hard way about that, being on her own with so much responsibility at a young age. "It is sad. She's a pretty strong person, and she managed to keep it all together. She's running her business as a naturopath and raising her little girl, Sadie."

"Wow. That's amazing. What about Dean? He's

a doctor, isn't he?"

He smiled slightly. "He is. He's also a rancher. He comes from one of the wealthiest ranching families in Montana, and he's also a doctor over at the hospital."

"He's not married?"

He shook his head. "Nope. He's pretty driven, career-wise. I don't even think he has the time for that."

"What about Tyler and Lainey?"

He smiled again. "That's a helluva story. Tyler left Wishing River nine years ago. Just picked up and took off. He was my best friend, and I was working at his ranch. His mother had died a few months earlier; they'd been really close. He and his dad had a big argument, and Ty couldn't deal with it. When he took off, Dean and I were pretty pissed at him. Martin, his dad, had a stroke last year, and when Dean managed to track Ty down, he came home. We gave Tyler hell, of course. But it was Lainey who got through to him, managed to repair his relationship with his father, too. Along the way, they fell in love…and got married."

"This is amazing," she whispered.

He glanced over at her. "Really?"

She threw her hands in the air. "All these lives, these friends. I mean, it's, like, *life*. I've been missing out on *life*. First it was the cattle drive, and being out there? That's what I always wanted, what my father did. Then tonight…your friends, their lives, the way they all care about one another, whatever it is that's going on between Dean and Hope…"

He turned to her sharply. "What? Who? Dean and Hope?"

She nodded. "Obviously, but you know that already."

Huh. News to him. "Obviously. So what's stopping you from going after what you want? You have more opportunity than most with that ranch. You're young. There's nothing stopping you from living, is there? I mean, you're a grown woman. Your parents are gone…if they're the ones who were holding you back. What's stopping you from living the life you want?"

She bit her lower lip. "Nothing. There's nothing stopping me."

"Good."

They drove in silence for a few minutes, and he wondered what she was thinking and if she was going to say anything about her family or her parents or exactly why they'd tried to keep her in a cage. This wasn't his business, so he wasn't going to ask. He also wasn't going to spend the night constantly looking at her, admiring how beautiful she was or how he liked the sound of her soft voice or the way she laughed or the way those green eyes seemed to catch and hold on to him.

He was already thinking about her way too much. Last night, after he'd gone home and showered and was happy to be lying on clean sheets in his bed instead of outside, he hadn't fallen asleep right away. Instead, he'd been thinking about Sarah. Replaying the cattle drive, the sheer will he'd witnessed in her. She was strong and capable and smart. She had been fearless. In fact, she'd appeared less afraid at the prospect of riding down that shitty, eroded section of the mountain than she did at Tilly's tonight. She was complicated. She was his boss. And she was so much more. The *much more* was giving him grief.

"I don't want to go home," she said as the turnoff in the direction of the ranch came into focus.

"What?"

Her hand clutched his shoulder, and he was shocked because they didn't usually touch. Or, as little as possible, anyway. The feel of her hand on him reminded him of why he shouldn't put himself in positions where it was just the two of them. It would only fuel the attraction he felt for her, especially with these conversations that told him more and more about her. "Don't take me home. I don't want to go back," she said, her voice whisper-thin, her eyes glued to the road.

Cade gripped the steering wheel tightly, and she dropped her hand. Hell. He kept telling himself he couldn't get involved with Sarah, but the more time he spent with her, the more he wanted to know her. "Why don't you want to go back home?"

"I've never been anywhere or done anything in the last fifteen years. I haven't lived. All those people at that party had real lives. I'm the same age, and I felt like an outsider tonight. I didn't know what to say, what to do. I was more comfortable on the sidelines. I… Don't drive me home. Take me anywhere but there. Please, Cade."

He clenched his teeth and knew he couldn't take her home. It couldn't be him to take her back there. Things he'd suspected about her, all those pieces were coming together. Her desperation clung to her words like fresh dew on the grass at dawn. "Okay. So where are we going?"

She turned to him and gave him a smile as though she'd just won the lottery. Her green eyes sparkled, and damn if her happiness didn't punch him in the gut. "Anywhere! The city! Billings. Where do people my age go? Where did you go when you were my age?"

His brows snapped together. "Oh, well, back in my day, we rode our horses to the saloon and made sure we were home before dark, since there was no electricity."

She burst out laughing, and he found himself smiling despite the fact that she thought he was from a different era. "I didn't mean it like that. So where should we go?"

"All right, let's head into the city."

"Road trip!"

He had no idea who the woman beside him was. Layer by layer, she was coming alive. The night she'd taken out that horse, it was as though something had snapped, shifted, and now she was trying to become someone new. Or maybe she was just trying to be the person she always wanted to be. "When are you planning on going back?"

"Well, you have the weekend off. It's only Friday. So how about tomorrow? That way you still have Sunday to relax and do whatever."

He ran a hand over his jaw. "I'm not sure that's going to look great," he said, trying to choose his words carefully.

"Who cares? I don't. I don't care what anyone thinks of me anymore. I have spent my entire life living by rules made up by well-meaning but horribly flawed people. They are gone now. I'm the only living person in my family. Do you care what people think of you?"

He cleared his throat. "Not particularly, no. But I wasn't thinking of me. I was thinking of you and the guys at the ranch." He was also thinking Edna was going to hang him on her wash line if he stayed away overnight with Sarah.

"No one is paying attention to what I'm doing, and everyone knows you aren't working. They'll assume you went away. I'll text Edna and tell her that I'm going away for the weekend with a friend and that I'll be back tomorrow."

"Sweetheart, you have no friends." Dammit,

he hadn't meant to use that endearment. That was reserved for…well, it wasn't something you said to a woman you were trying to keep your distance from, certainly not one you worked for. Then again, going on a road trip with that person wasn't exactly his smartest move, either.

"That's just rude. You're my friend…right?"

He smiled, despite the fact that he shouldn't be smiling. He should be frowning, wondering how the hell he had gotten himself into this situation. He was now Sarah's only friend. There were so many things wrong with that. "Yeah, I suppose I am."

His life had been fairly simple over at Donnelly Ranch. He'd worked for Martin, and then when Tyler had come home last year, sure, things became a little more complicated, but then they returned to normal again. He, Dean, and Tyler managed to mend broken fences and had picked up on their long-standing friendship quite easily. He didn't have any real or significant relationships with women. He liked women, loved women, and generally they reciprocated that feeling. But he was always very clear—Cade Walker was not a forever-after man. There had only been one woman who had ever made him come close to rethinking that policy, but even then, it was one-sided, and it had ended before it started.

But as he drove down the empty highway, with this woman beside him, he decided that complicating his life might be good sometimes. "All right, *friend*, so you're going to stay in a hotel room with me?"

Even in the dark cab of the truck, he could see the red flood her face. "Well that's what friends do. It wouldn't be a weekend away with a friend if we had separate hotel rooms."

It was going to be hell on earth. "Right."

"Oh, unless you don't want to share a hotel room with *me*. No, right. Of course. I mean, we're friends, like casual friends, not room-sharing friends. That would be uncomfortable. Awkward. Right?"

He ran a hand through his hair. Hell yes, "awkward" might be one word that came to mind. "Okay, we're friends, we've established that. Do you share rooms with guy friends?"

"I don't have any except you, remember? Do you share rooms with girl friends?"

He cleared his throat. "On occasion. But I don't really have women friends."

"Oh. Right. Obviously. I'm cool with that." She looked about as cool as a wildfire.

He kept his eyes on the road. "Anyway, let's just focus on this weekend and our arrangements. Ground rules because we have a professional relationship to maintain."

"Yes. Professional. So what are the ground rules?"

Hell if he knew. He'd never had to make any

list of platonic hotel room arrangements before. "No...clothing gets removed in front of the other person."

She let out a strangled "okay."

"Also, no drunk talking about feelings, attraction, or touching."

"You think quite highly of yourself, don't you, Cade?"

He choked out a laugh. "Hey, I'm just trying to be a gentleman."

"Well, thank you, and rest assured, I won't be peeling your clothes off you in a drunken stupor while professing my undying love and attraction for you."

He didn't know whether to laugh or cry because half that statement—the peeling-his-clothes-off part—sounded amazing right about now. "Fine. I promise not to do the same."

"Perfect. So here's what we can do—drink beer, eat snacks, and watch movies on those special channels."

He choked on his own saliva, then coughed. "What?"

"You know, like the latest releases you have to pay for at the hotel?"

He cleared his throat. Because that's what people meant when they said they were going to watch movies on the "special" channels. "Right. Sure."

They drove in silence for a while, which gave

him time to think about what he was getting himself into. Working at Joshua Ranch wasn't supposed to be him getting involved in someone else's personal life or involved in some kind of mysterious family history. But he *was* getting involved. He was interested in the woman beside him, and he didn't know what to do about it.

He'd driven this highway, all these country roads, alone, broke, and a different man. He'd driven these roads like a child in so many ways. He'd driven this road with friends, with different women, but of all the people he'd driven down this road with, he'd never been more intrigued by a person in his life. He glanced over at Sarah, expecting her to have dozed off, but she was sitting upright, a nervous energy emanating from her as her gaze fixated on the dark skyline out her windshield. "I think I'll tell Edna that I'm spending the night in town with my new friends," she said, digging through her purse and then pulling out her phone.

"Don't you think she'll find it suspicious that I'm gone, too?"

She paused mid-typing. "Well, she might not know because you don't really come around the house on weekends anyway."

"True," he said after thinking about it. "But I also don't want to feel like I'm a sixteen-year-old sneaking out of the house with my girlfriend."

"So let's stick to the original plan, and I'll say

I'm away with friends and you say nothing. I think I'll wait to text her. Maybe she'll fall asleep."

"Perfect."

"How much longer?"

He shrugged. "At least another hour. Of course, if this rain keeps up, it might slow us down a bit," he said, increasing the speed on the windshield wipers.

"Great. I'm starving. Do you know any good places to eat in Billings?"

"Not any places you'd like."

"Those are *exactly* the places I think I need to go."

He frowned. "You want to go to places I know you won't like?"

"Yeah. Those places."

"Why?"

"Well, I'm sure they aren't places I've ever been to, and I'm pretty sure they're exciting places, and that's what I need in my life right now."

His eyes narrowed on the sudden red taillights ahead.

"What do you think that is?" she asked, pointing at the windshield.

He eased his foot off the gas, noticing cars were reversing and pulling U-turns. He was getting increasingly concerned about the rain himself and was very aware of the fact that these country roads would often get shut down due to flooding. As they slowed to a crawl, a roadblock with the sign FLOODED ROAD shone against the headlights. Damn. "Looks like we have to go back," he said, stopping and turning the truck around.

"What?" she whispered.

"Sorry—" He'd been about to say *sweetheart* but stopped himself. He wasn't going to make that mistake twice.

"My one adventure and it's ruined by *flooding*?"

He cringed and racked his brain for something else to do. They drove in silence for a few minutes.

"Wait! There!" She was pointing to a random motel sign in the distance.

He swallowed hard, hoping he was wrong. "What?"

"The Highwayman Motel. Let's spend the night there!"

It was one thing to take Sarah out for an evening and show her some fun places; it was entirely another thing to just hang out in the *Highwayman Motel* for the night with her. It would be...uncomfortable. "Why would you want to spend the night there? Why don't we just go back to the ranch? We can do this any other time."

She didn't say anything for a moment. "Fine. I get it. No worries."

He knew *no worries* meant he should be really worried. "What do you get?"

"Nothing. It's just easier to blow me off like this. *Another time* will never happen, as if we're going to plan a weekend away together, Cade. It's fine. It's not like I haven't been anywhere for more than a decade or anything. It's not like I've basically been a prisoner on my family ranch and had a chaperone forever. It's not like we didn't already agree to do this. It's not like—"

"All right. Okay," he said, his voice sounding harsh to his ears.

Sarah huffed. "Well, don't make it sound like I'm twisting your arm."

He was pulling into the motel a minute later, wondering when he became such a softie. "You're not twisting my arm. There's nothing I'd rather be doing on a Saturday night than going to the Highwayman Motel."

"Really?"

He gave a stiff nod. It might have been that point in the night, when she smiled at him like he was the only person who had come through for her in a long time, that he knew he was in trouble. It wasn't the way she looked at him; it was the way he *felt* when she looked at him. Something he hadn't ever felt before.

And hell if that didn't put him on high alert.

CHAPTER NINE

"Okay, I'm ready," Sarah said.

Cade picked up a lousy bottle of whiskey from the grocery shelf and turned around to see Sarah standing there with at least five different bags of assorted chips, some toiletries for both of them, and a big smile on her face. He found himself smiling back. If they were dating, he'd think she was the most easily pleased woman he'd ever been on a date with. They were in a gas station convenience store after deciding they needed snacks and supplies and she looked as though she were holding an armful of gold. "Great. We just need to add some chocolate to that pile and water," he said, making his way to the refrigerated section.

"I didn't know you liked chocolate," Sarah said, the excitement lining her voice making him wonder what could possibly be interesting about what he'd just said.

He placed two one-liter bottles of water on the checkout counter along with the whiskey and then stepped back to take in the assortment of chocolate on the shelf below. "Yeah, chocolate is my weakness. Lasagna, too, but I'm not getting that here."

"There's no competing with Lainey's," she said.

He picked up three different bars and then

turned to her. "Do you want anything else?"

Sarah's mouth dropped open, and she pushed past him to reach for a bag of candy under the counter. She held it up like a trophy and beamed at him. "Peach Rings! Have you ever had these?"

He shook his head, not understanding the excitement at a bag of candy.

"These are my favorite. I haven't had them since…well, a long time. I have to get these," she said, adding the bag to the pile.

"I've got this," he said to the teenager behind the counter.

"No, I've got it," Sarah said, giving him a shove.

He refused to hip-bump her back and placed a twenty on the counter. "Nope, it's on me."

"But this road trip was my idea," she insisted.

"Yeah, well, I eat more than you do."

"You haven't seen me with a bag of Peach Rings."

The clerk let out a giant huff and rolled his eyes as he started scanning the items.

"Fine, well, the hotel room is on me," Sarah said as the clerk filled a bag with their things.

"We can talk about that," he said after grabbing the bag and holding the door open for her. The rain fell in straight sheets, and they both ran to the truck. By the time they got in, they were both soaked.

"The *one* time I actually do my hair, and it rains," she said.

He shot her a look as he pulled out of the

parking lot. "Your hair looks fine. Looks the same."

She frowned and then turned down the visor, snapping open the mirror. She let out a muffled scream and began finger-combing her hair. "*Really?* This is how I normally look to you?"

He shrugged and thought it best to keep his eyes on the road ahead. "I don't really notice hair."

"I used a *curling iron*. I had mastered beachy waves. I *know* this wasn't how I looked when you picked me up," she said, glaring at him.

He stared straight ahead, knowing he was going to regret speaking his mind. "You're beautiful. Beach curls or not." The long, awkward pause made him think she wasn't going to say anything back.

"Beach-*y waves*."

"Pardon?"

"Nothing. We probably should have packed some clothes or something," she said, rubbing her hands up and down her arms.

"Cold?"

"Freezing."

He turned the heat on.

"About all other expenses, I insist on paying. This whole thing was my idea, and I don't want you having to foot the bill for my adventure."

"Well, I'm going on the adventure with you."

"But only because I asked you. Maybe begged. Borderline begging for sure. This is not what you'd be doing right now. I have to insist, Cade. I'll write it off as a business expense," she said.

He laughed. "Are we talking business?"

"Have you met with the bookkeeper yet?"

Bookkeeper. Hell. He didn't want to think about that now. "Next week."

"Great. We just talked business," she said with an adorably smug smile.

"You're an excellent businesswoman," he said, pulling into the half-filled parking lot of the Highwayman Motel. The H kept blinking, and the M looked like it might fall off any second now.

"This place is perfect," she said as he parked.

"You really need to get out more, Sarah," he said as he shut off the ignition.

"I know. This is perfect. One night at the Highwayman. What could go wrong?"

"All right, let's go," he said, not wanting to burst her bubble and tell her all the things that could go wrong.

By that point, the rain had turned to a light drizzle. She let out a tiny squeal as she opened her door and hopped out of the truck. He was torn between rolling his eyes and laughing or maybe both. Somehow she got under his skin, and he had this irrational need to want her to be happy. He grabbed their bag of junk food and met her around the front of the truck, where she was staring at the $99 A ROOM PER NIGHT sign as though it were the Ritz. "This is going to be so great," she breathed, looking up at him.

Fifteen minutes later, Cade was holding open the door to the motel room for Sarah and wondering how the hell he'd gotten himself into this mess. The double bed loomed large, in his opinion. Typical to roadside motels, which he'd had more than his fair share of experience in, the room was utilitarian but looked reasonably clean and fresh.

"Wait!" he yelled as Sarah looked like she was about to do a backward dive onto the bed. He strode across the room and flung the neatly made comforter off the bed. "I saw this *20/20* documentary years ago about the cleanliness in these places. Fluids neither of us wants to think about are on that."

She scrunched up her nose and took a step back. At least he'd gotten through to her.

"You can thank me later. Also, don't touch the remote or go barefoot."

She lifted her index finger, raising her eyebrows. "Do you have a hazmat suit in your truck?"

He almost laughed, except he was busy placing the remote in the shopping bag from the grocery store. "You know, it's all fun and games until one of us ends up with some nasty rash."

"Ew."

He tossed the protected remote onto the bed. "You're welcome. This would also be a good time to keep that strawberry hand sanitizer around."

She rolled her eyes. "Okay, well, I'm going to wash up. We're allowed to use the bathroom, right?"

He shrugged. "I'd advise against touching the door handle once you've washed your hands."

For some reason, she thought this was funny, because an endearing smile took over her face and her eyes sparkled. "I had no idea you were such a germaphobe."

He shoved his hands in his pockets. "It's called reality. Not some kind of phobia."

"Mm-hmm," she said as she took off her boots.

"No bare feet on this carpet. Keep your socks on."

She clasped a hand over her mouth, doing a bad job of hiding her laughter.

He frowned. "What?"

Her smile was wide and so damn carefree that any regret he had in coming here vanished. "I'm just so glad because I thought I was the one with all the issues. You're making me feel so much better."

He wasn't sure whether he was insulted or happy. He rolled his shoulders and walked across the room. "I'm glad I can provide assistance with your lack of self-confidence."

"Oh, I don't have self-confidence issues. More of a lack-of-life issue."

She disappeared into the bathroom, and he let out the deep breath and relaxed his shoulders. He leaned against the dresser, taking in the small room and the reality that he'd agreed to spend the night with Sarah. There was no avoiding the bed.

Because the room was so small, there wasn't any other place to sleep except the hard-back, upright chair by the window. He'd rather saw off his arm with a dull knife than sleep on the carpeted floor, so that left him with no other options.

Sarah emerged from the bathroom a moment later. "Okay, your turn. I'm sure you'll want to scrub down. You'll be pleased to know that the towels are fresh and clean."

"Thanks," he said.

"I left the toiletries we bought spread out on Kleenexes so they didn't touch the counter. Also, I accidentally dropped your toothbrush in the toilet, but it was still in the package so I'm sure it's fine."

Her eyes were sparkling, and she was barely holding on to that gorgeous smile because her lips kept twitching. She was a horrible liar. And if she'd been any other woman in the world, he'd have crossed the room and kissed her until they were both laughing. But she was Sarah, so hands off. "Thanks. I'll be sure to return the favor."

He walked into the bathroom and closed the door, laughing, as she screamed from the other side that she'd been joking.

Sarah was pretty sure this was the wildest thing she'd ever done, with the hottest man she'd ever known. Snacks with gluten and sugar and a bottle of whiskey…it may have taken her twenty-six years to get here, but she was certain she was living her best life right now. She just wasn't sure how this was all going to pan out. There was a giant bed in the room that wasn't giant at all. She was pretty sure Cade's feet would be dangling off the end. And what would Cade sleep in? What would she sleep in? This hadn't been the most carefully thought-out plan. There was no going back at this point, though.

She leaned against the dresser and quickly messaged Mrs. Casey. After a few stops and starts, she settled on: *Mrs. Casey! I met a wonderful friend tonight at the party and decided to spend the night.*

There. That wasn't an outright lie. Cade was becoming a wonderful friend to her and she had decided to spend the night. With him. Before she could even put her phone back in her purse, it vibrated.

> *I don't think that's a wise idea. I urge you to come home at once.*

> *Sorry, I can't do that. I'm having too much fun. I'm twenty-six, remember? I'll see you tomorrow; have a good night. Shutting my phone off now…*

> *I will pray for you.*

Sarah frowned at the message and dropped her phone in her purse. No more of that thinking now.

She riffled through the bag of snacks and brought it over to the bed. Cade was a little more than her life situation had prepared her for. Maybe a man who was a little less...everything would be a better fit. She looked up as he walked out of the bathroom and strode across the room to the whiskey. Her gaze took in the long, muscular length of him, the stubble on his handsome face... and knew she was in over her head. She needed someone a little less manly. Someone who used strawberry-scented hand sanitizer without giving it a second thought. Someone who didn't make her squirm with a long stare or with the brush of his hand across hers.

Cade left her breathless. Breathless was dangerous, and she wasn't quite ready for that level of danger.

He poured them each a glass and handed her one. "To a road-trip detour."

She clinked her plastic cup to his. "To my first night away from home in ten years."

He grimaced.

She tilted her head. "Was that too sad?"

He lifted one shoulder. "Slightly. But also, this whiskey is really bad."

She laughed and raised her glass. "To new friendships."

Something flashed across his eyes, and she

hoped it wasn't surprise. He'd agreed they were friends, after all. "To new friendships."

"So what do we do now?"

He shrugged, leaning back against the dresser. "What do you want to do?"

"Me? I don't know how to have fun, remember? Why don't you lead the fun charge? What would you do right now for fun?" The second the words escaped her lips, she became frazzled because of how that sounded. What would Cade do for fun? She could imagine all the things he might do for fun with someone else in a hotel room. Well, no, she probably couldn't imagine *all* the things, but just the bare few things were enough to make her feel giddy and embarrassed.

He cleared his throat and walked across the room. "How about we find a movie and start eating our way through this pity party of junk?"

She nodded, relieved that he hadn't answered her question in a different way. "Perfect," she said, joining him on the bed. He sat on one side of the bed, making a mountain out of the food between them. He looked comfortable enough, with his legs stretched out in front of him and one ankle crossed over the other. The only thing was, it looked as though he went out of his way to make sure they were as far from each other as possible.

He was currently flipping through channels and drinking his whiskey. "What do you want to watch?"

"Any movies?"

He shook his head. "Unfortunately, the High-wayman doesn't have any new releases."

He was pointing the shopping-bag-covered remote at the television and mumbling something under his breath as the plastic crinkled.

"Oh, are you having problems through the hermetically sealed plastic?"

He slowly turned to look at her, and she smiled.

He pulled the plastic tighter, and finally the television turned on, the nightly news filling the screen. "Not that. Anything but the news."

He smirked. "Right. You wanted adult movies."

Her face burned. "No, I meant"—she cleared her throat—"like, movies. New releases. Not... *other* things."

He finished off his whiskey but didn't turn to her. The television suddenly went black.

"What!"

He groaned and tossed the remote to the foot of the bed. "Well, there goes that idea."

"I'm sure someone at the front desk will be able to fix this."

Giving her a look, he rolled over, yanked a tissue from the Kleenex box, and used it to pick up the phone and dial. She held back her laugh when she noticed he didn't put the receiver right to his ear. She was trying not to notice the forearms that were roped with muscle that led to more muscle as her eyes wandered up the length of his body. She downed her whiskey, even though it may not have been the wisest of moves, but it really seemed like the only move she could make in a situation like this.

He sat up. "So Carl will be over soon. Maybe. If Carl's wife brings him dinner. If not, he can't leave the desk. But, according to Carl, his wife is pissed at him for not going home last night. She's also mad at him for never spending time with her and the kids and doesn't think he respects her role as a stay-at-home mom."

"Oh. Well, he should do better. Not good. I can understand her position," she said, fluffing up a pillow behind her back to make sure she was sitting upright. He refilled both their glasses while she spoke. "Don't you agree?" she asked when he didn't answer.

He frowned. "About Carl?"

She rolled her eyes. "Uh, yeah? You should have said something to him."

He shook his head. "Uh, no. And I'm not qualified to give marital advice to a stranger. Considering Carl's T-shirt was stained and it looked like he hadn't showered in a week, his wife might be better off with him *not* going home."

He had a point. "See, you already know half of what's wrong with Carl's marriage. Do you have cards?"

He raised his eyebrows. "Cards?"

She nodded, crossing her legs. "I'm good. A

shark."

His mouth curled up slightly, and he leaned on his side so that he was facing her. "You are probably the worst liar I've ever met."

She inhaled sharply. "What? I've mastered my poker face."

He gave her a full-on Cade grin, and it should really come with some kind of warning. "Your face goes red."

She shook her head. "No."

He pointed at her forehead and cheeks. "Yep. Blotchy, too."

She clenched her teeth. So while she was thinking about how his smile was deadly good, he was thinking about her blotchy face. This was her life now. "You're just saying this because you don't want to play poker with me."

He rolled his eyes and flopped back on the bed, tucking one arm behind his head. Dear God, he was like some kind of model, just lying there casually beside her. *Don't look anywhere but his face.* Unfortunately, his face was all kinds of perfect, too. There was nowhere safe to look. "You gotta work on that poker face," he said gruffly, staring at the ceiling.

Oh no, what did that mean? *He knows.* She had ogled. Never in her twenty-six years had she ogled. She needed Carl to hurry up and get here so she could stop being so awkward. "Is there more whiskey?"

"Maybe we should just go to sleep. It's late enough, and tomorrow if we leave early, at least the entire day won't be wasted."

"Oh." If it had been freezing temperatures in here, she bet she would have been able to see the cold form an *O* around the word as it whispered out of her mouth. How was she going to save face? It was a Friday night and she had dragged this man—*this* man of all men, a man who could probably choose to spend his Friday night with almost any woman—to a motel in the middle of nowhere, with nothing but liquor and candy and the offer of a card game. How had this become her life? At least her old life was pathetic only to herself. With this new life, Cade was witnessing it.

"But what about Carl?"

"Ten bucks says his wife isn't giving him dinner."

"Can you pass the bottle of whiskey?"

He refilled her glass.

"Thank you. Listen, I'm sorry I dragged you into this anyway. It sounded like it was going to be an adventure, and now you're stuck here wasting your Friday night with me."

She downed her glass and watched as he stared at the ceiling.

"It's not a waste." His voice came out clipped and not at all like the warm, sexy voice she'd heard all night. Fine. Well, there was no point in sitting here crying over this cowboy. She had a giant pile of food that she normally never allowed herself to eat, and the whiskey was making it very easy to speak her mind and indulge her cravings. He didn't say anything, so she helped herself and grabbed the bag of Peach Rings. Maybe he'd fall asleep right then and there.

"Are you going to stop crinkling that bag soon?"

She made sure she crinkled it extra-loud and extra-long for being so rude. The bag finally opened, and she tossed one of the sugar-coated rings into her mouth. Then she remembered the last person she'd shared these with, and a wave of loneliness swept over her, even though she wasn't alone.

"All done crinkling," she choked out, cringing slightly at the way her voice sounded. It was either choke on her own tears or choke on the Peach Ring. Josh would always end up eating way faster than she would, and then she'd get mad at him for eating most of the bag.

The memory and the ache left her sitting there with her hand in the bag and her mind in the past. At least she didn't have to worry about actually crying in front of him. When she finally raised her eyes, it was to witness the hottest man she'd ever known punching his pillow before settling back down on it, his back to her. Was it sad that she really wanted him to say something? Anything so that she wouldn't feel so alone? She shoved another Peach Ring in her mouth and stared out the window into the parking lot.

"Are you also going to keep making that smacking sound with your mouth?"

That was it. Hot or not, he was being a jerk. "These are chewy candies," she said, her words garbled because of the amount of candy in her mouth. She threw a Peach Ring at his head.

He flipped over, looking at her. "Did you just throw candy at my head?"

She rolled her lips inward and started to slowly shake her head and then turn it into a nod. He let out an exasperated sigh.

"I think it's rude of you to just check out on our plans just because Carl is having marital issues. If I had hired you as an escort, I would have fired you by now. Also, I get that your Friday nights are probably filled with lots of…lurid things and this is really tame and boring for you, but you should at least try and be polite."

His eyes were wide, and for a second she didn't know what he was going to do. But he burst out laughing. A really deep, throaty laugh that almost made her smile. Except she didn't because she was mad at him and he was laughing at her. "Lurid?"

She shoved a few more Peach Rings in her mouth and washed them down with whiskey. The whiskey really did make everything better. "That's it? I tell you all that, and all you can do is point out my vocabulary choice?"

"I haven't heard that word since I watched a black-and-white movie when the cable went out."

"You're funny, Cade. You know what I mean," she said, hating that she'd used the dated word. *This is what happens when your only friends are over seventy-five, Sarah.*

"Why don't you tell me what you think I do on Friday nights?"

"Uh, this isn't a game show. I'm not going to sit here guessing what you do for one hundred points." She grabbed a Peach Ring and carefully placed it on the tip of one finger, then continued to do the same until each finger had a Peach Ring on the tip, just like she'd done when she was a kid.

He stared at her and then laughed again. She had never seen him laugh so much. He grabbed her hand, and she stopped breathing as he dipped his head, pulled a Peach Ring off one of her fingers, and ate it. *Dear God.* Nothing in her life had prepared her for Cade's mouth on her finger, and even though it happened so fast, she was pretty sure she'd never be the same. She was also pretty sure her face was as red as a tomato. "That was mine," she managed to say, waiting for him to laugh.

"I'm not wasting my Friday night," he said in a voice she hadn't heard from him before; it was deep and gravelly and stirred something unknown within her.

She peeled her eyes off his face and stared at the contents of the bag. She was reassured that even if she choked on the Peach Ring in her mouth, the opening would prevent her from suffocating to death. "Thank you for saying that."

He shrugged and sat up. "Are you sharing?"

She nodded, holding the bag in his direction, torn between relief and disappointment that the moment was over.

"I've never had these."

"Really? They used to be my favorite as a kid. I haven't had them in years."

He refilled their glasses. "So. Why don't you tell me why you didn't want to go home tonight?"

"Because that's the only place I ever go," she said with a shrug.

"Why?"

She put down the bag of candy and traded it for the whiskey. "My parents were extremely overprotective people, and I wasn't really allowed a social life unless it was one they orchestrated."

"Like how?"

"I've been out with three different guys, each one worse than the other. But all three were from families they thought were suitable."

He grabbed a handful of Peach Rings. "So they set you up on dates? What was the criteria for these dates?"

She held up her hand. "Money, ranching family, upstanding citizens."

He looked away for a moment, his jaw clenching. "And what was wrong with the guys?"

She shrugged, knowing exactly what was wrong, everything that was missing in this scenario. Not that she'd tell him that, but the buzz that was rippling through her that had nothing to do with the liquor she was drinking was exactly what had been missing. "Well, they were kind of boring. Remember, I'm the girl who had no life, so if *I* think someone's boring, they're definitely boring."

One corner of his mouth tilted up, his eyes sparkling with something. "For someone who hasn't had a lot of freedom, you're not boring at all, sweetheart."

Her mouth dropped open slightly, and her stomach swirled at the endearment and how softly he said it, how deep and rich his voice sounded. She frantically thought of something to say to him, knowing that she was one of many who'd probably been on the receiving end of that endearment but not wanting to dwell on that. For now, this was her night with him, and he made her feel more alive than she ever had as an adult. "That's sweet."

"I'm not being sweet; I'm just telling you the truth. This is…fun."

Her heart started beating frantically in her chest. "So what was the last fun night you had?" she blurted out, wanting to know more about what he actually enjoyed doing.

He ran a hand through his hair. "I, uh, I'm not sure."

"Liar."

"Hey, I may be lots of things, but I'm not a liar. Fine, let me think. I didn't know I'd have to come up with an actual example. Oh, I've got one. Tyler and Lainey's wedding."

Her mouth dropped open again.

He frowned. "What?"

"That's also really sweet."

He shut his eyes and lay his head back on the pillow. "Clearly you're getting the wrong impression of me."

She picked up the square decorative pillow at the foot of the bed, intending to smack him with it, but without even opening his eyes, he'd anticipated her movement and grasped her wrist. "That had better not be one of those decorative pillows that are filled with germs."

She laughed, but her voice came out breathy because the feel of his hand wrapped around her wrist was making it hard for her to breathe normally. "I cannot get over how much of a germaphobe you are. No wonder you carry hand sanitizer. Not many cowboys I've met do."

He let go of her wrist, and she put the pillow back down, flustered and giddy at the same time. "If you knew what I knew about motels, you'd feel the exact same way. Can I ask you something?"

She nodded, trying to hide her embarrassment and disappointment that he was distancing himself. "Sure."

"We've worked together for a few weeks now, and you've kept up with all of us, have worked hard and haven't backed down from anything.

I was worried about you on the cattle drive, and I didn't need to be—you were amazing. Why wouldn't your family let you get involved with the ranch? It couldn't really just be that you're a woman?"

A pang of remorse stabbed her in the heart. She hated talking about this. It was one thing for it to be there in the back of her mind, but it was another to have to talk about it aloud. But he was the first friend she'd had in years. The first person who listened to her without shooting her down or mocking her. He brought her here, just because she asked him to. Cade was so much more than the most attractive man she'd ever known.

Suddenly, all those years of holding everything in, of keeping it all together, seemed so wrong, seemed so heavy, and she wanted nothing more than to rid herself of all of it. She wanted to share it with someone.

She stared at him, the pile of junk food between them on the bed, and knew that once she opened up to him, she was going to let herself fall for him. Even though she sensed he wasn't a man who was going to give her happily-ever-after, maybe all she needed was right now.

CHAPTER TEN

"*I*t's a long and complicated story," Sarah said, ripping open his Snickers bar, breaking off half, and offering it to him.

He shook his head. He shouldn't be asking her this. But none of this should be happening tonight—not that he'd ever let them get further than this…sharing of stories. This crap-ass hotel room felt too small, too intimate, for two people who had no business being together to spend the night in. Especially not when, over the last two hours, he'd found himself craving the way she laughed, the way she got irritated with him, the sound of her voice.

This wasn't what he wanted. He never tried to get to know about people's lives other than his two best friends. Except he found himself wanting to know what had turned this intelligent, capable, gorgeous woman into someone so sheltered and introverted. He wasn't going to care about the fact that when she was with him, she didn't seem introverted at all. He also was only going to look straight into her eyes and keep that pile of food between them.

His first mistake had been letting himself touch her, to pull that stupid Peach Ring off her finger, even if it was just to keep himself from getting that pillow on him. His second mistake was taking in her features up close as she spoke, teasing her and laughing with her.

All around, this entire night was a mistake. And yet, here he was, the guy who never wanted to know anything about anyone, wanting to know everything.

"*Long and complicated* sounds just about perfect for two people sharing a room with no television."

She popped half the chocolate bar in her mouth and shut her eyes, making some moaning sound that had him pouring himself another whiskey and looking out the window at the view of the parking lot. At least his truck was still there.

"I can't believe I've been missing out on this all these years."

"You don't eat chocolate?"

"No dairy, no gluten, no sugar."

He blinked. "Is there a point in living?"

She shrugged, her hair falling around back in a cascade of honey-colored curls, and he smiled watching her. "It was worth it, I guess. Maybe not, jury's still out. But that's a story for another day."

"So I think you were about to tell me your long and complicated story," he said, swirling the whiskey in his cup.

She leaned forward. "Here's the deal I'm willing to make: If I tell you, then you're going to have to tell me something."

He sat up a little straighter. "All right. One question each, no more."

"Fine. Deal." She balled up the empty chocolate wrapper and attempted to chuck it toward the garbage, but it floated not far from the bed.

"Okay. So what's the real story behind you being kept away from the day-to-day on the ranch? I know what you told me, and I believe you; I just have a feeling there's a hell of a lot more to it."

He sat there, waiting, watching while her eyes changed as rapidly as a storm passing across the open sky. Every ounce of laughter that she'd been brimming with vanished, and now she resembled the woman he'd first met that day she'd hired him; she was reserved and nervous, looking inside her almost empty glass of whiskey.

"I had a brother."

He didn't want to let on that he already knew that, so he gave her a nod to continue. His heart broke just a little when her hand shook as she tried to open a bag of Skittles.

She cursed under her breath. "My hands are too slimy."

He silently took the bag, opened it, and handed it back to her. She didn't meet his eyes and dug her fingers into the candy.

"His name was Joshua. He died when I was ten and he was twelve. My parents changed the name of the ranch after it happened. Josh was my best friend. He was funny and wild and loved life so much. He was one of those people who, when they woke up in the morning, hit the ground running, always into mischief. We would follow my dad around every day and were even allowed to help out on the ranch on the weekends. We took the bus together to school, and he was never embarrassed by his little sister tagging along. He got into loads of trouble with my parents—but not the bad kind of trouble, the kind that left them rolling their eyes and laughing at his antics. They were very different people when he was alive. They were happy. They would hold hands, kiss, have friends over for dinner, and go on vacations. One Saturday night…" She stopped talking and scrambled off the bed abruptly.

His gut was already in a knot, and a part of him regretted asking her about her past. He regretted the promises he'd made to himself about keeping his distance from her. Because if he hadn't made those promises and there weren't those restrictions, he wouldn't have let her walk across that room alone; he wouldn't have let her tell this story by herself. He would have held her and let her know without words that she wasn't as alone as she thought she was.

She stood at the window, her back to him, her shoulders rigid. "Our parents were entertaining guests, and Josh came to my room and said he had a great idea and wanted to go build a campfire. It was stupid, though; it was so stupid, what he did. I knew better. If I could go back and replay that night, I wouldn't have let him. But I thought he could do anything."

He'd sat in many motels, with many different women—he'd have never brought a woman back to the Donnelly ranch—but this was the first time he'd spent a night just talking, and it was the first night he never wanted to end. He'd known the moment he met Sarah that she was different...different from anyone he'd met, completely different from him.

He'd been told by parents, grandparents, relatives, teachers, adults that he was worthless, stupid, and insignificant, and he'd believed it for so long. Until he was old enough to realize that the people spewing out the trash talk were the ones with the issues. It wasn't until he'd come to Wishing River and was given a real home by the Donnellys that he found his self-worth, knew that he had nothing to prove to anyone but himself and that the world he'd grown up in—the one that didn't give a shit about a kid like him—wasn't the entire world. There were better people out there.

As he sat there, waiting for the most incredible woman he'd ever known to confide in him, he knew...Sarah was better people.

She turned around and crossed the room, leaning against the dresser and staring some place beyond his shoulder. "He was so sure, always so confident that nothing would happen, that I went along with it. I will never forgive myself for that," she whispered.

He threw his legs over the side of the bed, tension in his muscles building, making it impossible to lie still anymore. His stomach churned as he waited for her to continue.

"When we got down to the river, he said he was going to take a quick swim. I told him not to. I mean, we knew you don't swim in that river when the currents are high. It had been a rainy spring. There are rapids at certain points. Rocks. He was a good swimmer, strong, and big for his age. I stood on the bank and told him to hurry up, but he wanted me to time him to see how long it would take to get to the next clearing. But…but I lost sight of him and ran down the river, and he wasn't there. I ran and I remember thinking that he couldn't be far. And all of a sudden, I caught a glimpse of his red shirt. He was being carried downstream. By that point, we were far from my house, and I had to make the decision of whether I should help him myself or go back for help. I knew that by the time I ran back and got help, he would have no chance. I was a good swimmer, too, but I…I waited to jump in because the rapids were carrying him too fast and…"

She covered her face with her hands. "I jumped in when I saw the blood. I almost didn't make it. The rapids almost pulled me under, except they started slowing, and I managed to grab on to him and climb onto the bank. I flipped him over and...he was bleeding everywhere. His head. He must have hit his head. He wasn't breathing. I was screaming. I remember screaming and I didn't know if it was for help or because I knew he was gone. His blood was all over my hands; I felt the way his neck was bent, and I knew it was too late. I didn't want to leave him. I couldn't. I wanted to hold on to him. I couldn't let him go, even though on some level I knew he was gone.

"But they were all coming, running with flashlights. And that was it; just like that, he was gone. I could hear...I could hear my mother's scream forever. It was the kind of scream that you would think would shatter windows, but it shattered my heart, it shattered her, all of us. It was like I inhaled it and breathed it every night. I couldn't speak. I didn't speak for months after he died. I was in my head. Deep in my head. I had night terrors for years."

Hell. His hands were clenched tight into fists, and he gritted his teeth. He'd known, obviously, because of Tyler and Dean and the ranch hands, but he hadn't realized how bad. And he hadn't known Sarah then. Now...he knew her. He could feel how this had broken her. But everything, all those missing pieces came clicking in perfectly. The way she could ride, the freedom she'd felt that night he'd gone chasing after her, only to find her watching a sunset without anyone hounding her—it was the childhood she'd lost. Cade didn't know what to say, but the emotion in her voice made him want to close the distance between them, to offer her comfort.

"I'm so sorry," he said finally.

She was staring out the window, and he didn't know what to expect, but when she turned back to him, her eyes didn't show an ounce of tears, and her features were so controlled that he wouldn't have thought she'd just told him the story she had.

"Thank you," she said. "The rest of it is just people coping after a tragedy, going through the motions, never really expecting to come out on the other side, time not really healing any wounds. Time made the wounds bigger in my family because no one talked about him. No one even spoke his name. Every ounce of happiness that existed in our family was buried with Josh, and my parents destroyed their relationship. Tragedy can bring people together or tragedy can tear people apart. That's what happened to my parents. I cried that entire first year, and then I never cried again. I never wanted to feel again. I never wanted to love someone like that again. I withdrew... I became this person who doesn't know how to talk to people or have friends. Those... Your friends tonight... I couldn't...I didn't know what to say; I didn't know how to act. I don't fit in anywhere anymore."

He stood up, his thoughts going a mile a

minute. Everything she was telling him was painfully candid and hard to listen to. He took a step toward her, and he could have sworn he saw a flash of panic in her eyes. He didn't know if it was him or the fact that she'd revealed so much about herself. He knew he probably should have stayed on the bed, given her distance, but he didn't want to. There was something about her, the detachment in her voice that called to him. "You fit in," he said, knowing that she just needed more time around people her age.

She shrugged. "I felt awkward. Anyway, my parents were very overprotective after that. They didn't care about anything else I did, but they didn't want me in any kind of danger, and the ranch, to them, was a danger. I started getting debilitating migraines after he died. I would lose my sight for a period of time before the intense pain would hit. They were terrified the first couple of times it happened, and that basically solidified their plans to keep me in a bubble so I'd be 'safe.' That's why I was homeschooled."

Were her migraines the "medical condition" Edna had been talking about? And hell, the older woman must have seen all the family at their worst. Even Edna's behavior made sense now, how overprotective she was. "That sounds like it must have been a pretty frustrating way to live for a kid. Do you still get the migraines?"

She nodded. "Every now and again. Much

less than when I was a child. Now I can usually predict when one is coming. They're most often caused by severe stress or if I haven't been taking care of myself, drinking enough water, or eating some trigger foods, namely sugar, chocolate, and gluten," she said with a sheepish half smile.

It didn't feel right, just having her standing there. He wanted nothing more than to pull her close to him, to make her feel safe and loved and to ease that ache even just a little. But that was the worst possible thing he could do.

He placed his hands in his back pockets and racked his brain for the right words. "Basically everything you ate tonight?"

She nodded, the sparkle coming back in her eyes, and he was relieved to see it again. He didn't realize until it came back just how much he'd wanted to see her smile again. "I'll be fine. It's just one night. How could one night undo everything?"

Neither of them said anything, and he couldn't turn away from her. There was this energy between them that only seemed to get stronger the longer they spent together. He wanted her like he'd never wanted anyone, but he knew better than she did that one night could change *everything*.

He wasn't willing to risk everything for one night. And he wouldn't do that to Sarah. "Did your parents ever come around? Before they died?"

She crossed her arms over her chest. "No. They became different people and stayed that way for years. We used to go on picnics by the river—that had been my favorite thing to do on the weekend—but it was just gone, all that fun. That family stopped existing. It's not that I didn't forgive them, but the trust was broken. I don't think they wanted to go back to the people they were before. I stopped trying to look for the parents I knew. My dad's gambling was out of hand."

"Gambling?" Cade repeated. His mind raced as he thought back to what he'd found in the spreadsheets, the inconsistencies, the large sums of withdrawn cash, the random infusions of cash without a paper trail. Shit.

She nodded. "My mother didn't know about it for a long time. The drinking was easy to spot. That's what took us from a normal family to a completely dysfunctional one. He used to be a religious man—when times were good, when my brother was alive. But it tested his faith, and it crumbled. My mother, on the other hand, leaned in hard to her faith, except she didn't go to church anymore, which only widened the gap between them. I bought this locket with Mrs. Casey after he died and placed his picture in it. It made me feel like he was always with me." She stopped talking abruptly and winced. "This is boring, isn't it?"

He shook his head, this incredible weight on his chest making it hard to breathe. "Not at all."

Her fingers toyed with the delicate locket. "When my father found it, he took it and hid it in their room. No reminders."

She folded her hands tightly. "Anyway. I guess there's not that much left to tell, except that the gambling and drinking got completely out of control, and one night he stumbled into the house drunk and told my mother he'd lost everything. I was hiding upstairs in the hallway, listening. My mother lost it on him. I heard glass shatter, and even though I'd missed my brother every day since he died, at that moment I would have given anything to have him there hiding with me. I had never felt so alone. He would have known what to do; he might have even gone down there and broken it up. I didn't. I sat in the shadows and watched as their marriage unraveled, this horrid display of grief and anger and rage. God, the things they said…"

This time, when her voice trailed off, he didn't stay on the sidelines—he reached for her, tugged her to him, and the initial contact of her body against his robbed his breath, robbed all memory of why this woman was off-limits to him. Sarah's hands went to his waist, and she tucked into him with a trust that no one had ever given him. She fit against his body like she belonged there, with him. He'd never belonged to anyone, and here he was, wishing to belong to her, wishing that all of this wasn't as complicated as it was.

When she leaned her head back, every ounce of loneliness, every piece of sadness was revealed to him in her eyes. The need to make that change, to make that disappear overtook him, and for the first time in his life, he wanted to step up and go all in with someone. Sarah brought out this need in him to be more than he was, to want more than the life he was used to. He held her face in his hands, one thumb gently grazing over her cheekbone, his gaze on hers, waiting and wanting.

Her lips parted, and her hands slowly traveled up his chest in a light, torturously gentle motion until one hand gripped the back of his head.

He clenched his teeth tightly, waiting until he felt that faintest tug; that's when all bets were off, all walls came down, and all sense of rules and boundaries shattered. His mouth came down on hers, and he kissed her with every ounce of longing and desire that was in him. He kissed her with an abandon and feeling he didn't know he was capable of. She tasted like candy and chocolate and better than anything in the world. Every hollow and curve was pressed against his body, and he memorized it, knowing it couldn't happen again.

She clutched the back of his head like she was holding on to him for dear life, and he felt the same way. He needed to stop everything that was happening. He told himself that over and over again as his hands left her face and traced the sides of her breasts and her waist and hips, as his mouth left her impossibly soft lips and trailed kisses under her ear and down her neck. But when she whispered his name, her voice thick with desire, reality crashed over him. He dropped his hands and raised his head, finding the self-control he'd always prided himself on, even though he hated it right now.

He knew he couldn't sleep with Sarah. He knew that would be crossing lines and would make both their lives hell. He pulled back slowly, his body throbbing, and stared into her eyes. The desire and disappointment in them made him almost rethink pulling back. So he took a physical step away from her. "I'm sorry."

She blinked a few times and ran her hands through her hair. "Why?"

He clenched his jaw and forced himself to maintain eye contact with her. "I… We can't get involved like that. It will make your life difficult."

She frowned at him and crossed her arms. "My life? How?"

"If any of the guys at the ranch knew we were involved, it would look bad."

She shrugged. "That has no effect on my life. Besides, how would they know?"

"They'd know. Trust me," he said, turning his back to her because he needed more distance. He flopped down on the bed again and stared at the ceiling, noticing a few questionable splotches.

"I think you're just trying to get out of this. Maybe it would make *your* life difficult."

He kept his eyes trained on the ceiling, refusing to feel anything. "What? No. I couldn't care less what people think of me. Never have."

"Neither do I."

"Yes, you do."

She crossed her arms. "So you know me better than I know myself?"

He shrugged.

"Can you give me more than shrugs or one-line answers please?"

"Fine. I don't want you to get hurt." So much for keeping emotion out of things.

"Hurt? By you?"

The way she said it was almost insulting, but he chose to ignore the tone. "Yeah. By me. Because you deserve the rancher who's going to come in and sweep you off your feet and give you everything you could ever want. Then you can get married and have kids or whatever…" He thought it wise to stop talking when her eyes narrowed and she slowly started walking toward him.

"You're really lucky I'm not prone to violence, Cade."

He almost laughed, but she was looking even more pissed, and her face was turning red. "You wouldn't hurt me."

"Y-You should at least be sitting at attention or something when someone walks toward you with their hands fisted," she sputtered.

He crossed one ankle on the other and tried

not to let his gaze wander over her, because he hadn't touched her in all of two minutes, and he was already longing for her, not just for the moment or the night, and that was why he linked his hands behind his head and took on the role he'd once been most known for—troublemaker.

Her gorgeous mouth curled into a half smile, and damn if he actually physically responded to the sight. Except she ruined the moment by picking up one of the decorative pillows he'd already removed from the bed. There was a dangerous gleam in her eyes as she approached him slowly.

"Hell, Sarah, put down the damn pillow. We already went down that road with the dangers of upholstered fabrics in here. No need to get crazy," he choked out, scrambling into a sitting position.

She laughed. *At* him. And raised her arm with the filthy pillow.

"You wouldn't."

She raised her eyebrow, an adorable—if not slightly evil—smirk on her lips. "People think I'm boring and I don't take risks."

He swallowed hard, his gaze darting from the pillow to her dancing eyes. "You don't have friends, remember? No one knows if you're boring or not. I don't think you're boring. You're very dangerous, you take lots of risks, and you're the scariest person I know."

She laughed.

He took no chances. He grabbed her wrist and she half screamed, half laughed as he pulled her onto the bed, but she still managed to hold on to that damn pillow. They were laughing as he tackled her gently and rolled until he was on top of her. She kept her arm raised, the pillow dangling off the bed. He didn't think he'd ever laughed so hard in his life, certainly not as an adult. He was still laughing when he lowered his head to kiss her.

Wait. Hell, what was he doing?

He stopped himself before their lips touched and pried that pillow out of her hands with as few fingers as possible. She ran her now-free hands down his shoulders, over his arms.

He sat up. "You're killing me."

"But I'm a lot of fun. Admit it."

He smiled. "You are. Which is why I'm getting up now," he said and forced himself to stand up and cross the room.

"I think it's your turn," she said finally.

Right. "Okay. Go ahead."

She fixed her green eyes on him. "Where is your family?"

The pounding on the door came at the perfect time. "I'll get that," he said, opening the door to find Carl standing there with a toolbox and wearing the same dirty shirt.

"Hi, folks. I'm here to fix your cable," he said, walking in when Cade opened the door wider for him.

"Miss," he said to Sarah with a nod. "I'll fix this in a jiffy so you two can get on with your night."

"Oh, take your time; we're not having a night," Sarah said, her face red.

Carl gave him a look that pretty much said, *you poor bastard*, before banging his hand on the side of the television a few times.

"So is your wife helping you tonight?" Sarah asked as he picked up the cable box, turned it over a few times, and then tapped the screen. Carl had no idea how to fix anything.

"Yeah. She came by eventually," he said with what Cade was pretty sure was an overly dramatic sigh as he put the cable box down and leaned against the dresser. "We've been having a few problems lately."

Please don't ask why, Sarah.

"Oh no, I'm sorry to hear that," she said. "I'm sure all marriages go through rough patches."

He shrugged and again made no move to fix the cable. "I guess. She says I'm not trying anymore."

Maybe he should wear clean clothes.

He watched Sarah smile sympathetically. She was too nice, and that was going to be their downfall. "That's something you can fix, don't you think?"

"Yeah. Buy a magazine about relationships or something. Thanks for your help, Carl," Cade said. Sarah frowned at him before turning back to Carl with that sweet look of sympathy.

"Why don't you sit down for a minute and let's brainstorm. Can I get you a coffee?"

Carl nodded, and Cade watched with disbelief as he sat on the corner of the bed. "That would be great. Mary Beth said I should be making my own coffee."

Sarah started the coffeepot and folded her arms, turning to Carl. Now, she'd let him have it. "Well, she's right. You're capable. Please don't tell me you rely on Mary Beth to make you a simple cup of coffee."

Carl squirmed under Sarah's stern gaze. Cade was inexplicably pleased. "I guess I shouldn't, right?"

"Of course not! Think of everything Mary Beth has going on, what with the kids, the house, and then helping out here. You have to step up. She can't do it all. I bet she feels so unappreciated. Okay, let's see what we can do," she said, handing him his coffee.

"Do you have sugar?" Carl asked, looking up at her like a lost puppy.

"Carl, this is your motel," Cade snapped.

Carl nodded and scurried over to where the sugar and creamer were. Sarah shot Cade a warning glare. Once Carl sat back on the bed, this ridiculous conversation continued. "Let's think," Sarah said. "Did she bring up anything else that's bothering her?"

Carl stirred his coffee and let out a forlorn sigh. "I think I should try and take her out for dinner every once and a while. Just the two of us. She said something like she's tired of feeling like a slave."

"That's a pretty good warning sign," Cade said with a snort.

They ignored him.

"Yes. Of course you need alone time with Mary Beth, and you need to help out. Tell her how much you appreciate everything she does for you and the kids."

"Why don't you bring her here?" Cade said.

They both frowned at him.

"Something a little more...romantic," Sarah said.

"I'm not very creative," Carl said, slurping his coffee.

Cade wondered if he should tell him to stop slurping coffee and making that noise. It might be contributing to his marital problems if Mary Beth had to listen to that every morning at the breakfast table.

"Okay, let's see. Do you know her favorite flower?"

Carl shook his head.

Cade let out a *tsk*ing sound.

They ignored him. "Okay, well, roses are always a good bet if you don't know. Think of the things you used to do in the beginning of your relationship. Did you bring her flowers? Did you...um, dress up a little more?" Cade almost cracked a smile at her diplomatic rewording of *wear clean clothes*.

Carl shrugged. "I guess I did. I just never realized that that was important stuff, you know? She's home with the kids, and then she tries to help me here…"

"Do you help her at home?"

"I guess I could do more," he said.

"Great. Problem solved. Do more at home, say thank you once in a while, make your own damn coffee, buy flowers, and change your shirt. Can you fix our cable now?" Cade said.

Carl nodded and stood. "Thanks for that advice, kids. I'm going to take it. Tomorrow I'll be a new man."

Sarah beamed at Cade as Carl's back was to them. The man did nothing more than pound the television a few times and then turn it on. Somehow, it was working again. "Well, you have a good night. The Highwayman appreciates your business. If you need anything, you just call me at the front desk."

Cade walked him to the door. "Thanks."

"Good luck, Carl," Sarah called out.

Cade locked the door after Carl left. Sarah was already picking up the remote. "Poor Carl. Hopefully he takes our advice."

He was thinking more like *poor Cade*. He was alone in a motel room with the most gorgeous, sweetest woman he'd ever known, and it was hands off. Carl was the lucky one. "He'll be fine," he said, joining her on his side of the bed.

He was relieved she seemed to have forgotten about her question. If there was one thing he'd never shared with anyone, it was his family. The deeper he got with Sarah, the more he wanted to keep his past to himself.

CHAPTER ELEVEN

Cade looked down at Sarah, who'd fallen asleep, her head against his shoulder, one hand in the bag of Peach Rings, and smiled. He kissed the top of her head and slowly pulled her hand out of the bag, wincing at the crinkling sound in the quiet room as he placed it on the nightstand.

He had no idea how it was almost three o'clock in the morning. He also had no idea how they'd made it to almost three o'clock in the morning fully clothed without any whiskey left.

"Can I ask you something?" she whispered.

He craned his head back to see her—he'd assumed she'd fallen asleep. The parking lot light streamed through the curtain, a thin ribbon in the dark room, reminding him again how different this was. He'd never noticed the small details of nightfall, the sound of the woman next to him breathing, how soft and intimate a voice could be in the darkness. As much as motels were a part of the man he used to be, this lying here with a woman, talking and sharing, was a part of him that he wished had existed earlier. Or maybe not, because that would have meant it was another woman. But the intimacy of this, of Sarah's hand on his chest, of her soft body pressed against his or their secret-filled whispers, could have only been with her.

"Sure," he said, brushing his lips against the top of her head as she spoke.

"Did you do this a lot?"

He kept his gaze on the ribbon of light, as all the times, nights he'd spent in places like this danced along that ribbon. He wanted to make her understand that he'd been a different man, one she didn't know and one he really didn't want her to know. But this was about honesty tonight, about letting walls down, and he'd answer as much as he could honestly answer. "This?" he said finally, wanting to be sure he knew what she was asking.

She shifted, perching her chin on her hand and turning to him. "With…your girlfriends. Were there lots?"

He wished that ribbon would disappear and he wouldn't be able to see the flicker of insecurity in her eyes as she watched him. "I've never had a girlfriend. I've never had a lasting, committed relationship." Maybe that was the way to explain his lifestyle. It sounded better than admitting he'd only ever had sex with people he barely knew and would rarely ever have to see again.

"Sooooo…" she whispered, her voice trailing off as she continued to look at him.

He put one hand behind his head and stared up at the ceiling. "So, I've been with women I barely knew because I never wanted anything more than that."

"Why?"

"I've never had a reason to want more." He wanted to add *until now*, but he wasn't naive. Just because this wave of regret and longing was hitting him hard tonight, he knew it wouldn't still be there tomorrow or next week. This thing he had for Sarah wasn't ever going to go anywhere. It couldn't.

"Did you spend the entire night with them?"

"Sarah…"

"Never mind. None of my business."

He spread his palm against her back. "I've never done this. I've never held on to someone during the night or shared my thoughts."

He let that sit out there, wondering if she'd say anything, wondering why he'd even revealed that. He'd always assumed that revealing his true thoughts would make him vulnerable. In the past, they had. At home, as a kid, they had. Tears and sadness meant that the adults could cut you apart for not being strong enough. The world was no place for a man who wasn't strong. So he'd learned to be strong and to fake it even when he didn't feel it. But Sarah made him feel…safe.

"I used to lie in bed at night, in a house full of people, and feel completely alone. I could hear voices and footsteps all around me and yet I'd never felt more alone."

"I know what that's like." He wanted to keep speaking and share all the times as a young kid he'd hide somewhere in the house. He'd never really had his own room, but he'd always managed to find a secret spot where he could hide a blanket and flashlight, sometimes a snack. That would make him feel safer—his own little spot where no one could find him.

"Do you have any brothers or sisters?"

He shook his head, not wanting to offer any more. "How do you feel right now?" he asked, because it was important, and because he didn't want to talk about himself.

"This is the safest I've felt in a long, long time. When Josh was alive, the world was this big, safe, exciting place. I thought I had it all. And when everything just…exploded, I learned that good stuff can't last forever. That's what I think is so hard to take. It's scary to think that at any moment, when you're living the life you've always wanted, it could be ripped away from you without warning."

Shit. He pressed his lips to the top of her head. "It's scary as hell. But what choice is there? Live in fear the rest of your life? That's not really living. And then there are those lucky ones, the ones who get to grow old after having really lived and come out okay in the end."

"And maybe that's why we can't take things or people for granted. Or situations like this for granted."

He stilled. He didn't say anything. He should

pull away. But he also knew on a deeper level that he would always have a hard time keeping his hands off her now. What he felt for her was completely different. "Sarah," he said in a choked whisper.

"Don't say no to me. We're here. It's just the two of us. What if it wasn't an accident that you applied for the job? What if you were meant to? What if we were meant to meet each other?"

Hell. No way. "I don't believe in that."

He was glad the lights were off so that he couldn't see the disappointment he knew would be on her face. The silence was enough of a confirmation, and soon he was pretty sure she'd fallen asleep for real.

He adjusted the pillows. She didn't even open her eyes as she curled into him, her head against his shoulder. He placed his hand on top of hers that was resting on his chest, and then he slowly picked it up, kissing her smooth skin before laying it on top of him again.

This was a night unlike any other for him. It felt like the beginning of something he didn't know he'd ever find. He'd longed for things in the past, different ways, a different life, but he'd never found anyone to make him want to jump in headfirst. He'd spent his life drifting from home to home and from person to person. Women he hadn't wanted for more than a night, women who didn't want him for more than a night. That had been his way…and it had been pretty damn lonely.

Then Sarah walked into his life, or he'd walked into hers, and suddenly one night was nothing. One night would never be enough. This was his one night with her, and despite both of them being fully clothed, he'd never felt as close to anyone as this.

Sometime before dawn, he drifted off to sleep, a smile on his face as he pictured Sarah holding the damn throw pillow over him.

Sarah opened one eye, and it took her a minute to figure out where she was and who she was with. The Highwayman. Cade. She was half on him, her head on his chest and her hand… She slowly pulled it out from under his shirt, off his hard abs, careful not to disturb him. But she couldn't quite force herself to move away just yet. She wanted to hold on to this moment for as long as she could. She didn't want to be alone again. She wanted to lie here forever with him; she wanted to watch him forever, to run her hand over his cheek and feel his stubble against her fingertips. She wanted to feel the safety of his strong body against hers.

She wanted this weekend to be the rest of her life.

Last night, she had finally broken free and lived. She had kissed Cade and hadn't wanted to stop. He had been incredible. He'd made her feel alive and safe at the same time. She had talked to him about things she never talked about, things she could never mention to Edna. He had sat there and listened, the warm reassurance emanating from his eyes making her feel like she could go on talking for hours.

But when he'd crossed the room and held her, nothing had prepared her for what it would mean to be held by him, kissed by him.

She closed her eyes as a wave of nausea hit. Alarm gripped her for a moment, and she forced herself to calm down. It wasn't a migraine. That would be too cruel after the night she had. One night. She slowly opened her eyes as the sensation passed, only to find the telltale visual blurriness of aura confirming that she was getting a migraine.

This couldn't be happening. Moving slowly, not wanting to wake up Cade and not wanting to jostle her head, she made her way to the shower. Maybe she could fight it off. She opened the bottle of water and downed as much as she could before going to take a shower.

Twenty minutes later, Sarah emerged from the bathroom, feeling like a train wreck. She'd hoped that a shower and brushing her teeth would have made her feel like a human again, but it was no luck. She squinted against blinding sunlight streaming through the windows and clutched the doorframe as two waves floated across her sight line. *Oh, crap.*

She opened her eyes again to see Cade standing across the room, only half dressed, staring at her. Thankfully her vision hadn't completely gone before she could admire that sight. There was something incredibly intimate about sharing a room with someone, especially someone like him. Wherever he went, he had a presence. Here, his presence took up an entire room. It wasn't just how he looked—his face, the ripped and lean body—it was him.

"You don't look well," he said, concern lacing his deep voice as he crossed the room.

She clutched the door tighter as he turned into a blur. Not wanting to speak, because it would take too much effort, she just stood there. She knew she had minutes until her vision would be gone. He leaned down, holding her shoulders and staring into her eyes. "Sarah, what's wrong?"

She forced the words out. "I'm getting a migraine. I…have medication in my purse…"

"Okay. I'm going to help you over to the bed, and then I'll get you the pills."

"I can do it," she whispered, because it hurt to speak normally. She cursed when her foot hit the toe of the bed, but Cade's hand gripped her arm.

"I think you might be more stubborn than me, and that's not a compliment," he said as he guided her onto the bed.

"Thanks."

"I'm getting the pills," he said, and she could hear him rummaging through her purse. He was back a minute later, sitting beside her on the bed. She forced herself to open her eyes, and he placed the pill in her hand and held the cup to her lips for her. She swallowed it and lay back down with a sigh. She was in so much pain, she couldn't even be embarrassed. "Thank you," she whispered, squeezing her eyes shut.

"I'm going to close the curtains; will that help?"

She nodded. "Please."

A moment later, the light was gone and the room was shrouded in darkness. She turned on her side, curling her legs up, praying that nausea wouldn't hit before the medication could kick in.

"I'm going to call Carl and get the room for another night," Cade said, his voice sounding like he was speaking from a tunnel.

She tried to reply, but she wasn't sure he could hear.

A moment later, his deep voice spoke in hushed tones, and the sound of him was reassuring. "Okay, just do what you need to do. We don't have to go anywhere. I'm right here if you need anything. I won't leave," he said.

The throbbing pain finally hit full force, and his words barely registered. "I'll be okay. I just need to sleep it off," she said, willing herself to speak. She kept her eyes closed, praying the medication would kick in, that she wouldn't humiliate herself any further. She wasn't going to think about how unfair this was, how embarrassed she was at being seen as so weak, and how this proved that Mrs. Casey had been right about her.

Cade stood by the bed, never feeling more useless than he did right now. The fact that Sarah was in a fetal position was making him downright nervous, even though she'd mumbled she was fine. He'd had a handful of headaches in his life, usually the kind after a night of too much drinking when he was young, but barely even remembered having to take something for one.

He carefully pulled the sheet and blanket over her, relieved that she didn't flinch. Maybe the medication was working.

He stood there for what must have been ten minutes, his hands in his pockets, his mind drifting back to places and memories he hadn't visited in years. It was the pulling the blankets over a sleeping form, a still form, and even though Sarah wasn't drunk passed out, it triggered the memory of him pulling one of the dirty blankets off the ground and covering his mother at the age of four. He remembered the panic in his stomach when she'd pass out, the anxiety of not knowing how to function in the house alone. But he always found a way. Usually when she slept he'd go around and try and clean up; that made him feel useful, made him hopeful that maybe she'd keep him instead of give him away to the dealer on the corner like she always threatened when he'd be bad.

Cade blinked, wishing the moment away, wishing that it wasn't part of his past. He'd come so far, yet in an instant he could be taken back to when he was helpless.

He crossed the room and grabbed the vinyl-backed chair and, after wiping it down with a towel from the bathroom, sat down. He carefully propped his feet on the end corner of the bed, vigilant so as not to disturb Sarah. Maybe he'd fall asleep. But the chair was pretty damn uncomfortable, and the thoughts wouldn't stop; he didn't know why. He was pissed that he was being plagued by them now, after a night with an incredible woman.

He swore silently and crossed the room, deciding to make himself a cup of coffee. Luckily, the cups were disposable and new, so he didn't have to clean them out. As the coffee brewed, the dark liquid pouring into the cup, he thought of the coffee he'd made for his grandfather. Even though his grandfather had been negligent, at least he'd never hit him or gotten drunk or high when Cade was there.

But Cade knew by the age of ten that if he didn't make himself useful, he might not have a bed the next night. He made his grandfather breakfast before he went to school, and he'd clean up the little house every day after school and give his grandfather dinner. His favorite nights were when they sat on the same couch and ate cheese sandwiches and watched *Little House on the Prairie* reruns.

His grandfather had loved that show and so had Cade, not that he'd ever admit that to anyone. He'd always wondered what his grandfather had liked about it, because he was so different than the dad. Cade liked to imagine that one day he'd wake up and his grandfather would start acting like Mr. Ingalls. Of course, that never happened, and before he turned thirteen, he noticed his grandfather having difficulty putting sentences together. Cade would have to help him walk and later wash and clean up. His grandfather refused to go to the doctor, and Cade had dropped out of school that year to take care of him. They finally ended up in a hospital when his grandfather had turned violent and tried to hurt Cade in his sleep.

Cade blinked when the ready light glowed on the single-serve coffee maker and picked up the steaming hot coffee. He didn't want to think about those days anymore. He didn't know who that kid was; he didn't want to know him anymore. He didn't talk about it with anyone and he didn't think about it. It served no purpose because he couldn't go back and change anything, and wishing things had been different would do him no good.

Except right now, he couldn't stop thinking about it.

Day bled into night, gently, eerily, as his past bled into his future, Sarah's deep, even breathing blending with his as he sat in the motel chair. He didn't know why all this stuff was surfacing now when he'd been so good at keeping that part of his life deeply buried.

He'd learned as a child that dreams were wishes that other kids made, not him. As he grew up, he learned that dreams could actually be goals, and the only people who could make those come true were the ones who worked for them. That's when he'd decided to turn his life around. But it stopped there. He'd been content in that place where his old dreams had been fulfilled—make enough money to never have to depend on anyone else, make enough that you had savings in the bank for a rainy day or could help a friend in need. Make enough for a roof over your head and clothes on your back.

Then last year, it was like he'd outgrown those goals, and this longing in his gut had begun, that maybe there was more. Maybe there was more that the people he'd been raised by had never known or been sober enough to even imagine. Maybe there was a woman, a woman who could challenge him, who could make him a better man. Someone he would want more than just physically, who would stir something deep down inside him, who would inspire him into wanting to be a better version of himself, a woman he could see an entirely different future with…and that scared the living shit out of him. He'd held on to this good-enough life as though he'd hit the jackpot, because ten years ago, it *was* the jackpot, and who was he to ever want more than this? He'd already surpassed everyone in his family by miles.

What was the kid cleaning up filth instead of going to school doing wishing for something with a woman like Sarah?

Spending this weekend with her made him wish his past were different, that his parents were different. He wished he had someone to bring her home to, something to offer her, another story to tell her. As it was, his wasn't a story he could share. He knew that the place he came from was nothing Sarah would have ever been exposed to. None of his friends would ever understand the dysfunction or the poverty.

When Tyler had come back after leaving Wishing River for eight years, Cade had been the hardest on him. He knew that deep down, he had issues with people just taking off on him. He swore he'd never forgive Tyler for just leaving them all in the dark like they didn't matter. It had happened too many times in his life.

Crossing the room, he made sure he was as silent as possible and that Sarah was still sleeping soundly. He sat back down in his chair and put his feet up, taking a sip of coffee. He stayed there for what must have been an hour before he started dozing. Just as he was nodding off, a text came in from the bookkeeper at Joshua Ranch: *I can meet with you next week when I'm back in town. Your suspicions were correct.*

Cade swore softly in the silent room. He didn't want his suspicions to be correct. He stared at the woman sleeping soundly in the bed, listened to her soft, even breathing, and he knew—he wanted more for her.

But even worse, he found himself wishing that he was the one who could give it to her.

CHAPTER TWELVE

$\mathcal{S}$arah slowly opened her eyes and blinked a few times. It was dark, and it took a moment for her to figure out that she was still in the motel room. She turned to find Cade sitting in a chair with his feet propped up on the bed, his eyes closed. The light on the alarm clock read eight o'clock. Panic filled her. She'd been asleep for almost ten hours?

She scrambled off the bed to use the bathroom. A few minutes later, she splashed cold water across her face and finger-combed her hair. At least the migraine was gone. She took a deep breath and tried to squash the embarrassment as she remembered what had happened this morning.

Slowly opening the door a few minutes later, she was surprised to see that Cade was now standing, the curtains open as he brewed coffee. "Feeling better?" he asked, looking rumpled, his voice slightly raspy.

"Much. Sorry. I feel horrible that this happened and you were stuck here, sleeping in a chair."

"Don't worry about it. I'll just use the bathroom, and then we can get going," he said, walking by her.

When the door shut, Sarah looked around the room. This had been her attempt at a real life, and look what had happened. Why couldn't she just be like a normal person and do what normal people did when alone in a hotel room with the hottest person in the world?

She flop-sat on the edge of the bed. What had she done? Oh, she'd become helpless and had to be tucked into bed. She didn't even have any friends to talk to about this. She groaned thinking about what Mrs. Casey would say when she returned. Well, at least she wouldn't have to lie. Nothing had happened. Nothing ever happened to Sarah.

"Ready to go?" Cade said, walking out of the bathroom.

She bolted off the bed. "Yup. I feel great. Like nothing ever happened."

He grimaced. "You don't have to lie. You were practically comatose for ten hours, and you don't exactly look great."

She crossed her arms. "Okay, I'm totally fine *now*."

He gave her a slow nod and then proceeded to rumple her hair, like one would do to a dog, when passing by. Humiliation stung deep, and she kept her back turned to him as he opened the door. She should just turn around, follow him back to the truck, and pretend like nothing was wrong, that it was normal to have a weekend like they just did.

"You look like you're ready to bash your fist through a wall," he said with a slight smile when she didn't budge.

Great. So now he thought she had anger management issues, too. "No, no. Everything's fine. I'm fine. You're fine. It was a great weekend."

She didn't know if it was the slightly shrill tinge to her tone that made even her cringe or maybe the panic, but he stopped, shut the door, and turned around. She wasn't going to lie to herself, but the man standing in front of her was probably the best thing she'd ever seen in her life; he was the best thing she'd ever experienced, and he was also the best listener and was funny and—

Disgruntled.

"What's wrong?" he asked flatly.

She tucked a few pieces of hair behind her ear and tried to look nonchalant. "Nothing. Nothing at all. Let's go." She took her purse from the chair and walked by him, angry with herself for not being able to articulate her frustration.

He grabbed her wrist, gently but firmly holding on. "Tell me what's bothering you."

His voice had softened slightly, but she stared straight ahead, reading the fire emergency plan on the back of the door because it was easier than facing him and telling him what she was feeling.

"Are you still sick?"

She shook her head and met his gaze. "No, I'm fine. I'm sorry, Cade. This was all so stupid. Thank you for putting up with this disaster of a weekend and basically sitting in the dark for the day. That was above and beyond, truly."

He dropped her hand and took a step so that he was standing directly in front of her. "Hey, it's not a big deal. It's not like I had wild plans this weekend anyway."

Wild plans. She wondered what kind of wild plans he had on other weekends. Her wild plans consisted of staying up until midnight. "Do you, um, normally have wild plans?"

He grinned, his shoulders relaxing and the sparkle in his eyes returning. "Sometimes."

"Oh. I see."

"Do you?"

"Yep. I have access to the outside world via social media, you know." The minute she said that, she regretted it. It made her sound even sadder than her questioning him about his wild plans. Who says they have *access to the outside world via social media*? She needed to leave this room and never see him again…until Monday morning. There was no escaping him.

"Sarah, what's going on?"

"I didn't expect our night to go like this."

"How did you expect our night to go?"

Heat burned up her neck and flooded her face. "Well, I mean— I just… Not like this."

"I don't think we can ever have more than this," he said, his voice thick.

Her gaze went to his mouth, and she wanted to kiss him again. Desperately. And then she wondered how many people he'd kissed, how many nights in motels he'd spent, how many women there had been. He hadn't answered her last night, and she didn't push because, really, it wasn't her business.

"Then why did you agree to come?" she asked.

"Because you needed a friend. You needed to go somewhere other than that damn ranch. You haven't lived a life, so as a friend, I thought I'd help."

Couldn't be any clearer than that. But he'd said he wanted her, he'd acted like he wanted her. Everything about last night had been so real. She hadn't been living in reality for so long. She'd been stuck in this place that avoided the harsh truth, and she never wanted to go back there. "What if no one knew? What if this was just our thing?"

His jaw clenched for a moment. "I'm not going to hide. So that leaves us with no options."

"You can just…shut off your feelings? That easily?"

He hung his head back for a moment. "No, I'm not shutting anything off, believe me. It takes a hell of a lot of self-control."

She clasped her hands together. "Really?"

"Obviously."

"Not so obvious. Like, um, yesterday? When you were crying about the pillow that I might throw at you—"

His lips twitched, but he stayed right where he

was. "Yes?"

"It looked like you had no problem lying on top of me and being really close to me and then rolling away. Is that what normally happens in motel rooms with you? You just…stop?"

This time, he did close the distance between them, and her back was to the wall, and the wall of Cade was in front of her. His lips were still slightly curled into a smile but his eyes glittered with the same heat she'd seen yesterday, the one that made her limbs feel heavy, that made her heart race. "What do *you* think?"

She quickly averted her gaze because, judging by the gleam in his eyes, he was torn between laughing at her and doing some kind of demo, which she wasn't entirely opposed to at the moment. Who was she kidding? She'd welcome the demo with everything she had. How had she gotten herself into this mess? Her big mouth, her inability to have normal, adult conversations with the opposite sex. Maybe it wasn't even the opposite sex; maybe it was just conversations with people in general.

She shifted her gaze back to Cade's and frantically tried to buy herself some time. "Did you, um, ask me something?"

This time, he gave her a slow, lazy grin, one that she was pretty sure must be illegal. "I believe you were asking me what I do in motel rooms, and then I asked you to tell me what you thought I did in motel rooms. Then your face went red, with a couple of white blotches here and here," he said, lightly touching two spots on her face.

She tried to swat him away, but he caught her hand, laughing, and kissed the inside of her palm. Her breath caught, words caught somewhere between her heart and her mouth. "So that's, um, what you do?" she managed.

"I don't have a set of rehearsed moves."

She pursed her lips. "I see."

"I don't think you do," he said, his voice husky, the teasing tone slowly leaving, being replaced by one that made her desperate to learn more about him. "If you had reached out for me, I wouldn't have been able to pull back. I wouldn't have been able to resist you even though we can never happen."

Her heart raced uncontrollably in her chest, and she was torn between clinging to her pride and laying it all out there. She wanted him in every possible way, and she didn't want to think about what that would mean for them tomorrow. She was tired of tomorrow. Tomorrow hadn't served her in more than ten years. Every single tomorrow was the same—a lonely, sad place that was filled with the past. "Just tonight."

His face went still. "What are you talking about? Be clear."

She frowned at him, because she wasn't thrilled with that tone or the demand. "I mean…I know you don't want to hide anything long-term, but maybe we can be more than friends just once and no one would ever have to know?"

He didn't say anything for a long while, and her heart was racing. "Tell me *exactly* what you want," he finally said.

"I want you. I want you here, in this dingy motel room, on the questionable sheets, to make love to me."

He ran both hands down his face, and when he looked at her again, it seemed as though he was being ripped in two. "Have you ever slept with anyone before?"

That wasn't exactly the response she was looking for. If this had been one of her romance novels, the hero would have closed the final step between them and proceeded to kiss her while declaring his undying need for her, and then they would have had sex and faced the repercussions later.

This…*this* was just humiliating.

She lifted her chin. "No."

He nodded. "That's what I thought. So no way in hell."

A jolt of searing heat blasted through her body. She wasn't going to beg. She just needed to get out of there and not see him again until she absolutely had to. Too bad they had a two-hour drive home. How was this even happening to her? Could there be a more humiliating way to be turned down?

"You have a wonderful way with words, Cade," she snapped. "You could have used a little more tact and less 'no way in hell.' Thanks so much." She stomped past him and whipped open the door. A part of her expected he might reach out to hold her back, to let her down gently. The other part of her wished that he'd lose all sense of propriety and kiss her, and then sweetly—in that deep voice—tell her how much he wanted to be with her but just couldn't.

"It's a 'no way in hell' because there are always strings," he said. "Two people who work together can't have strings. Think about this. You and I get involved, then things come to their natural end. You marry some rancher. He finds out we were together. Do you think he'd want me as foreman? Do you think I'd still have a job?"

His tone was harsh, and his words were so brutally honest and bleak. She didn't know how to respond. They were obviously thinking of two very different futures—because they were two very different people. She was silly and following her emotions. He was worried about job security.

She clutched her purse to her, like it was a shield of armor. "Okay. You're right. I don't know why I brought all this up. Well, because I felt silly and…I don't know. But now I feel even worse, so let's just pretend this conversation never happened. Better yet, let's pretend this entire weekend never happened."

"It happened. I won't forget it," he said, opening the door.

They walked out to the truck in silence, and she wondered if this was the end, before anything ever happened between them. She stared at her reflection in the window as Cade appeared behind her. He opened her door, and she mumbled out a thank-you before climbing into the truck.

A moment later, he was pulling out of the parking lot. She stared at the HIGHWAYMAN sign in the side mirror, watching as it grew smaller and smaller. Not wanting to deal with the awkwardness ahead, she shut her eyes and leaned her head back. She had just ruined the friendship they had established—for nothing. She was also going to have to face Mrs. Casey and her dramatic worry. If only it had been for good reason, she might've been able to keep her head.

A few minutes later, she heard Cade gruffly say her name, but she kept her eyes shut until she actually fell asleep.

Cade decided as they approached the ranch that he was probably the world's biggest jerk. The gorgeous, smart, sweet woman beside him had made it very clear that she wanted him, and he'd turned her down. Not only had he turned her down, he'd humiliated her—and he regretted that deeply.

But he'd been so close to giving in that being nice hadn't been an option. Because like he'd told her, if she'd reached out for him, he wouldn't have been able to say no. Being blunt had been the only way because he knew her pride would prevent her from pressing further. But now this also caused a whole new set of problems for them—namely the fact that they worked together and he worked for her...which was exactly what he'd been trying to avoid by not giving in to his fascination with her.

Really, he was damned if he did, damned if he didn't.

Gravel crunched under the truck tires as he pulled into the ranch driveway. Sarah still slept soundly, and he was glad. Even though she looked better than this morning, she was still pale and not herself. He turned off the engine and softly called her name. Her silky hair had spilled around her face, and he wanted to reach out and tuck it behind her ear. No, he wanted to kiss the soft spot under her ear as he moved the hair away and slowly wake her up like that.

He knew she was strong and brave, but the image of her lying in a fetal position on that bed for hours wasn't going to leave him anytime soon. When she'd started throwing up, he'd known this was what Edna had been referring to. It had scared the crap out of him when he'd had to help her to the bed because she'd seemingly lost her sight. He never wanted to be the cause of that, never wanted to be someone who triggered that kind of pain in someone else. A part of him agreed with Edna that maybe Sarah was doing too much; maybe she should be taking it easy.

He ran his hands down his face, exhaustion finally hitting him. He was in no position to tell Sarah he thought she shouldn't pursue her dreams of running her family ranch. It wasn't his business, wasn't his call to make. But he could start with some changes. He could alter some of the things they did around the ranch. Maybe he could say he really needed more help with the office end of things. That would be less dangerous. Hell, if that had happened on a cattle drive or even just during the day, dealing with cattle, what would she do? It was way too dangerous.

He glanced over at the house. The front porch lights were on, and he knew it was only a matter of minutes before Edna realized Sarah was back. He said her name again, this time more loudly, and she finally stirred.

She rubbed her eyes and then sat up straight, looking at him. "Sorry. I hope you weren't sitting here long," she said, her voice stiff and not filled with the warmth he'd gotten used to, that he was starting to love.

He shook his head. "No, just a minute. Are you feeling okay?"

"Yup. Thanks. I'll see you Monday."

"If you need to take the morning off, that's fine."

She raised her chin. "No, I'll be there at the usual time."

"I was thinking that I need some extra days to catch up on all the office work. I haven't put in any time over there. Maybe we can start there?"

She stared at him, and he could feel her evaluating him. After a long moment, she finally gave him a nod and unbuckled her seat belt. "I should probably start learning the business side of things as well."

"Great."

She picked up her purse, and he went to open his door. "Please. Don't get out."

"Sarah," he said, wincing when his voice came out sounding harsh.

She paused, her hand on the door handle. "Yes?"

He searched for the right words, hating that no matter what he said, he'd be hurting her. But he knew who he was, and he had no illusions about who Sarah was. She was his boss; he was her employee. She was the heiress to a ranching fortune; he was an heir to predispositions toward drug and alcohol addiction. He would always be the guy without a family, without a past, and it was best that he remembered that at all times, for both of them.

"I have a really good thing going here. I love this ranch, love working alongside those men every day. I like our time together and the fact that we are going to be building this ranch back up to what it used to be. I can't jeopardize any of that."

She turned to him, her green eyes glittering. "I understand that. It's very commendable and is exactly what I needed to hear. It was wrong of me to think or maybe make you feel like we had to be more. It's best that we go back to the way we were."

It took all his self-control to sit still and watch her leave. His teeth were clenched hard and his knuckles white in his lap. Sarah had no idea how much he'd wanted her, still wanted her. He knew he was doing her a favor by letting her go now before they got in too deep. And that's what would happen to them. He knew it, because he'd never experienced this before. He knew that he had the potential of falling hard for her, and he also knew what that meant—it meant opening up about his past, his feelings. He'd never had the luxury until this job came along of walking away, moving from one job to another. Sure, he could always go back to Tyler's, but it would be a pity job. He wasn't a man who had anyone to fall back on. There was no safety net for him.

He pulled away when Sarah entered the house and shut the door.

He drove down the gravel driveway, to the home he'd worked for, the only home he'd ever lived in based on true merit, and hated that he had no choice.

CHAPTER THIRTEEN

 $\mathcal{S}$ arah shut the door behind her, barely keeping it together, wanting to lean against it in exhaustion and sadness, but Mrs. Casey dashed into the foyer, her face white and her eyes wide. "Where were you?"

Sarah sighed. She needed to deal with Mrs. Casey first; then she could go wallow by herself in her room. "I was away for the night with a friend, just like I said in my message. Last time I checked, I was a twenty-six-year-old woman, not a child."

Mrs. Casey put her hands on her hips. "Cade was also away last night."

Sarah knew she couldn't lie. She shouldn't *have* to lie. "I was with Cade."

Mrs. Casey sucked in her breath and placed a hand across her chest as though she'd just taken a bullet to the heart. "I'm very disappointed to hear that. Your parents would be ashamed. Your father would have fired him immediately, and you should do the same."

Sarah rubbed her temples and forced her temper to remain in check. "*I* invited Cade, not the other way around. It wasn't some grand attempt on his part to seduce me. Quite the opposite." If she only knew just how true that was, she wouldn't be worrying about nothing.

"Why would you do such a thing? He should have refused."

"We're friends. Nothing more."

"Still, your father would have had him packing. Your mother, too."

Sarah glanced at the piano across the room, the family pictures lining the bookshelves, her gaze resting on the spot where Josh's picture should have been. "Please stop talking to me about my parents. I understand you're trying to protect me, but the guilt trips won't work. I don't need a chaperone or a nanny—I'm an adult. If I want to spend the night out, I can. But because I do believe this is coming from a place of concern, I will tell you that nothing happened between Cade and me. We are friends. He is, was, the perfect gentleman."

Mrs. Casey crossed her arms and shook her head. "I don't know what's happening to you, and I'm just so afraid I will lose you because you're going off in the wrong direction."

Sarah stormed over to the bookshelves, crouching down to open the closed cabinet doors on the bottom. She knew their pictures were in here somewhere. His school pictures and the ones of them together at birthdays, Christmases.

"What are you doing?" Mrs. Casey whispered as she stood beside her.

Sarah grabbed the stack of silver-framed pictures and pulled them out. "What I should have done as soon as my mother died. I'm putting

Josh's pictures back out on display so I can see them every day, so that I can remember the brother I had, not try and forget him," she said, making room on the shelves to nestle his pictures among the assortment of other family photos.

She braced herself, waiting for Mrs. Casey to tell her all about how wrong it was to defy her parents' wishes. She was startled when Mrs. Casey handed her a picture. "I agree with you," she said softly, her eyes filled with a rare show of tears. "I never thought it was right to not speak of or see Josh anymore. But I didn't want to judge. Loss is hard, and we all handle it as best we can, right or wrong."

Sarah paused, looking down at the last picture, the one of Josh and her the Christmas before his accident. He was making a face at the camera, and she remembered her mother reprimanding him, asking why at his age he still couldn't behave properly for a picture. She smiled and placed the picture on the shelf, then turned to Mrs. Casey.

"Thank you. I'm not a teenager; I'm past the age of wrong direction. You don't owe my parents anything," she said. "You can't let yourself be saddled by what they've burdened you with. Live your own life. You need to get out of this place, too. Maybe you should find a man!"

Mrs. Casey gasped again, that hand flying to her chest, this time taking a step back, another bullet received. "Child, the last thing this woman needs in her life is a man. One man for one lifetime is more than enough, thank you very much."

Sarah almost laughed, but Mrs. Casey didn't look as though she was joking.

"I know about men like Cade, Sarah. So good-looking that you forget why they're so wrong. Where are his parents? Why doesn't he have a family of his own? What, he just drifts from town to town without ever putting down roots?"

Sarah swallowed the worries because she knew Mrs. Casey was trying to get to her. "He's not drifting; he's been living in Wishing River for more than a decade, so... And as far as family, I think that's really low of you to say. We can't choose our families. He's a fine rancher, a hard worker, and one of the most caring people I've met in my life. When I got a migraine at the hotel, he took care of me, made sure I was okay."

"You had a *migraine* in front of him?"

If she wasn't careful, another one would be coming on soon. "Yes. A migraine. I didn't give a striptease."

Mrs. Casey made the sign of the cross, and Sarah almost felt bad. The most "scandalous" show Mrs. Casey watched was *Downton Abbey*—all this was way beyond her. But true to form, the older woman didn't stay down for long. She put her hands on her hips. "You come from a long line of wealthy ranchers, people with lineage, history, roots, and faith."

Sarah's breath caught, and her heart squeezed for Cade. "You have it all twisted. None of that means anything. Nothing real. You can't hide who you are behind a pile of money, Mrs. Casey. When Josh died, my parents fell apart—not for a while but for the rest of their lives. They destroyed each other, their marriage, and I was collateral damage. Nothing could save them. Even with all their resources, they didn't turn to their faith; they turned away from it and turned to gambling, drinking, and anger.

"When push comes to shove, when horrible things happen in life, all that status isn't what saves a person. It's something else, deep inside. Some people have that will to survive, to keep going, to conquer…and some don't. It can't be bought and it can't be faked.

"I don't hate them, and I'm not trying to dishonor them, but I am trying to shake that mentality. There was no life for them after Josh died. I can't do that. He wouldn't *want* that. I'm twenty-six, and I hope there's life for me; I pray there's a long life for me ahead, filled with good days and good people. I'm going to honor the life I've been given by living. I would love for us to be in this together, Mrs. Casey," she said softly.

Mrs. Casey's eyes were glistening, and Sarah didn't know if it was from regret or anger.

The older woman braced her hand on the piano. "We are in uncharted waters, Sarah, dear. I'm not sure I'm prepared for this. You were the child I never had. So was Josh. It was my biggest privilege to get to be a part of this family. And…I'm glad you took out that locket. Keep him close to your heart."

Sarah smiled at her, the lump in her throat making it hard to speak. "Thank you. Josh adored you. I'm going to change things up around here. As soon as I have a free morning, we're going into town. There's a great little diner, and I bet you'll meet a nice group of ladies to become friends with."

Mrs. Casey glanced away and patted her unmovable curls a few times. "Oh, Sarah, don't be ridiculous. Women my age don't go out with friends."

Poor Mrs. Casey. Sarah shook her head. "There's a whole other world out there."

"I can still pray that another man comes along for you."

Sarah reached out to give Mrs. Casey a hug, despite her comment. "I'm so happy you're here with me. Even though we may not see eye to eye about everything, I know you're only looking out for me."

Mrs. Casey patted her cheek. "Me too. Just remember that the next time I ask after your whereabouts."

Sarah almost laughed as the older woman walked away. She sat down on the bench, running her fingers over the smooth keys. Playing wasn't an option for her tonight, as it hadn't been for so long. What had once been a joyful, creative outlet for her had turned into a painful reminder of a life that no longer existed.

Sometimes, she'd imagined herself married with her own kids, picturing teaching them how to play the piano. She closed her eyes, her fingers on the keys to start her favorite song, but she couldn't make them press down. She let her head fall forward, exhaustion taking root deep inside, swirling with disappointment.

Maybe it was the disappointment that was more overwhelming. Maybe her parents had been right. Maybe she wasn't cut out for the real world. Maybe her reaction, her retreat inward after Josh died, meant there was something wrong with her. Maybe Cade sensed it, and that's why he pulled away from her.

Well, there was one thing she knew for sure—whether or not she was ready, life kept moving forward. It didn't matter how cruel or unfair, it kept going, and she had no choice but to move along with it. With or without Cade, she wasn't going to cower in this house.

She was going to *live*.

After a week of pretending as though nothing had happened between Sarah and him, Cade was at a breaking point. Besides the personal reasons for keeping contact to a minimum, there was now the stress of what he'd discovered about her dad. Cade was fighting the urge to walk over to the main house and tell her the truth about how bad her father's gambling had become.

But he had avoided any kind of conversation that didn't have to do with day-to-day operations around the ranch. There were two reasons, mainly—he regretted ever going away with her last weekend. It had been a moment of weakness on his part when he'd agreed to that. Never mind that it had probably been the best weekend he'd had in…forever. None of that mattered, because it could never go anywhere.

But he kept thinking about her, about how she'd let him in and told him about her brother and her family. He could hear the pain in her voice, could see the sadness in her eyes, and he remembered how she'd felt against him.

Which was his other problem—the attraction. It had been a PG-13-rated experience, and yet it had been one of the most memorable nights of his life. He wanted her with a part of himself he usually didn't put into the game—his heart.

He leaned back in the leather chair of Sarah's father's office and stared at the numbers in front of him. He had a stack of papers, bank statements, which he'd been going through for the last few weeks. Operating on a hunch, and with the proof the bookkeeper provided, he was pretty certain he knew why the last foreman had up and left.

The ranch was in the red and had been for years, thanks to her father.

His muscles protested after hours of sitting hunched over the desk as he stood. He needed something strong to drink while he came up with a plan. Obviously, he had to tell Sarah. He poured himself a whiskey, his gaze lingering on the handful of family pictures on the bookshelves.

His mind drifted to Sarah telling him about Joshua…and then to her migraines and Mrs. Casey's urgent warnings about Sarah's health. He rolled his shoulders and leaned against the bookcase ledge. That time, she said the migraine had been triggered by bad food. But she had also said that stress was a trigger when she used to have them frequently. How was she going to react when she found out just how deep in debt her father had gotten the ranch? She'd feel stupid, knowing her. She'd feel betrayed and panicked. That wouldn't be good for her health. As foreman, it was his responsibility to solve these kinds of issues.

He was going to have to tell Sarah eventually, but first, he needed to make sure there wasn't something he could do to make the situation a little better. The last thing he wanted was to ever inflict the kind of pain in her that he'd witnessed last weekend.

It was well past nine at night, a Friday, and this had been his routine for the last couple of weeks since starting on at Joshua Ranch. He'd put in a full day with the men, then shower, eat dinner with them, and put in an evening at the office. While the business side of ranching wasn't new to him and he'd done most of these tasks at Tyler's ranch, it was still a new operation to him, and he was essentially teaching himself.

He glanced at the clock and forced himself to get back to work. Time to stop daydreaming about Sarah like a teenager. He was hired on as a foreman, and he'd never disappointed any employer with his work.

The printer signaled it was out of paper and Cade sighed, standing. He was pretty sure there were a few more packs of paper in one of the rows of cabinets across the room. After looking through three and finding none, he came across a stack of printer paper. As he was pulling a bunch out, his gaze came across a stack of picture frames, leaning against the inside of the cupboard. He wasn't a snoop and it wasn't any of his business…but the people in the picture were Sarah and her brother. He gingerly pulled out one silver-framed picture, and Sarah as a child stared back at him, her smile wide and laughing. It was a smile he'd never seen on her. She was sitting confidently atop a horse, and her brother was beside her. He had the same blond hair and green eyes and the same smile.

A stab of sadness came over him. This wasn't his business. He slipped the picture back in the cupboard and shut the doors.

He was my best friend. He was funny and wild and loved life so much. Cade pinched the bridge of his nose, trying to quell the emotion that gutted him whenever he thought back to Sarah telling him about her brother. It wasn't fair, what that accident had done to her family, to her. She deserved more than to be held back because of fear. No one had held him back; he'd gone on to live life fully. Or so he thought. Maybe he had been missing out on the deeper connections, on the things that mattered.

He was attracted to Sarah on so many different levels that he'd never experienced before, and he'd barely touched her. Just one hot, very controlled kiss. Even after their disaster of a weekend, he found himself looking forward to his mornings, to seeing her smile, to listening to her soft voice as she asked him questions or having her by his side at the ranch. She was a quick learner and didn't shy away from hard work, never complaining that something was too difficult or that she was tired. She kept on going right along with the rest of them, never giving up.

The sound of his phone ringing in the quiet office jarred him, and he glanced over to see Dean's number on the display. For the last five or so years, he and Dean had spent most Friday nights together unless Dean was on call at the hospital. Now that Tyler was back home, the three of them had picked up where they'd left off before Tyler had left Wishing River.

He hesitated a moment before answering, for the first time in a long time not wanting to spend the evening at River's Saloon in town. River's was like a second home to him and home to many a cowboy in Wishing River. Everyone knew you went to Tilly's Diner for some real comfort food, but you went to River's when you were looking for the solace found in a bottle or fun for the night. He didn't really want either.

The ringing stopped for a moment, and a twinge of guilt hit him. He'd call his friend back. Dean had been there for him, and he knew that his friend's life was pretty stressful keeping up with the demands of his job at the hospital and the demands of his tough father at the family ranch. Dean's family almost made him glad he didn't have one of his own to worry about anymore.

The ringing started again, and this time it was Tyler's number on his display. All right. Maybe he should force himself to go. He smiled. To him, his best friends were family; they were the closest to family he'd ever get. Despite the fact that he really wanted to finish up in here and go to sleep, he picked up the phone.

Maybe a night at River's was exactly what he needed. Sarah would never go there.

CHAPTER FOURTEEN

$\mathcal{S}$arah leaned forward in her chair at River's Saloon, almost giddy with excitement. This place was amazing. She kept looking around, trying to soak in the atmosphere. The saloon was exactly like something out of a movie—rustic and old, with black-and-white pictures of Wishing River, dark tables and chairs, and what seemed like a mile-long bar with a polished but worn counter. The two levels of tables were completely full, and there was an area with pool tables, a stage for a live band, and even a floor for dancing.

This was the best thing she'd ever seen.

"So what's it like working with Cade?" Hope asked.

Sarah shifted in her chair, definitely feeling like she was in the hot seat and not really knowing what to say. She took a sip of the wine Hope and Lainey recommended, very aware she would have to drink this slowly and definitely not have more than one glass. They hadn't ordered food yet, but Hope had informed her that she'd made the owner add gluten-free-bread options for their famous burgers.

This morning, she'd received a text from Lainey out of the blue, asking if Sarah wanted to meet the two of them for dinner. She'd been giddy like a schoolgirl to receive the invitation and had looked forward to it all day.

Sitting across from the two of them, having easy conversation, she realized how much she'd missed women her age.

Before her brother's accident, she'd had tons of friends. She hadn't been shy and had no trouble fitting in with the kids at school. After Joshua, when her parents had pulled her from school, her closest friends had tried to keep in touch. She even remembered her best friend's mother coming over for tea with her mom and gently telling her that it would be good for Sarah to see her friends again. Her mother had been polite but noncommittal.

Slowly, everyone stopped trying. Sarah felt like they had become the weird family who didn't socialize anymore. They didn't go to town events, they didn't go to church events…they didn't do anything. She'd been so consumed by the loss of Josh that at first she didn't miss her friends. But as the months grew into years, she realized how wrong her parents had been. Isolation should have been temporary, but the company of good people and good friends could have helped them heal. Her parents had destroyed all her relationships.

Now, here she was at twenty-six, learning how to make friends again. And she *really* liked Lainey and Hope. She didn't want to blow this.

"Please tell me you're not going to leave us

hanging," Lainey said with a smile as she picked up her glass of wine.

Pushing aside what happened last weekend, she focused on their working relationship. "There's not that much to say, honestly. You guys probably know Cade better than I do. He's hardworking, and everyone seems to like him. It's been going much smoother than I could have hoped." Except between the two of them, but she couldn't get into that with women she barely knew. She didn't know what she and Cade were now. He'd been distant but polite the entire week, and she'd had to fight to keep focused on ranch tasks and not on how dejected she felt. He'd told her they could never go anywhere, but the reality of it was much harder to take.

There was so much about him that she admired, and having to work beside him all week as though they hadn't shared a room together was painful. She regretted divulging all that personal stuff about her family and Josh. Doubt started trickling in, making her wonder if it was easier for him to blame it on the job than admit he didn't have feelings for her. Maybe he was just letting her down gently— after all, she came with a lot of baggage, and she wasn't exactly fun, even though the whiskey had made her foolishly boast that she was.

"That sounds like résumé-ish stuff. Cade is great, don't get me wrong. But I could have sworn I saw a little spark of something at Lainey's party,"

Hope said with a mischievous glint in her eye.

"We both hate prying. But we just thought… or maybe hoped, since you came to my party together, that something might be going on between the two of you. Tyler claims he knows nothing about you and Cade and sadly, I believe him," Lainey said with a laugh.

Sarah toyed with the bowl of nuts on the table, trying to process her surprise that they noticed something between her and Cade. They were obvious? At that point, she hadn't assumed she had given off any vibes. Obviously he hadn't told his friends about going away with her that weekend, because then Tyler would have told Lainey. At least she didn't have to be worried about any of them knowing the extent of her humiliation.

She glanced up at the two women, wanting to be open and honest but not knowing how much to reveal because Cade was their friend, too, and he worked for her…but she also didn't want to shut them down and ruin this opportunity to have real friends. True friends shared things about relationships. "We… He's a really great guy and we work together. We both kind of agreed that nothing could ever happen between us," she said, hoping that would end the discussion.

Unfortunately, it seemed to pull Lainey and Hope deeper into it. Hope frowned. "That doesn't sound like Cade. I mean, okay, maybe the Cade we all knew, but I really sensed something between the two of you. He never brings dates to any of our events."

"Oh, it wasn't an actual date. Just him pitying me for not knowing anyone my own age."

Hope was tapping her chin. "Okay, but the fact that you two had this discussion means there *is* something between you. Wow, I'm being way too nosy."

Sarah cringed. She wanted to open up to them the way real friends did, but it felt so awkward, since they were *his* friends, not hers. "You're not. I get it. You guys go way back. Honestly, he totally bailed me out of a bad situation, and I don't know where I'd be without him. Obviously he's..."

"Hot," Hope supplied.

They laughed, and Sarah nodded. She didn't want to gush and come across like this was a high-school crush, but she also didn't want to not say anything and seem closed-off. These were women who had lived a lot more than she had. Hope had been married, had a child. Lainey was married and ran her own business and had even graduated from an art school in Italy. Sarah had just been... hiding. "Cade and I aren't really anything. I mean, anything other than coworkers."

"I always thought that Cade needed someone different from him to ground him a little," Lainey said before taking a sip of wine. Hope nodded.

"Ground him?" Sarah asked, leaning forward.

She was not above getting some insider info about Cade.

Lainey shrugged. "He was always kind of a loner, the guy who didn't really care about getting into trouble. He's stayed under the radar for years and has been best friends with Ty and Dean forever, but he just had an edge to him. It was like one day he just showed up in town with no history, no family, nothing. Tyler doesn't really say anything about Cade's past, and I think it's because he honestly doesn't know much."

Sarah processed that bit of information and thought back to the night at the motel. She had done all the sharing. Mrs. Casey had also mentioned that he said he had no family. None of this scared her, but it did make her heart ache just a little for him, and it made her wish that he felt she could be trusted enough to open up. "He hasn't said a thing to me."

Sarah took another sip of wine and forced herself to relax. She needed to learn how to open up to people, to share, to talk. *He's the best thing that ever happened to my ranch*, she would have added, but that would be premature, and she wouldn't want it to get back to him yet. "All the guys like him; it's as though he's been there for years. I interviewed so many and no one was right, and then he walked in…"

Hope leaned forward. "And?"

"He didn't patronize me, his references were

glowing, and he knew his way around the ranch right away."

Lainey smiled. "So you've become…friends?"

"I guess," she said. She was disappointed in herself. She should tell them. She didn't need to go into details, but she should admit that she had feelings for him. Putting herself out there was something she'd have to get used to if she wanted real friends. Maybe she could just swear them to secrecy.

"Okay, so maybe it's not Cade. We need to find you someone else," Lainey said.

Sarah cleared her throat, trying to shove away the awkwardness. "It *is* Cade, but he kind of turned me down."

Hope's mouth dropped open, and Lainey frowned. "What?"

Sarah nodded, deciding she might as well lay it all out there. "Yup. There was no mistaking it. It was a rejection."

"Did he say why?" Hope asked.

Sarah shrugged. "He didn't want to jeopardize his job at the ranch if things didn't work out well between us."

"That doesn't sound like him," Lainey said.

"Oh great, maybe he was just saying that as an easy out, then?" Sarah asked, taking another drink of wine. That's what she'd been worried about. From what they were implying, he didn't say no to too many women.

Hope waved a hand. "No, no, of course not. Maybe he does have feelings for you. Maybe he just thinks you want different things than he does. I never pictured him as the type to settle down."

"I look like that type?"

"It's not a bad thing! But maybe he wants someone for a night and that's all. He can't really do that with you, since you're his boss," Hope said.

Which was exactly what he'd said.

She must have looked as forlorn as she felt because Lainey jumped in. "It's not a bad thing. At least not about you. I know that Cade has always worked. Tyler's dad is always going on about how he was the hardest-working cowboy he ever hired. He has no family to fall back on, and maybe that's it. He can't afford to lose a job like that for a chance at a relationship."

Sarah nodded, knowing Lainey was right. "It makes sense. And honestly, the more I think about it, the more I realize we're probably not right for each other anyway. He's saving us a lot of awkwardness at work, and I should be grateful for—"

She sat up straight, feeling something shift in the room. She turned in the direction of where Lainey's gaze had drifted. Her stomach dropped as she spotted Cade, Tyler, and Dean walking toward them. "Great. Your new friend and foreman just walked in, looking about as hot as a man can get," Hope said with a wink.

Sarah held her breath. The last thing she wanted

was to sit with the man she'd just been talking about… But of course they would, she thought with a sinking stomach as Tyler waved at Lainey.

The three of them definitely turned heads as they made their way through the bar to where the women were seated. The guys pulled another table over once hellos were exchanged. Tyler and Lainey sat together, while an odd shuffling from Hope had Sarah sandwiched between Dean and Cade. After a round of beers were ordered among them, easy conversation started. Sarah tried not to turn too much toward Cade but didn't want to look obvious.

"Have you met Aiden?" Hope asked as the handsome server walked away.

Sarah shook her head. "I've never been here before."

"Aiden Rivers, the owner of this place, keeps a box of imported wine for us," Hope said with a smile. "I'm not sure if that's really sweet or really sad."

The three of them laughed. "Let's go with sweet," Lainey said.

She took another sip of wine, wanting to be done with this conversation. "I really like this."

"Well, he's…great, and so is the wine," Lainey said with a funny smile.

Hope let out a strangled laugh. "Yes, let's just say that Aiden is also responsible for drawing a crowd." Sarah looked at him again and noticed that as far as looks went, the man had something impossibly attractive about him, almost a roguish look.

Cade sat up a little straighter. "I never noticed anything special about him."

"Yeah, me neither," Tyler said, leaning back in his chair and putting his arm around the back of Lainey's. Lainey patted his arm and smiled at him. He leaned over and kissed her, and Sarah glanced away.

"How are you feeling?" Cade asked softly. "Are you sure that wine's going to agree with you?"

Heat stung her. She didn't want his concern or his pity, and she hated that he'd seen her with her migraine. "It's fine."

"It's actually organic and free of sulfites," Hope said.

"Oh, great. Yeah, because all these people in here are going to drop dead tomorrow because of sulfite poisoning," Dean said.

"Can you two not start?" Tyler said, shooting Dean a hard look. Dean shrugged and sat back in his chair, looking disgruntled but not disagreeing.

"I was thinking I might do some paperwork stuff on Monday. I'd like to organize that office. I have a long list of things to do. I probably won't get out there with you guys until the end of next week."

Something flickered in his eyes and his jaw clenched. "Okay, that's not a problem. Let me know if you need help."

"I won't. You have your hands full anyway."

He nodded. She was vaguely aware of the conversation floating around them, and Cade kept his voice low as he turned to face her. She wanted to reach out to him so badly and wished he felt the same way. "I'm glad you're out with Lainey and Hope."

Right. Because she needed friends. "I hope you don't mind. I know they're your friends."

"No, no. I'm glad."

"Great."

"Tyler, my favorite song," Lainey said loudly, drawing them out of their own private conversation.

Sarah pulled her gaze from Cade's, happy for the distraction. Sitting so close to him reminded her of their night at the motel, how that had been the closest she'd ever been to anyone. And as the days went by, she ached for him. Though she still saw him all the time, the wall was up. He wasn't approachable. That night, she'd had a glimpse of a man who was emotionally untouchable. But she still saw the sparkle in his eye as she teased him with the germy pillow, she still felt the strength in his warm body, his citrusy scent. She wanted it again.

Tyler grimaced and stood, holding on to Lainey's hand. "You know I hate dancing, right?" But he'd already started moving in the direction of the dance floor, the question obviously rhetorical.

"We hate watching you dance, too," Cade called after them, a small smile at the corner of his mouth.

Lainey tugged on Tyler's hand, and he put his arm around her as they both walked to join the others on the dance floor. The soft, sultry sounds of the music only added to the palpable connection between Lainey and Tyler. She found herself watching them, wondering what that was like, that obvious attraction and comfort with each other they both had. She couldn't imagine being that close, that connected to another person. Tyler bent his head and kissed Lainey. Sarah tore her gaze away, feeling silly and intrusive witnessing an intimate moment. That's when she noticed the odd dynamic at her table.

Dean was steadily drinking his beer like it was soda, while Hope was motioning to the handsome bartender that she needed a refill of her wine. Sarah was pretty certain that her wineglass had been full before the guys had walked in.

"Sarah, do you like dancing?" Hope asked.

Sarah finished her own glass of wine. Desperate measures. She really wanted to have an answer that a normal person her age would have, but saying that she danced in her room, in her childhood home, by herself, was sad. "Oh, no. I have two left feet. I avoid dancing at all costs," she argued.

"Cade loves dancing," Dean said before lifting

the glass to his mouth.

Sarah turned to Cade, shocked. He was sitting back in his seat, his legs stretched out in front of him, scowling at his friend. "We both know I'd rather be run over by a herd of cattle than dance."

Dean barked out a laugh. "I know; it was just worth it to hear the remark. I'm the only one of us who can dance."

"I can dance," Hope said, sitting a little straighter, her eyes narrowing on Dean.

"Sarah, would you like to dance?" Dean asked her, ignoring Hope.

Sarah's head was spinning. Something was happening here that was way beyond her knowledge base of these friends.

Suddenly, Cade stood. "No one deserves that kind of torture." He held out his hand to her, and her mouth went dry. "Sarah, care to dance with me?"

Hope smiled, her eyes twinkling, and Sarah knew her new friend had done this on purpose. Sarah stared at Cade's tanned hand in front of hers. As if she'd ever say no to a dance with him—well, a week ago that is. Now, things were different. She couldn't just jump up and eagerly nod like an infatuated tween. This was the guy who'd turned her down flat.

She crossed one leg over the other and idly picked up her wineglass and then put it down when she saw that it was empty. "I'm not sure I actually feel like dancing. It's probably too strenuous for someone with my delicate health issues."

She spotted Dean smiling and leaning back in his chair from the corner of her eye. Hope was watching the exchange, wide-eyed. When she finally glanced up at Cade, his face seemed a little ruddy. "I'll make sure you're taken care of."

"I don't need a caregiver."

"Fine."

"Wait. Okay, I'll dance with you for the sake of maintaining professional relations at work," she said, finally standing.

His jaw seemed to clench harder at the sound of Dean's laughter. She sighed loudly as she reached for his outstretched hand. Before they were out of sight, she noticed Hope standing while Dean had his head buried in his phone. As much as she wanted to think about her new friend, her mind was on the man who was leading her to the dance floor, the one whose large, warm hand was wrapped around hers as though he'd been holding her hand for years. She resented that he had this effect on her.

When they were enveloped by the crowd, he wrapped her up close enough that her body melted against his in a way that made her breath catch. His one hand grasped hers securely while his other wrapped around her waist. She wanted to rest her head in the crook of his neck or maybe, if she were someone else, would press her lips to the exposed, tanned skin of his throat.

She needed to stop thinking of him like this. Maybe if she looked up, they could engage in some kind of distracting conversation. He was probably irritated with her.

"I hope a herd of cattle doesn't trample you tomorrow because of this dance," she said.

"Right now, I'm thinking it's worth the risk." She felt his smile against the top of her head as he pulled her in closer. "I hope you're not overexerting yourself," he said, his voice laced with humor as his breath brushed against her ear.

She may have had a shiver run through her body. Maybe.

She cleared her throat and kept her head where it was. "I'm managing. If I didn't have to keep avoiding having my feet stepped on, it might make the situation less taxing."

"Taxing. Huh. There's another word I haven't heard in ages."

She stiffened at the reminder that she basically had no life and was out of the loop on how people their age spoke. "Oh, is that supposed to make me feel bad? Fine. If I had more time, I'd try and become familiar with some more colloquial slang that you're accustomed to."

She felt him smile against the side of her head. "You started this."

"No, you started this when you told me nothing could ever happen between us."

"Ah, so this is all about that. If there's one thing I could change, it would be that."

She sucked in a breath and pulled back slightly to look up at him. His features were hard, and his eyes glittered in that way they had at the motel.

She'd never once expected that he might reciprocate those feelings. Hoped, yes. Expected... well, that would have been more than she could have asked for. All the little things, the looks, the smile, that tip of his hat, that concern for her... She wanted it. But when he'd hinted at his life, she couldn't see her fitting into any of it.

She knew she was smart; she knew she was capable and strong even though that was not how she'd been living. It was the other stuff, the other areas she was so lacking in...like real life. Up until last month, the only woman she spoke to daily was a very conservative widow who was seventy-five. All of this, these new friends, this bar, this man... this was so *foreign* and so right.

Maybe it was that deep, sensual voice that made her discard her inhibitions, but she met his aqua eyes. "You have second thoughts?"

"Every second of every day. The moment you closed the door and walked away from me. Lying in bed that night. Waking up the next morning. Yes, I have a helluva lot of second thoughts. Seeing you sitting there with Hope and Lainey when I walked in? Standing up here, holding you, feeling your body against mine? Second thoughts, second thoughts."

"I thought it was just me," she said softly.

He stopped dancing and wrapped his hand around the nape of her neck. "Never."

He slid his hand down her arm and took her hand, then started walking back to the table. Her heart was beating so fast, she was grateful for the noisy bar. *Every second of every day.* So what was their plan? Was this what the rest of her life was going to be like? Falling for her foreman? It sounded like the name of a romance novel. Just before they walked up the steps to where their friends were, he stopped and turned to her. "What are you doing tomorrow afternoon?"

Stay cool, Sarah. "Things."

His lips twitched, and she would have loved to reach up and kiss that mouth. "Important things?"

She shrugged and brushed some imaginary dust off her shoulder. "Depends who's asking."

"A…close friend."

She tilted her head toward their table, not willing to let him off the hook. "I have lots of friends now, so…"

He laughed. "Okay. Me. Do you want to spend the afternoon with me?"

She needed some clarification so she didn't get her hopes up. "On the ranch?"

He shook his head, his gaze going from her eyes to her mouth. "Technically, no."

She hoped he couldn't see how fast her heart

was racing. "Fine. So we'll do *friendly* things together tomorrow?"

He gave her a smile.

She smiled back at him. "All right."

When they rejoined everyone at the table, the conversation was animated as they all placed food orders. She sat beside Cade as though he hadn't just told her that he wanted her. Every day. And tomorrow, they were going out somewhere. Instead, she had to try and concentrate on the conversation.

"Here comes Aiden. Sarah, I'm not sure if you noticed the"—Hope coughed and leaned forward—"mysterious scar."

Sarah's eyes widened, and she tried not to laugh. She glanced over at the men, who were noticeably silent. Dean was frowning. Tyler was rolling his eyes. And Cade just looked perplexed.

"He's so nice. He always does a little something extra for us," Hope said. "He's a great candidate for Sarah, and if not, maybe for me."

Dean scowled at the man, and Cade's eyebrows furrowed. "Is that so?"

"We don't really know the origin of the scar," Hope whispered, ignoring the men, her eyes a bit glassy from the wine.

"Oh, he didn't come to your office for a scar-fixing potion?" Dean asked, leaning back in his chair.

Lainey choked on her wine.

"I don't sell potions," Hope snapped. "I'm not

Gargamel."

Dean shrugged, but Sarah was pretty certain he was fighting off a smile.

"I'm sure it's no big heroic story," Cade grumbled. "He probably got the scar from shaving."

Tyler laughed. "Probably."

Lainey elbowed him. "Quiet, he's coming with our order."

Everyone turned to Aiden. Sarah had to admit, he was quite good-looking, and there was a particular charm he had that was indeed mysterious.

"Hey, guys. Here's your order. I don't have time to talk—I've got a bit of a situation I need to deal with," he said, efficiently passing their plates around the table.

"That's fine, no need to linger here," Dean grumbled.

"What's the situation?" Hope asked, leaning her cheek on one hand.

Aiden let out a sigh and ran a hand through his black hair. "It's live music night, and the band called in sick. I hate disappointing people, especially a full house," he said.

"You should do karaoke!" Hope said.

Dean made a choking sound. "Not unless he wants to put up a foreclosure sign next week."

Aiden laughed. "Yeah, I don't think this is the crowd, Hope, sorry."

Hope shrugged, picking up a fry. "No worries. Oh, wait, Sarah, didn't you say you used to play piano?"

Sarah's stomach dropped and she shook her head rapidly. "No...I mean, yes, technically I play, but I haven't played in front of a crowd in more than a decade and come on, this isn't exactly a piano soloist crowd," she said with an awkward-sounding laugh, looking up at Aiden, hoping he'd agree with her. Why had she even mentioned that she played? Oh, right. Because she was awkward and didn't know what to say to people.

Unfortunately, Aiden was already smiling. "Hell, that would be amazing. I'm sure you'll win the crowd over. Live music is live music. What do you say? Piano is tuned and sitting over in that corner," he said, nodding to the small stage.

Sarah put her elbows on the table for a moment, covering her face. She couldn't do this. Everything about her music was wrapped up in memories of Josh, of the family that no longer existed. All the joy in her music had been buried with her brother. She didn't think she could play without him.

She felt a hand on her shoulder and knew it was Cade. She turned to him, and he gave her a smile that made her forget their "nothing more than friends" arrangement.

"You can do it," he whispered in that voice that made her feel like the only woman in the room.

"You'll be great," Lainey said.

"I promise we'll cheer and give you a standing

ovation after each song," Hope said.

"I have to do more than one?" she croaked.

Aiden smiled. "You can stay up there as long as you want. But let's say at least one song. Let the crowd decide."

Great. How was this happening? Just a month ago, she barely knew a single soul besides Mrs. Casey, and now she had all these people in her life, pushing her out of her comfort zone. They believed she could do it. She turned back to Cade. "I'm going to make a fool of myself," she said quietly enough that she hoped he was the only one to hear.

He leaned forward and placed a soft kiss on the side of her temple. "Never, you could never do that. Just let go," he said in a voice so tender and so intimate that goose bumps flickered over her arms.

The only other person who mattered wasn't here, but she already knew what he would've said. Josh would have already blurted out that of course she could do it.

Sarah took a deep breath, gathered her resolve, and looked up at Aiden. "Okay."

"Yes! Thank you," he said. "Come and I'll walk you over there and introduce you."

Sarah stood on jelly legs. Her new friends all called out that she'd do great, and Cade gave her a serious nod, his gaze following her as she walked with Aiden. "You don't actually have to introduce me," she said as they walked. "Maybe I could just start playing and no one would notice. I'll start soft and get louder."

He gave a short laugh, his eyes sparkling with warmth. "Not a chance. I have a feeling you're a person who should be introduced."

"No, I'm really not. I'm more like the person who blends in with a crowd."

"Then you're short-changing yourself, darlin'. You're going to win this saloon over after one song, I know it."

She didn't even bother arguing. He was very sweet and very charming. She almost laughed, knowing exactly what Hope and Lainey had been talking about.

They stopped in front of the piano, and he ran his hand over the dark, dusty top. "It's a little beat-up, but it gets used regularly. Why don't you sit down and warm up? Give me the thumbs-up when you're ready, okay?"

Sarah nodded and pulled out the bench. She sat and immediately shut her eyes, then took a deep breath, the noise from the restaurant fading out. *Focus. Stop thinking, stop worrying.* She had been able to do that before with music. She could block everything out and only think about the notes in front of her. She could do it again. She could play for real.

She counted to ten and forced her eyes open. She placed her trembling hands on the keys, feeling the smooth ivory beneath her fingertips, letting the familiar sensation take her to where she needed to be.

A bead of sweat trickled down her spine, and she removed her hands, wiping her sweaty palms on the front of her jeans. She couldn't focus. Couldn't do this. Panic bubbled inside her, a wave of nausea hit her, and the urge to run gripped her.

Get it together, Sarah. Deep breath. You're an adult now—you can play for you, and you can play for Josh.

She glanced over her shoulder and found Cade's gaze, the reassuring strength in those aqua-blue eyes. The panic slowly eased. Turning back around, she reminded herself that she'd performed more than fifty recitals from the time she was five until…until Josh died.

Afterward, playing felt like grief, holding her hostage and weighing her down.

But there were other people here tonight, people she liked, people who were starting to care about her. As isolated as she'd been, she knew that *this* was right, being with people, with friends, caring about people. People needed people. Flawed and imperfect as she was, as they were, she needed them.

And she needed Cade. But right now wasn't about him. Maybe it was supposed to happen this way—playing the piano tonight. Maybe it was a kick in the pants for her to start living again. Sure, she'd blamed her parents, Mrs. Casey, but what was really stopping her now? Her mother had been bedridden for almost two years before she'd died. Sarah could have started reaching out to the outside world then. Instead, she'd stayed hidden away. Had she been that weak, that impressionable, that it took someone like Cade to draw her out of her shell?

A hand on her shoulder startled her, and she looked up to see Aiden standing there. She gave him a sheepish smile. "Sorry, psyching myself up. I'm good to go now."

He gave her shoulder a reassuring squeeze and walked to the podium.

As he introduced her, her stomach turned into a giant knot. Just as she feared, the boisterous crowd became silent. She didn't turn to look at anyone, because she knew what she needed right now had to come from the inside. She touched the locket for a brief second. A shiver stole through her as she depressed the first key, the second, and then let her hands and her heart do the rest. The crowd, their expectations, everything receded, and it was just her and the music that had once given her so much joy.

For the first time since Josh died, she played without sorrow threatening to overtake her, and instead played with an incredible lightness and freedom that reminded her of the girl she used to be.

She let the light guide her fingers and fill her

soul. She let her heart open to the people here with her.

When that first song ended, she sat still, out of breath, exhilarated, exhausted, but whole. The silence in the room seemed to get louder in her mind, to her ears, and she held her breath. And then the room erupted with cheers and whistles and the scraping of chairs against the floor. Sarah squeezed her eyes shut, knowing this was so much more than one song; she was reclaiming life. It was a different one than she ever would have imagined, without the people she thought would have been with her longer, but it was with people who made her happy.

Sarah turned in her seat, her eyes blurry, her gaze roaming through everyone to see Cade standing with their friends, clapping, the smile on his face, the pride in his eyes making her smile and solidifying that feeling deep inside that this was right.

CHAPTER FIFTEEN

*C*ade didn't even know who he was anymore. Only because he'd witnessed Tyler falling for Lainey last year did he recognize the warning signs.

The second he'd walked into River's last night, he'd known she was there. The air felt different when Sarah was around. Sure enough, she was sitting there with Hope and Lainey, looking as though they'd all been friends for years. It had made him so damn happy to know that she was out with Lainey and Hope. But the second he'd sat beside her, he knew he was a goner. It was why he'd tried not to get too close during the week—it was almost impossible to be around her and want to touch her or kiss her. He was attracted to her on so many levels that he hadn't experienced before. This was all new to him.

He'd been pissed off for most of the day because he was falling for a woman he couldn't have. Then, when he did see Sarah, he was even more pissed off because he had to pretend they were just friends. When he'd held her close again last night, he knew he was a goner, but he didn't know how to stop himself from wanting her.

So he was going to take her out…as a friend.

It was for the best. If things went too fast, he'd

get roped into…something. He wasn't okay with that—for her sake. She didn't really know him in the way she thought. She saw him as this great guy, but if she really knew who he was or where he came from, then she might realize he wasn't the one for her.

He pulled open the door to Tilly's Diner and swore under his breath when he saw his best friends sitting at the counter. Great. They were going to have a field day with this one.

The diner hadn't opened for the day yet, but Dean and Tyler were already there. Didn't anyone work on a Saturday anymore?

"Hey, Cade! Your picnic order's almost ready," Lainey called out, giving him a sweet smile, completely oblivious to the havoc she'd just unleashed. She disappeared into the kitchen, and Dean and Tyler turned around on the stools slowly, their smiles those of kids on Christmas morning.

"Picnic order?" Tyler said.

Cade shot them a look that normally would have shut them up, but clearly he didn't have that kind of respect anymore.

"Is it in a basket, Lainey?" Dean called out.

"My cutest one!" she yelled from the kitchen.

"How do you even have a license to practice medicine?" Cade grumbled, leaning against the counter, no intention of sitting down with them.

Tyler barked out a laugh at that one. "So you're taking Sarah out on a picnic? That's very…

charming…and very unlike you," Tyler said.

Cade braced his hands on the counter. "That's funny. Kind of like how you suddenly attend church on Sundays."

Tyler frowned at him.

"Well, you'll both be reassured that I'll never change a damn thing about myself for another person," Dean said.

"Yeah, you're really winning at life, Dean," Tyler said.

"Can you guys stop insulting each other?" Lainey said as she came out of the kitchen. Tyler and Dean burst out laughing when they spotted the basket, and Cade had to close his eyes momentarily at the sight of it. He didn't want to hurt Lainey's feelings, but it was a giant basket with red-and-white-checked lining that peeked through where she had a bottle of San Pellegrino poking out. Nothing he would ever be caught dead purchasing.

She placed the basket in front of him on the counter. He slipped her a large bill and grabbed the handle, wanting to take it and leave as quickly as possible.

Unfortunately, she plucked his hand off and opened both sides of the lid and insisted on giving him a walk-through. "Okay, so everything in here is dairy-free, sugar-free, and gluten-free."

She paused as Tyler and Dean snickered. Lainey turned to them. "Are you guys twelve?"

They both shook their heads quickly.

"This is for *Sarah*," she said to them.

"Sure, sweetheart," Tyler said.

Satisfied, Lainey turned back to face him. "I picked up this amazing vegan cheese from the Cheese Boutique, assorted imported cold cuts, along with these gluten-free crackers. Of course, there're fresh grapes and strawberries. Because it's for you, I did manage to pack up a single-portion lasagna," she said with a wink that made it impossible for him to be irritated. "For dessert, I baked a gluten-free chocolate chip banana bread. Oh! There's also a small thermos of coffee with dairy-free creamer, in case you want some with dessert and, of course, the San Pellegrino. I think that's it. Does that sound good?"

He cleared his throat. "Uh, yeah, you went above and beyond. Thanks very much, Lainey."

She beamed. "I'm so happy. I just love Sarah."

"Yeah, we love Sarah," Dean said, giving him a dumb smile.

"Oh! Shoot. I didn't even think of getting champagne!" Lainey said, leaning against the counter, a finger to her chin.

He rubbed the back of his neck and ducked his head. "Don't worry about it."

"Oh, Cade, what will you do without champagne?" Tyler asked.

Lainey turned around slowly, a hand on her hip. "Tyler, are you making fun of me?"

"No, ma'am," Tyler said with a sparkle in his eye and a slight smile that for some reason Lainey must have found charming, because she laughed.

Cade shut the lid on the basket, leaving the money on the counter. "Well, thanks again. I should really get going," he said, backing up.

"Make sure you get champagne," Lainey said. "It'll be perfect with the strawberries."

"Nah, Cade, why don't you bring that cheap beer you tried to pawn off on us last weekend?" Dean said.

Because Lainey was around, Cade didn't want to use his choicest words for his best friends, so he flipped them off...just as Father Andy walked through the door.

Of all the luck. "Morning, Father," Cade said, using his middle finger to scratch an imaginary itch on his cheek.

"Wonderful day for a picnic, Cade. And a wonderful day to take a special young lady out," Father said.

Lainey's face turned red, and she quickly ducked behind the counter.

Hell, sometimes Cade hated small-town life and the gossip that came with it.

Cade nodded and hurried out the door like he had a train to catch. He placed the picnic basket on the passenger seat beside him, then drove back to the ranch. Luckily, the farther from town he got, the happier he became.

He found himself thinking about spending the day with Sarah without anyone around. Of course, that led to other thoughts of things they could be doing without other people around. But really, if Tyler or Dean had told him a year ago that he'd be going on a picnic—one that he'd planned, with a woman he wanted morning, noon, and night but knew he couldn't actually have—he'd have laughed his ass off. Cade didn't think he'd ever even been on a picnic.

So why the hell was he doing this? Because Sarah had mentioned how one of her favorite things to do was go on picnics with her family.

God, who was he?

He pulled into the ranch thirty minutes later, and she was already walking down the front steps of the ranch house. Her dark hair shone in the sunlight, the wind picking up a few strands. Her red-and-white-checked shirt was tucked into her skinny jeans, and she was smiling as she walked toward him. He'd never had anyone look so damn happy to see him.

Maybe it was that, or maybe it was that he'd never been so damn happy to see anyone that it made him forget they were at the ranch, that they were just friends, that Mrs. Casey was probably peering at them while making the sign of the cross from her bedroom window, but he met Sarah halfway.

"Hi, friend," she said with an adorable smile

that made him want to pull her into his arms and kiss her until there was no doubt in her mind that they would always be more than friends. Sarah made him forget everyone else. Sometimes she even made him forget his past, because the present with her was so damn good.

"You're going to use that against me forever, aren't you?" he asked, holding open the door for her.

"You bet." She laughed.

As he rounded the cab of his truck, the idea of there not being a future with her struck him. Ideally, he'd work one ranch for the rest of his life and then retire. Would this be that ranch? If so, he'd work here until he was in his sixties and then…leave. What would happen to them during those years? One or both of them would get married? How would they go on with other people and then just pretend this thing between them had never happened?

He shoved all those thoughts to the back of his mind and hopped into the truck. It would ruin his day, thinking about her married to someone, having kids with someone.

"Where are we going?" she asked once he pulled out of the driveway.

He shot her a smile but kept his eyes on the road. "Three guesses."

"River's?"

"People don't go there during the day unless

they're really hard-luck cases." He didn't add that he'd been there a few days in his lifetime.

"Okay…Tilly's."

"Good guess, but nope."

"Uh…the Highwayman? We can check in on Carl."

He choked on his laugh. "I'm sure Carl is fine. And I don't think either of us ever wants to go back there."

"All right. Fine. Are we coming home tonight?"

"Uh, damn straight. Unless we want to dodge Mrs. Casey and the shotgun she'd have waiting for me when we returned." Again, who was this version of himself? Worried about an elderly chaperone/housekeeper and propriety? It was like he was living in the last century. But the woman beside him made it very hard for him to complain.

She sat back and let out a theatric sigh. "I give up!"

A few minutes later, he pulled off the road to the clearing he knew all too well. It was the winding road that led out of downtown, the one with the old red barn that Lainey had painted and hung in her diner.

The banks of Wishing River would make the perfect spot for their picnic. He hoped that she'd be happy and that it wouldn't spark any sadness as she remembered days with her family. If it did, he swore he'd make her happy somehow.

"We're here," he said, hopping out of the truck.

"Where?" she asked, rounding the corner of the truck to his side. He pulled out the picnic basket, and her eyes widened.

He grinned and slammed the door shut.

"A picnic?" she breathed. The image of her telling him she didn't cry at the Highwayman floated across his mind, because for a second, there was a sheen in her eyes before she blinked it away.

He nodded, grabbing her hand and walking.

"*You* planned a picnic?"

"I'm not sure why everyone seems surprised by this and if I should be insulted. Are you more surprised that I planned a picnic or are you surprised that I was *able* to plan a picnic?"

She laughed, the sound making him smile, and he squeezed her hand. "You just don't strike me as the picnic sort of guy."

He didn't think he'd ever felt so comfortable with another person or so at peace. He didn't know how she did that. "Well, I'm open to new experiences. You…told me about your family and that you loved picnics, so I thought…"

They had stopped walking, and he almost felt awkward or bad or guilty somehow because she was staring at him as though he'd just given her a million dollars. Then she threw her arms around him, and he immediately hauled her up against him.

"Thank you," she whispered against his neck.

He slowly put her down, her soft curves gliding against his body. He reached for and squeezed her hand, then kept walking in the direction of the clearing. He didn't want to get too close to her; he didn't want to ruin this or push too hard because he didn't even know what was happening.

"I never would have guessed you were such a softie," she said.

He glanced over at her, his eyebrow raised. "I'm not."

She gave him a mischievous smile. "I think you are. Everything you've done for me, our night together. I mean, I may have been pretty isolated and lonely, but I'm not completely delusional. You don't exactly strike me as the type of man who stays up eating candy and talking in a motel room or going on picnics and holding hands all day."

He stopped at the clearing and busied himself with spreading out the checked picnic blanket Lainey had lent him, purposefully not answering her. He had no idea what to say. Of course this wasn't how he spent his time with women. But with Sarah…it wasn't like that. He wanted to do this stuff because she wanted to do this stuff. That made him happy. All of that was an entirely new concept for him.

"What do you think of this spot?" he asked, sitting down on the blanket and taking out the containers of food.

"This is absolutely gorgeous. The river, the flowers,

the mountains. All of it," she said, sitting down opposite him.

"I hope you haven't had lunch, because Lainey packed this thing to the brim," he said, opening the San Pellegrino and pouring two glasses. "Everything is gluten-, dairy-, and sugar-free. Except the lasagna—she knows I'm kind of obsessed with it. But I don't have to eat it now."

She was staring at him with that same expression again, her eyes slightly glazed. "That's really sweet. You go ahead and eat it; it won't bother me."

He shrugged. "I'll save it for later. There's other things—crackers, some kind of vegan cheese, fruit—but that can sit. Oh, she also made banana bread, I think, and coffee with dairy-free creamer."

"Uh, talk about hitting the jackpot in the friends department," she said, reaching for the cutlery and napkins while he pulled everything else out.

"I know. You guys seemed to be getting along," he said as they helped themselves to the food.

She beamed. "They texted and asked if I wanted to meet them at River's the night you saw us there. Luckily, Wishing River is so small, I knew where it was. I hear you're a regular?"

He took a long drink of water. He had no idea what Lainey and Hope had told Sarah about his... dating life. But the fact that she was still smiling was a reassuring sign. He shrugged. "There's not a lot of places to go in a town like this, so Dean, Tyler, and I hang out there a lot."

She nodded, popping a grape into her mouth. "I guess that's where single people in town go to hook up?"

This was the last conversation he wanted to be having with her. But he also didn't want to lie. "It's sort of known for that."

She nodded, looking toward the river. "I always love how Wishing River can look like it has diamonds sparkling on it when the sunlight hits it perfectly."

Hell. "Sarah, I know that we both have different lives..."

"I don't have a life, remember?" she said with a smile that was too tight to be a real one and a tone way too chipper to be believed.

"Is that what's bothering you?"

"Omigosh, what am I doing? Never mind. I'm fine. Let's just enjoy this lunch that you went to so much trouble getting."

"It was no trouble," he said.

"But it was so thoughtful. You remembered. You took the time to do this for me even though you've probably never done anything like this before." She smiled, a real one this time. "I've been getting the vibe that you're not the 'Sunday night roast beef dinner and meeting the parents' type of guy."

He didn't even know what that was. He only

found out about Sunday night dinners when he lived at Tyler's place. That had been the first place he'd ever had a home-cooked meal. Before that, it had been just putting together whatever he could find. When he'd lived with his grandfather, he'd been the one responsible for cooking—and he didn't cook. Over the years, he'd learned a thing or two, but he mostly ate at Tilly's or the canteen at whatever ranch he worked at. So Sunday night dinners weren't his thing, with or without the parents. "That's true," he said, knowing he was going to have to expand on something.

"But that's okay because even though I've met parents before, it's really not important."

"Right. Those guys you dated."

She rolled her eyes. "We never came close to anything like the Highwayman experience."

That was just sad.

"Oh, that's pity in your eyes, isn't it?"

He ducked his head. "Guilty as charged. You've been missing out on life."

"You haven't." She said it matter-of-factly or maybe with a tinge of awe.

"Let's just say we've lived different lives."

"And I guess that means I'm the only one here who's had no life. Or sex life. You seem to have mastered that area of life?"

He choked on his Pellegrino. He was as far from virgin territory as the San Pellegrino was from Italy. "Of all the things you were going to say, that wasn't one I'd bet on."

She shot him a smile. "Well, you're very evasive. I'm just trying to get some insight into your life before…we met. I feel like you know everything about me and I know nothing about you."

That was true, and it wasn't a coincidence. He shrugged. "I've never had a serious relationship with a woman because in my younger days, I had to work really hard to have a roof over my head, and now… I don't know. I never saw a point in commitment or anything like that. I don't let people in very easily. I don't talk about my past. It's nothing I've ever wanted to share. The women I've been with haven't wanted that, either, so it was a mutual understanding."

She nodded like she understood, even though he caught that flash of disappointment, or maybe hurt, in her eyes. She smoothed her hand over the blanket. "So, just like, sex in a motel room like the Highwayman?"

His stomach dropped. "It's not the same thing. Those are two entirely different things."

She waved a hand. "No, no, I get it."

She didn't get it. She wouldn't get it because he didn't even. He didn't understand how he could feel more intimately connected to Sarah after a night in a dingy motel, fully clothed, with barely a kiss. "I don't think you do. But…I haven't been with anyone in a long time. And I've never done this. I've never talked to anyone other than Tyler,

Tyler's parents, and Dean for this long. I've never gone on a picnic. I've never taken a woman out more than once."

She tilted her head.

"I mean, it's not that I don't want that," he hurried to say. "I see what Ty and Lainey have and…I think…he has it all," he said, his voice fading at the end as he stared into her eyes.

He thought he'd known who he was. His entire life he'd been figuring it out, wanting to be more than that poor kid but never really believing it was possible.

"They seem so happy," she said, picking at the remains of the strawberries on her plate. "Were your parents happy together?"

He stopped eating. Just thinking about his early years robbed him of his appetite. "No," he said flatly.

She stared at him expectantly, and he took a deep breath, trying to tell her what he never told anyone, even his closest friends, even when piss-drunk in their youth. He wanted to tell her all of it; so badly, he wanted to share it with her.

"Uh, no," he tried. "They weren't really together for long."

She gave him a sympathetic smile. "I'm sorry."

He shrugged and put the plate aside. He wasn't good at sharing his past, but there were other things he was good at, and he'd rather concentrate on those. He leaned across the plates to place his hand at the nape of her neck.

She met him halfway. "I don't think you answered any of my questions. And the whole Lainey and Tyler angle was a really great way of getting out of answering my relationship questions."

"Who wants to talk about old relationships?"

She shrugged. "It just says a lot about a person, I guess. It's also how you build trust. You can't go any further without trust."

"True. I'm not good at it, Sarah. It's not personal; it's just a fact," he said, hoping that was enough.

She searched his eyes, and he felt like she was waiting for something from him, looking for something in him, and he prayed like hell that he didn't come up short. "Well, since I'm the blabbermouth, I can tell you all about my past relationships."

He smiled, pouring coffee for them. "Did I tell you that's one of the things I really like about you, that you're so honest? What were your relationships?"

She groaned and pulled back, resting her palms down behind her, and he couldn't help letting his gaze roam appreciatively over her, the way her shirt strained against her breasts, her small waist, and then back up to her eyes. But it was the look in them that was the biggest turn-on of his life. There was this sexual chemistry between them that he'd never experienced before, this want, this ache that filled him, and yet they'd barely done anything.

She turned her head away from him for a moment, and he saw the shyness in her expression, in her needing to break his gaze. "So, yeah, my experiences were probably a little different from yours."

"Well, I'm anxious to hear," he said with a smile, handing her a cup.

"Thanks," she said, taking it from him and adding a bit of creamer. "They were prearranged. You know, like, preapproved financing?"

He bent his head and laughed. "That sounds bad. So your parents were the lenders?"

She nodded, some of the sparkle back in her eyes. "Something like that. I shouldn't be mean, I guess. The guys were…well, they *meant* well. They were nice."

Her voice hung on the word "nice" for a moment, but he didn't say anything. He was waiting for more. Maybe he was slightly uneasy, thinking about these men her parents approved of, knowing he'd have never made the list.

"They just had some pretty strong beliefs of how relationships were supposed to play out and how marriage and kids and all that would go."

"Seems like pretty intense conversation for a first date?"

"Oh, none of them got to the relationship phase…or the kiss phase…or the anything phase," she said with a laugh that sounded awkward. Then the laugh stopped and he realized what all of

that meant. That their time together in that dingy
motel room was the most intimacy she'd ever had.
Even that kiss. That had been her first.

He ran a hand over his jaw and tried to mask
his shock. He didn't want her to feel embarrassed,
but hell…that was sad.

He swallowed hard. He had known she wasn't
experienced, but he didn't really think that anyone
in their mid-twenties would have that little experience in the relationship…or kissing department.
"Why not?"

"I knew my parents were pretty traditional, and
I mean, on the whole, I didn't mind that—it's not
like I was dying to have any kind of…relationship
with anyone. But I have my own ideas, too, and my
own goals and ambitions, and I wanted more than
to just be someone's wife. I wanted to run this
ranch, and there was no way in hell any of those
guys would have been okay with that. So I would
have been on the sidelines watching, not because
I chose to but because that's the way it would be
with one of them. I want to be able to make my
own choices."

"You don't give yourself enough credit. With
all the problems in your family, the fact that you
could turn these guys down even though you
knew it disappointed your parents… You should
be proud of yourself."

She picked at some grass on the edge of the
blanket. "Thanks. That's the first time I've heard

that or had someone get it. I have no regrets."

"And you shouldn't. I wouldn't ever want to be stuck living by someone else's expectations or have to commit to the person I'm supposed to be with for the rest of my life because of anyone else."

"Exactly. My parents were pretty irritated with me, but I knew there was no point in continuing any of those relationships. One date each was more than enough. By the fifth guy, I told them I was done."

"Five?" He shook his head. "That's persistent. What'd they say about that?"

She shrugged. "We argued a lot, but they sort of led their separate lives, and soon after, my dad had a heart attack and was gone before we knew it. In a way, he was gone as quickly as Josh."

"I'm sorry." Much like when she'd told him about her brother, he had the urge to reach out and hold her or comfort her, but she took on that distance she had that night. It was a hands-off vibe that felt so unlike the person he thought she was. It almost reminded him of himself. They were so different but so alike in so many ways, and he wanted more for her. He didn't want her to be like him. He didn't want her to have the walls that he had. She needed more than that.

Maybe he did, too.

"It's strange, because he'd changed into someone I didn't know anymore," she continued.

"The father who raised Josh and me was happy, encouraging, and fun to be around. I mean, he was still pretty strict, but he was a different man. I lost everyone when Josh died—" She winced. "I'm sorry. It's like every time we're alone, I unload all my old baggage on you."

He cleared his throat past the lump that had formed there, that always seemed to be there when she talked about her brother. "Please. Keep going. You're not unloading."

She hesitated. "I want more. I've always wanted more. I want the ranch," she said quietly. "Josh and I had plans for that place. We were going to be partners; we were both going to have our families and build houses and all work together."

The longing and pain in her voice filled his chest. "I'm sorry."

She blinked a few times and gave him that brave smile he was coming to care about so much. "I can still keep my end of the deal. Thanks to you."

His chest swelled, but he shook his head. "It's not thanks to me. You would have found your way, Sarah."

She gave him a teasing smile. "Ah, but then I wouldn't have met all those escorts."

He gave a short laugh. "Well, I'm not going to argue with you there."

They lapsed into silence, picking at their food

and drinks.

Eventually, Sarah spoke. "Have you ever had perfection? Lived perfection?"

She was perfection. But he couldn't tell her that. He shook his head.

"I have," she continued. "I had it and I lost it and I became afraid to ever wish for it again, because I know it's fleeting, that in one moment, it can all be taken away. So what's the point of wanting something so good only for it to be ripped away?"

His stomach turned because he knew she was talking about her brother and her childhood. He knew the scars it had left. But it was wrong for someone like her to keep hiding from life and dreams. "Because maybe even a short time of bliss is worth the heartache. Maybe this state of not really living, this half-baked attempt at life, will wear you down until you wake up one morning, eighty years old, and realize that you wasted your years alone and afraid, but hey, you still made it to eighty. You made it to eighty without a person to love, and maybe that's a helluva lot worse than loving and losing."

None of this was stuff he dreamed he'd ever say to anyone, let alone a woman. Then again, had it been any woman but Sarah, this conversation wouldn't have even happened. She made him think about things he tried to avoid on a daily basis. She would just throw these thoughts, these truths, out there and make him dig deep to really figure out what he believed.

"I'm not sure I agree with you, but it's a nice theory," she said with a polite nod.

He tried to hide his shock. "Really? I thought that was a damn fine convincing argument."

He was rewarded with a soft laugh that pleased him inexplicably. "It was. Except for the fact that there are no guarantees anyone makes it to eighty."

He shrugged. "I'd take ten amazing years with the right person over fifty years of sitting on the sidelines, afraid to live."

Her fear and hesitation were reflected in her eyes, but damn it if he didn't want to be the one to take that look away forever.

"*A*re you happy?" Sarah asked, fighting the nervousness and leaning closer to him.

The afternoon had been one of the best of her life. Sometimes when she was with Cade, she felt like she didn't know herself, but now she was beginning to wonder if this was the real her, if being with him brought out the side of herself that she'd hidden away. She hadn't shared her real feelings with anyone in so long, yet it came so easily to her when he was around. There was something about him that made her think that he would have her back, that he'd be strong enough to take whatever she threw at him. He hadn't ever tried to shut her down or end their conversations about her family or her brother. He understood her dreams for the ranch when no one in her family besides Josh ever had.

She looked into his aqua eyes, searching for the answer, desperately wanting him to say yes, that he was the happiest he'd ever been in his life. Lying on the picnic blanket, his hands linked behind his head, he managed to make the gorgeous landscape less interesting by comparison. One leg was drawn up, and he looked like the poster boy for the cowboy life.

He turned from gazing up at the clouds to give his full attention to her. Sarah's breath caught in her throat at the tenderness in his eyes, that sweetness that always took her by surprise, that was such a contrast to the hard man he presented to the world.

This was her Cade. The one she saw, the one she was falling for.

He reached out for her, his hand coming to rest at the nape of her neck again. "With you, here, I'm the happiest I've ever been in my life."

Warmth seeped through her, and she leaned down to kiss him as though she'd been doing this for years. Her body pressed against his hard one, both his hands tangling in her hair, and all thoughts of Cade being sweet vanished. He kissed her with a passion that she understood, that was always lingering between them, one that made her forget reason, and one that left her hungry for more of him. But he rolled her off him gently, his hand still on her face. He looked at her with a mix of fire and tenderness. It almost made his rejection not hurt at all.

"Why'd you stop?"

He pulled his hand away and ran it through his hair. "For all the reasons we said before. Plus, you're not the only one who can have morals."

"Hey, who said I needed to exercise those morals right now?" she asked, scrambling up.

He let out a choked laugh. "Yeah, well, I'm not enough of an ass to not make promises and then just sleep with you. There are rules."

She wanted some kind of reassurance that he would be here tomorrow, or next month, or next year. Of course, he'd signed on to be here, but she wanted the promise that he'd be with *her* next month. That was ridiculous, of course, because what were they? What was this?

He'd been on his own a long time—did he want to stay that way? In all the ways that Cade made her feel alive and free, he also made her feel safe. He gave her the freedom to reach for what she wanted, to not place limitations on her, yet his presence always made her feel like he'd be there to catch her. That had never happened to her before. Every person who'd loved her had stifled her or had left her alone.

She had been buried so deep inside herself, so far under the blanket of grief, that she hadn't wanted to reach for her voice. She'd craved silence, not empty, meaningless words. But nothing seemed meaningless with Cade. She was done being silent.

"I think my parents would have liked you," she said, touching his hand.

He leaned his head back and stared at the clouds as the sky turned overcast. "I'm not so sure about that."

"No, they would have," she said, frowning.

"Maybe as a foreman, but not as your boy-friend, not anything more than that. I didn't have a family in the way that you did," he said. Something about his demeanor changed. He was suddenly aloof, pulling away and standing.

"I'm sorry," she said softly.

He shrugged. "I'm fine with it."

Everything about his posture and the stiffness in his voice told her that he wasn't fine with it at all. It was also very clear he didn't want to talk about this. "What was your family like then?"

He shoved his hands in the front pockets of his jeans. "I was a mistake. My parents weren't the type to want kids or commitment or anything like that. They were alcoholics; they couldn't hold down a job or make rent. It got to the point that I had to look after them in order to stay there or, uh, they'd send me out on the street. They eventually did get rid of me.

"I was passed from one low-functioning relative to the other. My last stop was my grandparents. My grandmother died shortly after I came to live with them, and then it was just my grandfather. He, uh, he needed help, so I helped him as best I could. Spent almost ten years there. I'd attend school when I could, but most days he really needed me around. He died when I was fourteen. I slipped under the radar and just left town, and I've been on my own since then."

She knew that if she showed emotion or pity, he'd close off even further. His voice was choppy, his face rigid, and she wondered if he'd ever told anyone even these small details. Pride and defiance were stamped on his strong face, and she took a deep breath, searching for the right words, trying not to convey the ache in her heart.

He had opened up to her, had laid it all out there, and she wanted to offer the comfort he obviously never had. She scrambled, standing, not about to just sit there when he was standing alone. Knowing he might push her away, she wrapped her arms around his waist and looked up at him. His eyes glittered, and his jaw remained clenched. "Every good gift and every perfect gift is from above," she said, the bible verse jumping into her mind.

He took a step back. "You think I'm different than I am. That's why I told you all this, so that

you could see where I came from. How different
we are."

"You are exactly who I think you are. Better,
maybe, because I had no idea. You don't wear that
hurt on your sleeve, you don't walk around with a
chip on your shoulder." Maybe it was silly because
he was a man who looked like he needed no one,
and for so long, he hadn't. Maybe it was silly of her
to think he might need her as much as she needed
him. "You've come a long way. There are so many
people who have a start like yours who can never
escape that life, and who end up repeating the
mistakes their parents made."

"I haven't been a saint. I've done things I'm not
proud of when I was desperate, things I can't take
back, things I'd be ashamed to admit to you."

She swallowed past the lump in her throat, not
turning from his hard gaze. She didn't know if he
was trying to scare her off or warn her. Standing
on her tiptoes, she placed a light kiss on his lips,
hoping to crumble the massive wall that he was
trying to build between them. Her heart ached
at the slight flinch she caught as she reached one
hand up to touch his face. "Yet you made a life for
yourself. You have friends who'd have your back
any day. You have made more of a life for yourself
in this town than I have. You've shied away from
no one. You are a good man—I know it, and I'm
so lucky you walked onto my ranch that day."

"Sarah," he said in a tortured, raspy voice. His

jaw clenched repeatedly, and his eyes glistened as he gave her an almost imperceptible shake of his head. There was nothing childish or immature about Cade, nothing soft or mushy, but for the briefest second, she caught a glimpse of that hurt, unwanted boy, and she wanted to reach out to him, to comfort him.

"You could tell me anything and it wouldn't change what I know to be inherently true about you—you're a good man, a strong man, one with deep emotion. You're the only man who's ever really listened to me, who believed that I knew what I wanted, who was willing to take me on a road trip and sit up all night eating junk food in a crappy motel room, and who acted like a complete gentleman."

One corner of his mouth curled ever so slightly. "I can't lie and say that my thoughts were entirely gentlemanly."

"Our thoughts are one thing, our actions another," she said, taking her own words and letting her hands slide down the hard, hot skin of his chest and rest on his waist.

He threaded his fingers through her hair, grasping her gently, tugging her forward slightly even though she didn't need any encouragement.

She stared up at him and knew, deep inside, that she was falling in love with him. That seemed impossible to her. A month ago, she didn't even know he existed. A month ago, she'd been buried inside her parents' home, living a life she didn't want. A month ago, she thought she'd be alone forever, that she'd never let anyone in again. And now this man was here, telling her everything she wanted to hear.

Except they could never be anything other than what they were because of his position. So where exactly did that leave them?

CHAPTER SIXTEEN

*T*wo weeks later, Sarah left the barn after finishing a ride, feeling like she was finally living the life she wanted. She couldn't wait to find Cade. She hadn't felt this free since Josh was alive, and it was all because of Cade.

She had a smile on her face, and instead of walking back to her house, she decided she'd surprise him because she knew he was working in the office today. The last two weeks had been the best of her entire life. Her days were bursting with ranch work, her new friends, and Cade.

The six of them had gotten together once at Tyler and Lainey's house, and she and Cade had seen each other every day. While Mrs. Casey could tell something was up, she hadn't interfered or tried to stop her.

The ranch work had come easy to her, like second nature. The men were slowly coming around and treating her like one of them, and things were becoming more relaxed.

Sarah slowed her pace and took a moment to appreciate the skyline and the clouds that rolled through with a speed that suggested a change in weather. They tucked around the mountains, and it was a sight that she'd seen so many times growing up, one that usually resulted in rain. But there was never a bad skyline in Wishing River; there was always beauty to be found in it.

This was the same view she'd had all her life. It was the same ranch, the same sky, she'd shared with her family, but she wasn't the same person, and it wasn't the same life. They were gone, and for some reason, she was the one still standing here.

A shiver ran down her spine as a cooler wind blew in and the feeling that her life was going too well, too picture-perfect right now, came with it. She tried to shrug it off as she made her way to the office.

Her footsteps faltered outside the office door as she heard a familiar male voice. She stood still, not wanting to eavesdrop but not wanting to be unprepared. Holding her breath, she listened carefully and shut her eyes as she confirmed who the voice belonged to—her old foreman Mike Ballinger. What was he doing here? Why hadn't Cade told her he was coming? Maybe he'd just shown up?

She straightened her shoulders and fixed her ponytail, wanting to look as polished and self-assured as she could. She still had a lot of resentment for Mike just up and leaving them, but he probably hadn't taken her seriously at all, because she'd barely been involved in the ranch before.

Sarah knocked on the door once and walked in.

Cade and Mike stood up. She could tell right away that Cade was upset about something. His posture was stiff, and he didn't have his usual smile for her. His handsome face was drawn, without any warmth in it.

"Sarah, good to see you," Mike said.

"Hi, Mike. I'm surprised to see you here after the way you left things," she said, crossing her arms.

Mike hung his head for a second. "I regret the way I left. I didn't handle the stress of everything that was happening well. I'm sorry. I'm glad Cade called me here, and I'm glad to help and explain myself."

A jolt of alarm hit her as she looked at Cade. He'd called him? Cade hadn't mentioned anything to her. Cade's jaw was clenched, but he didn't say a thing. She wasn't going to assume why he would do that. There had to be an explanation, but she still wasn't happy about the surprise. "I see," she managed to say, feeling stupid for not knowing what was happening on her own ranch but not wanting Mike to know that.

"Well, thanks for coming by, Mike. I think we're done," Cade said in a clipped voice as he held out his hand.

Mike shook it and picked up his hat. "Sarah, good luck to you," he said with a nod before putting his hat back on and leaving.

Sarah turned to Cade once the door was shut,

trying to quell her nerves and keep her voice neutral. "What was that all about?"

He didn't answer her immediately, just began gathering papers on the desk. His jaw was clenched, and he looked nothing like the man she'd come to know in the last couple of months. "I needed to ask him some questions."

She crossed the small office, trying to figure out why none of this was making sense and why Cade was being so standoffish. "Oh, like some ranching stuff?"

He gave her a terse nod.

"I would have liked to know that you'd invited over the guy who stiffed me. I would have liked to be prepared when I saw him."

"You're right," he said, running a hand through his hair but still not making eye contact with her.

"Why are you acting weird?" She touched his arm. His muscles flexed beneath her hand, and his body was almost rigid.

"I need to talk to you about a few things that I've been looking into. Do you want to sit down?"

Her stomach dropped at his tone and the fact that he'd never mentioned that he was looking into anything. "No. I'm fine standing right here. This is feeling pretty formal for the two of us."

He still didn't warm up to her. "I called Mike here because I noticed some weird things when I was looking through the books and bank statements."

She frowned. "Why didn't you ask me first?

Why would you trust him? I told you he quit without notice and left me hanging."

He nodded slowly, finally bringing his gaze to meet hers. "I know. I realized, though, that he might have discovered the same thing I did. I also knew that he knew your father, that he might be able to confirm my suspicions and give me some insight. I spoke with the bookkeeper, who also confirmed everything, but I wanted to hear if Mike had anything to add."

A wave of nausea swam through her as he listed everyone he'd discussed this with—except her. "You thought he could give you more insight into my father than I could? I don't get what you're implying. Confirmed what?"

"That when your father almost lost everything ten years ago, he nearly lost this ranch. He tried to dig himself out of massive debt and leveraged everything. He was this close to going bankrupt," he said, leaning against the desk and holding up two fingers to indicate how close.

Sarah clutched the back of the chair but kept her features neutral. "Then how are we still operational? How did he save this place?"

"He sold off ten acres of land, laid off half a dozen ranch hands, and stopped gambling."

She crossed her arms, trying to process everything he was saying, but even more that he hadn't told her a thing about his suspicions until now. "Then why did Mike leave?"

"Because you haven't been operating in the black for a while. Instead of trying to figure things out, he took off. He said he was too old for this kind of stress. But I can fix this. It isn't a disaster."

She could barely grasp what he was saying, her mind racing. "When did you begin to suspect this?"

He glanced away for a moment. "A while."

"How long?"

"Weeks."

"Before the Highwayman?"

His jaw clenched, and he gave a stiff nod.

Her chest suddenly felt heavy, and she had a hard time taking a deep breath. "So all that time, these weeks, our conversations…you never thought to tell me? You brought an old foreman out here to talk to *him*? The bookkeeper…you didn't think I should be included in that meeting?"

"I didn't want you to be worried for no reason. I wanted to make sure before I told you," he said, his voice thick.

Alarm bells were going off. "So you get to decide when and why I should be worried?"

He frowned. "No, it's not like that."

She crossed her arms, trying to keep her temper in check and give him the benefit of the doubt. "Then explain it. I offered to meet with the bookkeeper. How many times did I tell you I wanted to look at the books with you? We see each other every single day. We spent a weekend together where I told you everything about my family, but you never said a thing about your suspicions. Tell me why you wouldn't include the owner of this ranch on these details."

He shrugged, shoving his hands in the front pocket of his jeans. "I don't know."

"*I* know," she said, trying to speak past the ache in her heart, the heaviness in her chest. "Because you didn't think I could handle it."

He glanced down at the desk, and that was more than enough confirmation for her. "Sarah…"

She stepped forward, bracing her palms on the desk, her chest aching with the knowledge that he thought she was so weak. It was humiliating and hurtful. "I told you everything. *Everything* about my family. You know I was treated like this delicate flower who couldn't handle the stresses of life. You know I was dismissed and shut out of the ranching life. You know all of that. You know how much it hurt me. Yet you sat there and listened to me and…and what? You were secretly agreeing with my parents' decisions? With Edna's?"

"No," he said roughly. "It's not that I think you're weak. I just didn't want you to be stressed for no reason if I was wrong."

"Wrong answer!" she yelled, throwing her arms in the air and walking toward him. Betrayal sliced through her in a way that she'd never experienced. She hadn't expected this from him. "Cade, you can't decide what I'm allowed to be stressed about. You can't filter news for me. I…I can't believe you would do this to me. Of all people. I laid it all out there. You know everything. You helped me. I thought you believed in me; I thought you believed I was strong enough to do all of this."

"I do, sweetheart—"

"Don't 'sweetheart' me," she said, holding up a trembling hand as he took a step toward her. She hated how he was trying to justify this and hated even more that she was wishing that he actually could.

"That morning at the motel, when you had that migraine…I've never seen someone so sick. It killed me to sit there and watch you like that, Sarah. I didn't want to be the cause of that."

"So you wanted to prevent a migraine? By doing *this*? This kind of stress is great."

He grimaced. "Obviously I wasn't going to tell you like this."

"What, were you going to spoon-feed me the message over candlelight and wine?"

Something flashed in his eyes, and he gave an almost imperceptible shake of his head.

She gasped. "Oh, you weren't going to tell me at all, were you? That was the plan. You were going to somehow fix everything and never get me involved."

He didn't say anything, but for the first time since she met him, she saw his cheeks go red.

She wouldn't back down from this, from getting the truth out of him. "Admit it."

"Fine. I wanted to fix this for you and not have you deal with any more pain from your family. I didn't want you to know just how bad it got with your dad."

She shook her head and turned away from him, feelings of betrayal and hurt and humiliation coursing through her all at the same time, making it impossible to breathe. She squeezed her eyes shut and rubbed her temples. He couldn't be doing this to her, too. Not Cade. He'd been her champion. The one encouraging her this whole time. But he was like the rest of them. He thought she was too weak to handle the realities of life.

"Sarah," he said in a tortured voice that any other day would have made her forgive him, but not today, not with this.

"So you're the big man, just like my dad. You tell me what I can and can't handle and I'll just sit here, trying not to get too stressed about life. I thought I'd proven myself. I worked alongside all of you guys, I went on the cattle drive, I learned my way around here. But I'm still not enough. Maybe I'll just go and do some cleaning in the kitchen and then paint my nails—"

"That's not fair. I never once treated you like that," he said roughly.

An image flashed across her mind, a memory, and she stared at him, wondering how she couldn't have seen any of this before now. Was she really this naive? Really so trusting? Maybe Mrs. Casey had been right about her. "You wanted to call the shots in this relationship, and you have been this entire time, but I was too infatuated by you to realize it. I actually let you lead the way and I was acting like this little schoolgirl."

His brows snapped together. "What are you talking about?"

"Everything. You even decided we weren't going to sleep together because I couldn't make my own decisions!"

He thrust his hands in his hair. "Are you kidding me right now?"

She nodded, on the verge of a total meltdown. "You have slept with I don't know how many women—maybe that's something else I'm too sheltered for you to tell me—and that's perfectly fine. But you refused to sleep with me because you think that's the wrong decision for me. You *lied* to me."

Cade ran a hand over his jaw. "It's not like that."

"Hiding information from me and only telling me things if you can come up with a solution isn't your job. We are talking about things my father did—*my* father. My old foreman. This is my ranch. I asked you from day one to keep me informed. It's not up to you to decide what information I can and can't handle."

"It's not that I thought you couldn't handle it."

"Then what?"

"I don't have a black-and-white answer for you. When I first started having my suspicions about the debt, I thought I'd just do some digging on my own. I never expected to find that your dad was responsible for this. I had no idea gambling it all away was even a possibility. By that point, I was in too deep, and I knew how hard you'd take it. You told me about how your family fell apart. I didn't...I couldn't throw even more on you."

She rubbed her temples, trying to ease the throbbing pain that was starting in her head. "Why wouldn't you have come to me and we could have looked into it together?"

"That was early on. I was still trying to prove my worth around here," he said.

"Worth! You were priceless around here right from day one. The point I'm making is that you didn't think I could handle it. You thought I was too weak to deal with what my father had done."

He didn't say anything, but his jaw was clenched tight, and she saw the affirmation in his eyes. "It's not as easy as that."

"So then tell me."

"When I first came here, Edna told me you had some...health issues and that maybe you needed some extra care."

"That's bull. You know me now. I've told you everything, so that means you agreed with her. If you didn't, you would have told me then and there, that night I opened up to you about my parents, my brother. That would have been the perfect time. Or that night we were working together and you were going through the books with me—how about then?"

He scraped the side of his face with his nails. "I should've told you."

Her shoulders relaxed slightly. "I thought you understood me when I explained why it was so important that I know how to do all this myself."

"You're right. I just thought when I spoke with Tyler—"

Hurt slashed through her. "You talked to *Tyler*? As in your friend, another rancher, a *guy*… basically someone who has nothing to do with this ranch, over me."

He gave a nod.

She threw up her hands. "Do you even realize how patronizing and demeaning that is? So what, the big, capable men talked about my ranch without me even there?"

"It wasn't like that, Sarah. It came up in conversation one night over drinks, that's it. I didn't plan a meeting with him. I've worked with Tyler for years, with his father for years. They're like family. They're trustworthy, and they know what they're doing. They never would have said anything to anyone. It has nothing to do with me thinking you aren't capable. I…I did want to fix this for you, but if I couldn't, I wanted to be able to present you with solutions."

Everything he was saying was bouncing off her, hitting all her insecurities along the way. She had been silenced and dismissed so many times; she couldn't handle it from him, too. "You decided I'd just sink into a pile of nerves and fear if I knew. Admit it."

He shook his head, his jaw clenched. "No, I'm not admitting that. It's not black-and-white like that. I didn't think you'd just fall apart if I told you. But I did know it would hurt you and stress you out and if I had the power to prevent that, then I would."

"It's more. Admit that you don't think I can handle stress."

"Fine! I admit it. Yeah, you came on the cattle drive with us and worked just as hard as any of us, but then a day later, I'm watching you in agony in a motel room in the fetal position where you passed out for ten hours. Do you know what it's like to watch someone you care about in pain? I don't see the problem here. Yes, I think that you can't handle a lot of stress and as someone who... cares for you, I didn't want to be the cause of that agony."

She blinked a few times, the unfamiliar sting of tears in her eyes alarming her. She wouldn't cry in front of him. "So I'm this fragile flower you need to protect from the harsh realities of life?"

"I know you're not fragile. It was hard to watch

you in that kind of pain, and I made the decision to not put you through that again."

"Your decision again. You decided. That's where you're wrong. And that wasn't triggered by the stress of the ranch, it was triggered by too much bad food and alcohol. If this had been any other ranch, and I had been a guy, would you have done this?"

*S*hit. Cade didn't know the answer to that.

He stared into Sarah's eyes and questioned everything he'd done, the reasons behind it, whether or not his intentions were good. Did everything she'd revealed about her past, her migraines, her shutting down emotionally play into his subconscious? Why *hadn't* he told her? He didn't actually think she was weak or incapable. He knew this was her ranch. He knew she deserved to know major problems like this one, even more so because they involved her father. But he also knew that part of his job was finding solutions, making himself valuable. If he wasn't of value, there was no reason for him to be on this ranch, let alone to stay once she was ready to start running it herself.

But her question—would he have withheld this if she was a guy? No. No, if this had been Tyler, he'd have told him in an instant. But Tyler was different. Tyler didn't shut down and pass out for hours. Tyler…wasn't Sarah. He wasn't in love with Tyler.

He was in love with Sarah.

That knowledge punched him in the gut and left him standing there, staring at her, wondering how the hell this was going to be okay. "I…I don't know."

She took a physical step back from him, her eyes flashing with betrayal. "I haven't asked for much. Just that you treat me like an equal."

"You can stand there and be pissed, but I was doing what needed to be done. I'm your foreman, Sarah, the hired help, and I needed to prove my worth. I wanted to come to you with a solution."

"You're not just the hired help. Don't say that."

If there was one thing he did know, it was himself. He had always been the help, hired or not. That was his place in every home he'd ever been in. If he didn't help, there was no roof over his head. If he didn't solve problems for people, there was no home for him. If he couldn't work, he was nothing. "It's true, though. It may make you uncomfortable, but it's never far from my mind. It's why we haven't slept together."

He didn't know if she was going to take a step forward to hit him or a step back because she was repulsed by his comment.

"Don't do this," she whispered. "Don't make yourself into some asshole."

"It's the truth."

"So what, you held back because you're the hired help, which gives you all the power in what happens in our relationship? C'mon. How do you know I would have slept with *you*?"

He didn't say anything. He just stood there and watched her as her cheeks turned red.

"Oh…" she said after a second. "Oh, maybe… maybe you did all of this. Maybe this was a fake romance between us to keep your job. Maybe you're not attracted to me at all. Fool the stupid, naive rancher's daughter into thinking she was falling in love."

It hurt to speak. She had it all wrong. "Sarah…"

"Yes?" Every last ounce of pride glistened in her eyes, waiting for him to tell her she was wrong, that he loved her, that he hadn't been faking, that not sleeping with her had been hell for him, that he'd wanted her from day one. But he didn't. It was easier this way. It was easier than having to admit to her that he wasn't good enough, that he'd never have anything to offer her, that he couldn't fix this problem for her and he didn't have the money to fix it, either. Not that she'd ever ask let alone allow it—because he was the hired help, regardless of whether she'd admit it—but that's something *he* wanted do.

"I'm sorry."

She let out a small laugh and dropped her hands to her sides. "Okay, well, so am I. I'm sorry

I ever met you, sorry I ever took out that ad. But most of all, I'm sorry I let you in. I'm sorry I trusted you."

"This whole thing needed to end anyway," he said, walking back over to the desk, racking his brain for a way to wrap this up swiftly. He could do the hiring for a new foreman. He would make sure that he took the steps to keep the ranch running the way it should. By the end of the year, she'd be running it anyway and wouldn't actually need him. It was time to find a new place to go. All he needed to do now was go along with her idea of whoever she thought he was.

"What does that even mean?"

He looked into her eyes, his chest painfully heavy. "It means that whatever was started between us needs to end. It was wrong, and I should have stopped it before it turned into something…more serious."

She crossed her arms. "That is so insulting on so many levels. Once again, you're the big man in control of this relationship and *you* should have stopped it? Care to let me in on any other life decisions you've made on my behalf?"

"Fine. Do you know how this will look? People will assume we're together because I want to get my hands on the ranch." He put up a hand before she could argue. "I don't give a shit what people think about me, but I care what they think about you. I don't want people whispering behind your back that I'm screwing you to get to your money. I don't want to give them any reason to disrespect you."

She folded her arms across her chest. "So you're going to end our relationship because of other people?"

"It's not just that. Your father wouldn't have approved of me. Edna can barely stand me. You're the landowner here, the ranch owner. I'm just the hired cowboy."

"So? Is this a male ego thing? Is that what this is about?"

He ran his hands through his hair. "You wouldn't get it."

"Because I'm a woman?"

He gave a terse nod.

"Try me."

"It's going to sound old-fashioned and politically incorrect as hell, but yeah. I'm supposed to be able to bring something to the table. I've got nothing except money in a bank account that wouldn't even put a dent in ownership of a ranch this size. It bothers me that the only way I'd have owner-ship of a ranch like this is because of my wife."

Her eyes flashed as she marched toward him. "How do I own this land?"

He shrugged. "Your family."

"Exactly," she said, poking his chest. "I didn't do anything to become an owner of this ranch. I inherited. You probably deserve this ranch more than I do, because you've put in more hours here than I have."

He snorted. "That is an idealistic way of looking at things. It's not the way the real world works."

"Thanks for explaining the real world to me, Cade. Were you attracted to me because of this ranch? Because of the money in my bank account?"

"Of course not."

"You want to know what you've brought to the table? If I needed someone when I was down, you're the guy I wanted by my side, because I know you would do anything to help me. I know you'd have my back, just like I would have yours. Millions don't make a man. It's his heart, his courage. How wrong of you to think your self-worth is tied up in your bank account."

He shook his head. He loved her heart and that she actually believed all that stuff, but he knew it didn't matter. "That's a really great, naive way of looking at things."

"You're impossible. Okay, then—what was your plan? Find a woman who has less money than you to make yourself feel better? Is that what you'll do now? Are you going to take out an ad?"

"Don't be ridiculous," he snapped.

She pointed a finger to her chest. "*I'm* being ridiculous? Right. Oh, I guess you don't need an ad, do you? You can just walk into a bar and pick up whomever you'd like. How's that been working for you all these years? Last time I checked, you were single."

"Because I *choose* to be single." He shook his head. "I feel worthless, Sarah. I feel like shit when I think that I've got nothing to give to you."

She rubbed her temples, and he hoped to God she wasn't getting a migraine. He wouldn't forgive himself if he caused one.

Finally, she dropped her hands to her side and leveled him with a look that set his body on fire. "You're so worried about being a man? Then why don't you be a man and actually *act* like one?"

He stilled, disbelief and anger pumping through him as he stared at her, not really believing he heard what she said to him. Her chest was heaving and her face was red and he knew she was just as pissed as he was. "What did you say?"

She lifted her chin, defiance and challenge glittering from her eyes. "Come over here and act like a man."

He cursed under his breath, knowing he was walking into a trap, knowing he was too weak to resist. Yanking her against him, he kissed her with every ounce of frustration and anger—and every ounce of love—he had for her. He backed her into the door and she peeled his shirt off him with the same impatience he felt.

She ran her hands up his arms and around his shoulders, her breasts pressing into his chest, and he removed his mouth from hers only to kiss that sweet, soft spot beneath her ear. She whimpered as his fingers quickly and deftly unbuttoned her shirt, his knuckles grazing her breasts. He pulled back only to see what he'd imagined many, many nights—and she was even more beautiful than he'd thought. A pale-pink, sheer lace bra did nothing to hide her full breasts. He slipped the straps off and quickly unclasped the flimsy fabric, catching her gasp with his mouth, and despite his anger, his hurt, and his unabashed want for her, slowed it down and kissed her with that same wonder he had the first time. Because Sarah would never be just any other woman to him. If this was the last time he kissed her, then he didn't want it to be in anger.

He ran his hands over her smooth skin, feeling every sweet curve he'd imagined, hearing every sound in his ear, and knew he couldn't keep going. But it was when she whispered, "I love you," in his ear that he shut down and pulled back. He kept his hands on her waist to hold her steady, to wait for the reality of what kind of an ass he could really be to sink in.

She blinked up at him. "What are you doing?"

He picked up her bra and shirt, handing them to her. "This isn't going to go anywhere," he said, stepping back.

Hurt slashed across her eyes, and it was just as bad as the red humiliation that streaked across her cheeks. He knew he was going to regret this for the rest of his life.

"Cade," she said in a voice that he'd never heard before.

He backed up a step. "I think we're done here."

"What?"

She had told him she loved him. There wasn't a person in the world who had ever told him that. She turned around and got dressed quickly while he turned away, wanting this torture to be over. He couldn't have her in love with him. She was angry with him for what he'd held back; she couldn't love him. How could she? He'd screwed up badly.

There was only one way this could go.

She turned back around, her eyes glistening, and his gut twisted horribly when he saw the sheen of tears in her eyes, knowing she never cried. "I hope you've humiliated me enough now. That was the goal, right? You're so in control, you can pull away from me so easily. You can decide when everything ends."

"I'm leaving. I'll hand in my resignation. I'll find a new foreman before I go."

She shut her eyes, and when she opened them, the hatred there was enough to make him wish he'd never come here, never met Sarah, never laughed with her, fallen in love right alongside her.

"I hope you have a good long laugh about this when you leave town. I hope the next woman you screw in some crappy motel room gets treated better than me," she said, opening the door and walking out.

The minute she left, he kicked his foot into the desk, cursing out loud in the silent room. He gripped the edges of the desk until his knuckles were white. There'd been low points in his life, plenty of times he hated himself, but this was the ultimate.

She loved him. Sarah had told him she loved him, when not a damn person in the world had. And he'd treated her like she was meaningless to him. He'd treated her like she was a nobody, when she was everything.

CHAPTER SEVENTEEN

You're a worthless little shit, Cade.

Cade drank straight from the bottle of whiskey and leaned back on the sofa, hoping he'd just fall asleep instead of listening to the stupid voices from his past. Except the problem with sleep was that it filled him with thoughts of Sarah. First his dreams would start with good thoughts…Sarah laughing, Sarah passing around strawberry hand sanitizer, Sarah helping Carl with his marital problems… Sarah kissing him, Sarah telling him she felt safe with him…and then it would change to their last conversation, when she was against the door, half naked, and so sweetly telling him that she loved him, and him shutting her down callously.

The knock at the door didn't prompt him to get up. He wasn't in the mood to talk to anyone, and if it happened to be Edna Casey, he couldn't be drunk, because she'd run circles around him with her arguments.

He cursed under his breath when the knocking didn't stop, and he knew exactly who could knock so relentlessly and obnoxiously. He stood slowly and crossed his messy living room.

Cade opened the door, not looking forward to an interruption from his wallowing, to find Dean and Tyler standing there holding a bottle of whiskey.

"I have to say, I'm surprised you lasted this long," Dean said, walking in without Cade actually inviting either of them inside.

"I have no idea what you're talking about," he said, torn between kicking them out and actually admitting he was glad to see them.

Tyler put his feet up on the coffee table, and Cade didn't even care. "We're referring to us being surprised it took you this long till you screwed up your relationship with Sarah."

Oh. He crossed the room and sat down on the opposite couch. He knew they'd never get it, because as much as his best friends hadn't had the perfect life, neither of them came from nothing. Neither of them had been kids tossed around like a worthless nuisance or knew what it was like to have nothing to offer a woman. Neither of them knew what it was like to spend your life thinking that you wouldn't ever own anything. Tyler had his family ranch to offer Lainey, and while he wasn't loaded, it was a damn fine ranch and a solid income with the potential to grow into something even bigger. Dean had been born into major money and had been able to do whatever he wanted. Hell, he was the perfect guy with his career and his ranching money.

"How do you know that I screwed things up?"

"Lainey."

He accepted the glass of whiskey Dean poured. He wasn't so intoxicated that this bit of information wasn't of interest to him. He wanted to know anything about Sarah. He was going through withdrawal. "What, uh, did she say exactly?"

"Well, first off, you should know that Lainey went to bat for you. Saying all the reasons you're a great guy—things that never would have occurred to me," Tyler said, pausing, a slight smile on his face.

He cleared his throat. "Thanks. What did Sarah say?"

"She's pissed off because you acted like a jerk is what I gathered from the conversation. Something about you not telling her her father gambled away the family fortune?"

Cade cringed and hung his head. He was an idiot. "There was more to it than that. It was what we were talking about that night, about her dad and the missing money. I wanted to find a solution before I dumped it all on her."

"So you wanted to decide what she could handle and what she couldn't about her ranch, her family. And you basically decided she couldn't deal," Dean said, sitting back on the sofa.

Sometimes he hated having friends. "I know it looks bad, but that's not the way I thought of it. I don't expect either of you to get this, and you're not aware of all the details anyway. When I moved in here, their housekeeper basically gave me this warning that Sarah was sheltered because of health issues and a family tragedy. I saw her migraine firsthand, and it was bad. I didn't want to cause her stress."

Dean shrugged, lifting his feet onto the coffee table as well. He accidentally touched Tyler's feet, and they started shoving each other. "If you two could stop playing footsies, I'd like to get on with my night," Cade grumbled.

They immediately moved their feet to opposite ends of the table. "That's funny, Cade, considering. I'm sure your plan didn't cause any stress at all to Sarah."

"Are you guys here to make me feel better or worse?" Cade snapped, grabbing the bottle of whiskey on the coffee table and refilling his glass.

"Right," Tyler said, shooting Dean a look. "*Now* we'll help you."

"I don't need your help. I know what I'm going to do. I'm going to pack it up and move back to your place," he said, leaning back and putting his own feet up on the coffee table and shoving Tyler's off.

"What? No. You're going to stay here and fix this," Tyler said.

He hadn't wanted to get into his own family history. Sure, they knew bits and pieces, but they would never understand why leaving Sarah's ranch was his only option until they told him more. "I don't belong here. I don't belong with Sarah. We would never be able to make this work because of our backgrounds."

Dean leaned forward, straight-faced. "What? Your background as an alien who isn't allowed to stay on Earth?"

Cade held up his hand, scowling. "Okay, enough with the sci-fi, please, Dean."

"Agreed," Tyler said, shoving Dean's feet off the table with his own.

"I'm not... I've got nothing. Nothing except the money saved from years of work, which in the ranching world is a trivial amount."

"So?"

Cade ran his hands through his hair and stood up, marching across the room and looking out the window even though it was dark. The lights were on at the main house, and he wished more than anything that he was there right now with Sarah. But the main house on a ranch had never been his home. That big stone house with the wraparound porch, the flowers, the grandeur...that would never be his home. He would never fit in with that kind of a home. He'd feel like a fake.

He didn't take handouts, and he wasn't just going to change. "You can't say that. Both of you have families, have family ranches, money that goes back generations."

"My ranch wasn't even in the black when I came home last year," Tyler reminded him.

Cade turned around. "Don't even give me that crap. You owned the land, the house, the business, and you can't compare a ranch going through hard

times to me. I will never be able to get into the
ranching business on my own because it's just not
doable. I will always be the hired help."

"I think that's a pathetic cop-out," Dean said.

"Coming from a guy born into the wealthiest
family in the state. I'd keep your opinions about
that to yourself."

"Sure. So we'll just leave you here feeling sorry
for yourself and let you ruin your life," Dean said.

Cade looked at the ground. He'd known they
wouldn't understand. They couldn't. Just like Sarah
wouldn't be able to understand. They'd all grown
up in real families, with parents who'd loved them,
imperfect or not. None of them had had to clean
up their parent's shit or be worried about whether
or not there was food to eat. None of them knew
what it was like to be the weird kid in school who
only came on days when he wasn't needed at
home, never making friends, always on the sidelines. "Maybe I'm doing the right thing. Maybe I'm
making sure I don't ruin Sarah's life."

Dean shook his head. "Yeah. I don't think so.
What does Sarah think about all this?"

Cade leaned against the wall. "Obviously she's
pissed. But that's because she doesn't get where
I'm coming from. She won't. Which is why we
won't work."

"You're messing things up bad, Cade. Did
you tell her about your family?" Tyler asked, his
expression hard.

Though he'd kept the details about his life before he came to Wishing River to a minimum, he knew Tyler and Dean had managed to piece together enough. "Yeah. I told her. She knows. She knows enough. I don't need people feeling sorry for me. That's what would happen. She feels sorry for things…people…animals. You know. I don't want to be grouped into that. The last thing I'd want is the woman I'm in a relationship with to feel sorry for me. That's a real turn-on."

Tyler leaned back on the sofa, spreading his arms across the back cushions. "You're looking at this all wrong as usual. As the only one of us who's married and managed to remain married for a year—"

"Maybe because Lainey's been living on another continent," Dean said with a smug grin. Cade almost laughed.

Tyler shot him a look before continuing. "You're going to have to get used to talking about your past, your feelings, and all the shit that goes along with it. Sarah will expect that, and it will also allow her to figure out why on certain occasions you act like an ass. You need to tell her more, apologize, and find a solution, otherwise she'll just see you as this jerk who does dumb things for no good reason."

He tried to filter out the stupid shit in Tyler's advice and focus on the relevant information. He jammed his hands into his front pockets. "I don't know that I can do that."

"Has she shared stuff with you?"

He gave a nod, his gut automatically clenching whenever he thought about that night, her story, and then the migraine.

"A real relationship can't be one-sided. Lainey makes me talk about all kinds of shit that I never even thought about. And it feels good to have someone to talk to about that. To have someone you trust with all your thoughts who won't judge you. Don't screw this up because you're afraid you're not good enough for her. Wise words someone told me once," Tyler said, reminding Cade of the advice he'd given Tyler not that long ago.

"I believe you might have also said it didn't matter if I was good enough for Lainey. So maybe you don't have to be good enough for Sarah, either. Maybe she just wants you, man."

The hard knock on the door had them all staring at one another. Tyler and Dean were his only friends in the world. The only other person would be Sarah, but she'd never knock like that.

"Did you order pizza?" he asked. They shook their heads. With a rough sigh, he went to answer the door. Tyler's father, Martin, was standing there, cane in one hand, frown on his weathered face.

"I thought the three of you might be here," he said as he scanned the room.

Cade opened the door wider and reached out

to make sure he could cross the threshold steadily. Of course Martin brushed him off, determined to assert his independence. To his credit, the man had made an almost miraculous recovery. Cade was pretty sure that once he'd repaired his relationship with his son, he'd had a reason to get better again.

Martin shook his head at the three of them. "I'm surprised you're not hiding cigarettes," he said, walking with a limp into the family room.

Tyler laughed. "We're not sixteen. We also don't smoke, Dad," Tyler said, referring to the time Martin had caught them smoking when they were sixteen on the Donnelly property. It had been Cade's fault, of course.

Martin sat down and pointed his cane at him. "Now, tell me how you managed to mess things up with that sweet Turner girl, Cade."

Cade groaned and sat on the couch. He never could figure out how news traveled so fast in this town. "Martin," he said, not wanting to get into this all over again but not wanting to dismiss him, either. He was surprised he was here. And touched. Martin was the closest he'd ever come to having a father.

"Cade has problems expressing his feelings, Dad." Tyler smiled at Cade.

Martin gave a snort and then pointed to the whiskey. "Pour me a glass of that and I'll give you some advice."

"As your doctor, Martin, I'm going to have to

say no to the whiskey," Dean said with a chuckle.

Martin frowned. "I think I liked you boys better when you were getting in trouble as teenagers. What's a little whiskey going to do?"

"I'm sure a small glass wouldn't hurt. Does anyone really know if Dean graduated med school?" Tyler asked, laughing, and Cade actually joined in.

"Fine. Half a glass, followed by a glass of water," Dean said, shooting a glare Tyler's way.

Martin waved a hand. "That's fine; let's not panic. This cowboy has been drinking this stuff for years. It might actually be more harmful to my health to eliminate it completely," he said, giving Dean a pointed stare as he picked up his half-filled glass.

Dean shook his head and lifted his own glass as a salute. "Most stubborn family I know," he said.

Martin chuckled. "Back to you, Cade. I know you're a proud man, and it's humbling to admit to a woman that you got nothing to offer her, especially a woman who comes from a successful ranching family."

Was this for real? How the hell did Martin know all that? "Who told you that's what the problem is?"

Martin put down his empty glass. "I know you, boy. And I know cowboys. I know the pride that runs through your veins, and I'm here to talk some sense into you."

Cade swallowed past the lump in his throat. "That's pretty old-school thinking, but I can't help feeling that way. I was hired. I work for her."

"But you're not just the hired help who can be tossed out. You are invaluable, just as you were at our ranch, and you are good at what you do—take some damn pride in that, son. And love doesn't care about those things. Love doesn't care about where you came from or how much money you have. If that girl loves you, then you don't let her go. I'd give anything to have one more day with Tyler's mother, but I can't. So don't waste this time being stubborn, being apart from her. None of us know how long we have here."

Cade leaned forward, his forearms on his thighs, feeling Martin's words deep in his gut. He knew how in love the man had been with his wife.

Luckily, the whiskey had loosened his tongue, and even though he hated an audience, he loved Sarah more. If Martin could tell him something that would convince him that maybe this could work, he'd take the awkwardness. "It's not that simple. I feel like I'll never be enough. I don't want the guys around here to talk about her. It would kill me to think that people are thinking I'm just trying to get with the rich woman."

Martin shrugged. "I can't say that some won't think that way, but who cares? You can't let other people's opinions ruin your life."

"It's not me I'm concerned about; it's Sarah.

She's the one who's gotta run the ranch."

"Or maybe you're concerned that when you really tell her everything, she won't love you."

The room grew silent, and Cade knew in his gut that what Martin was saying was true. He didn't feel like he was good enough for her. There were some days he found himself putting in longer hours to prove his worth, to prove why he needed to stay here.

"I don't expect you to admit any of that to us, but think on it yourself. As for the rest, she's an adult. You can't decide for her what she can and can't handle. In my experience, people who are going to talk are going to talk. No matter what you do. Those are the people who have nothing better to do than look down their noses at other people in order to make themselves feel better. You going to make your life decisions based on what the rest of the world might think of you? Or you going to live the life you want, with the woman you want? Do you love her?"

"Of course I do," he said without hesitating. He knew he loved her. The night she told him she loved him, he'd known he felt the same. But he'd also known he couldn't admit it to her.

"Have you told her?"

He shook his head.

Tyler and Dean both made frustrated noises like they were relationship experts.

"Well, start with that," Martin said.

"It's not that simple, Martin. Our last argument was bad. I said and did some shit I regret, and it's beyond just an apology. How the hell do I fix that?"

Martin slapped his knee. "I can't go fixing all your problems. You boys need to learn how to figure out all your own love lives. I'm not going to be around forever giving you advice. Take a break from the whiskey, grab a shower, and get a good night's sleep. Then wake up like a new man and you'll find your answer. Cade, you gotta examine what's in your heart, and then you've got to show it to Sarah if it's her."

They all fell silent, and Cade soaked up Martin's advice. He made it sound so simple. He'd never known the man to discuss hearts and feelings, but his advice was pretty spot-on.

"Thanks. I appreciate it."

Tyler helped Martin off the sofa. "Now, don't drink too much," he told them. "Tyler, your wife won't want to go to bed with a drunk, so mind yourself."

Tyler let out a choked laugh. "Thanks, Dad. I wasn't planning on getting toasted."

"Good to know. Can't hurt to have a reminder. I love that daughter-in-law of mine," Martin said, opening the door.

"I know," Tyler said, ushering his dad out. "So," Tyler said once the older man was gone. "Did we get through to you?"

Cade put down his half-full glass of whiskey, resolving to get cleaned up, sobered up, and go after the life he really wanted, with the only woman he wanted. "Yeah. So how am I actually going to convince Sarah to give me a second chance?"

*C*ade knocked on the Turners' front door and held his breath. He felt like he was sixteen years old and ready for his first job interview.

He already knew Sarah wouldn't be here, because he'd watched her ride off onto the trails, but he was counting on talking to Edna. This morning, he'd woken up with a hangover the size of Joshua Ranch, and it had taken a cold shower, Tylenol, and black coffee to get his ass in gear. But he was motivated. He had a plan. After he made a phone call, he was relieved to have his plan in place. Now he needed to execute the first portion of it.

A minute later, the door opened, and Edna gave him her scariest frown to date. She stared at him without saying hello, and he was glad he'd put on one of his best shirts and newest jeans for the occasion. Her eyebrows were pinched together so severely, they looked as though they'd been sewn there. Deep lines framed her thin lips, and he braced himself for a scathing lecture.

He cleared his throat. "Good morning, Mrs. Casey."

She stood even straighter, and Cade wouldn't be surprised if she eventually reached his height. "You had better tell me you're here to fix this catastrophe you have created with your looks and your charm, young man."

He forced a smile as she held open the door and sort of invited him in. "That's what I came to talk to you about."

"Well, I would not be opposed to having you sit on the couch while I listen to your explanation," she said, gesturing to one of the matching dark leather couches.

The room was filled with sunlight, the high, peaked ceilings like something out of a magazine. The traditional furniture was centered on the floor-to-ceiling fieldstone fireplace. He swallowed back the nerves that threatened, the feelings that told him he didn't belong in a place like this. It didn't matter. Sarah didn't care about that.

Cade's gaze landed on the shiny piano across the room and the polished silver frame with a picture of Sarah and her brother, and his chest felt heavy. He wasn't going to let her down. He wasn't going to be one of the people who left. He was going to give her the life she deserved, and he was going to be the man she deserved.

Once Mrs. Casey was seated in one of the armchairs, he sat down on the couch opposite her.

"How is Sarah?"

She raised an eyebrow. "Oh, do you mean today? Or do you mean the day that you broke her heart and I found her on the front steps, unable to see or get into the house because she'd been stricken by a migraine, brought on by heartache, no doubt."

Hell. He dug his nails into his palms. He'd been worried Sarah would get one of those migraines, but the thought of her, helpless like that on the porch, made his gut churn. He never should have let things go that far. "It wasn't my intention to hurt her. I thought I was doing the right thing. I believed that I wasn't the right man for her, that she deserved…more than I can offer. But I was wrong. I want to make things right between us."

"I don't see how that will be possible. She hasn't told me the details, just that I was right and that you weren't the man for her."

His stomach dropped. At this point, if this had been anyone else, he would have gotten up and left. Mrs. Casey's words, the words he'd grown up hearing, would have followed him out the damn door and he wouldn't have looked back. Hell, he would have agreed. But he'd come too far, and he loved Sarah too much not to try.

"I'm here to ask for your help. I know you may not like me very much, and I'm sure after what Sarah's told you, you like me even less. But there were details I kept from her that I discovered about her father's gambling and I wanted to solve the problem. I didn't want her stressed about something in the past. I saw her sick, and I never wanted to be the person to inflict that kind of pain on her." He paused, taking a deep breath, not looking away.

"Go on," she said, not exactly softening but her eyes warming slightly.

"I understand what you were telling me when I first came to work here—about Sarah. When I saw her with that migraine, it clicked. Everything you'd said."

She sighed and shook her head. "I'm sorry that I somehow contributed to this."

"It's not your fault. It's mine. I know what she's capable of. And she is capable of way more than anyone has given her credit for, including me. I need to make it up to her. I need to find a way to show her that I do trust her."

She stood. "I don't know how to help."

"I love her," he blurted out, standing. He didn't care anymore whether or not he was good enough, if he had her approval, or what Sarah's parents would have said. None of it mattered, because it was like Sarah had said—it was letting other people make decisions for him. She had been right about all of it. Even when he'd mentioned the reasons they couldn't have a relationship, she had known that living to avoid other people's gossip was no way to live.

Mrs. Casey didn't say anything; she just gave him this long, evaluating stare that was almost worse than Martin Donnelly's and practically made him squirm.

"I can't really blame you for making the same mistake I did. I can't blame you for loving her and wanting to keep her safe, either. I was also quite harsh when I told you about her condition, and that can't have helped your worry about her."

"There is something else," he said, wanting to get it all out there. If Sarah actually did forgive him and they were together, he wanted Mrs. Casey to know about his background.

"Go on," she said, her eyes clouding slightly.

"The other reason I told Sarah we couldn't be together was because of my past. I don't come from a good family. I didn't have a dime to my name, and I dropped out of school and started working very young. I've always been a hard worker, but I've always worked for someone else. I...I know Sarah's parents would have wanted her to marry someone with the same kind of wealth, and I felt insecure. I didn't want people talking, and I wanted to bring something to the table."

He felt a sense of relief once he got that out, even though Edna didn't say anything for a long moment. She finally let out a long sigh and folded her hands. "I came from a situation similar to yours. But I made the mistake of marrying someone when I was far too young because I was desperate for love and for a real family. He turned out to be a rotten man, and I was grateful I never had children with him. I worked until my hands were blistered, and I was thin as a rail when he left me. I happened upon the Turner family and was immediately brought in as one of them. They were good people, treated me like I belonged. I knew them before their son died, and the man I knew Sarah's father to be, before Joshua died, would have approved of you, Cade. I know it deep down. They changed, they destroyed themselves, and I witnessed all of it. But that girl held on when her entire world crumbled before her young eyes. It wasn't fair the way we all sheltered her, and I feel responsible for that.

"Sarah always had a light about her, an inherent happiness, a uniqueness. Wherever she went, she lit up a room. That light went out the day her sweet brother died. I hadn't seen that light again until you came into her life, Cade. And it worried me. It kept me up at night. Because I didn't know if she'd survive if that light went out again. Or if I would, for that matter. I think you've proven yourself to be a good man, and I trust Sarah's instincts. I know you haven't taken advantage of her kindness or her feelings for you. I believe you were acting in Sarah's best interests. So now, we find a way to get her back to you," she said with a wink.

He cleared his throat past the lump that had formed there. "I have your blessing?"

She put a thin hand on his shoulder, giving it a pretty strong squeeze for someone her size. "You have my blessing and my support. Now, let me make us some tea and let's get started with a plan."

He followed her to the kitchen. "Mrs. Casey?"

"Yes?"

"I really hate tea."

"I know, child. That's why we add a little bit of whiskey to it. It makes it go down much smoother. Now, follow me and let's figure out how to get your girl back."

CHAPTER EIGHTEEN

"*I* don't see why we need to go out for breakfast. You know I love cooking, and really, you have no idea the types of ingredients that these places use," Mrs. Casey groused as Sarah pulled her truck into an empty parking spot outside of Tilly's Diner.

Sarah had wanted to do this for her ever since Lainey told her about the older ladies who came to the diner every morning. The only thing that was keeping her going after Cade's rejection and lie were her friendships. She had no idea how she could have missed out on this part of life for so long. She wanted Mrs. Casey to have the same experience.

"I know you can cook. This isn't about the food. But I do happen to know the owner, and I know she uses great local ingredients and has tons of options that I can eat. Now come on and try something new," Sarah said, grabbing her purse and giving a pointed look before getting out of the car.

Mrs. Casey stood on the steps, not looking like she was planning on budging any time soon. Sarah opened the door and gave Mrs. Casey a gentle shove. The diner was bustling but not packed, and Lainey was smiling at them from behind the counter. "Good morning! I'm so glad you could make it," she said.

Mrs. Casey gave her a strained smile, but her shoulders seemed a little more relaxed. "This is my friend Lainey. Lainey, this is Edna Casey."

Mrs. Casey gave her a nod. "This looks like a fine establishment you have here, dear."

Lainey smiled warmly. "Thank you so much. It was my grandmother's, but I'm happy to be running it now. If you don't mind, I'd love to introduce you to some regular customers of mine—they're also friends," she said, pointing to a table by the window that was filled with ladies who looked to be about Mrs. Casey's age.

"Oh, well, that's very kind of you, but I should sit with Sarah. And I'd hate to intrude on their conversation," she said, her eyebrows raising as the ladies at the table erupted into a fit of laughter.

Sarah smiled at the sound. "They seem like a great group, Mrs. Casey. It looks like they're having lots of fun."

"They are," Lainey said, rounding the counter. "They come here every morning after church."

That piqued Mrs. Casey's interest. "Church?"

Lainey nodded. "All different churches in town, but they all meet here after. Usually for pie. They've been coming for years, and their table gets bigger and bigger as they add new friends."

Mrs. Casey stood a little straighter and smoothed her already impeccably ironed navy dress. "All right. Then maybe I should try and meet some of them."

Lainey winked at Sarah and then linked her arm through Mrs. Casey's. The three of them walked over to the table, and the chatter died slowly. All the women fixed their gazes on Lainey. "Ladies, I have someone very special for you to meet. This is Edna Casey, and she's new to Tilly's Diner."

"Well now, come and sit with us, Edna. I'm Marjorie Busby and I'll introduce you to all the girls. I hope you like pie," she said, motioning for Mrs. Casey to sit in the chair that Lainey had brought over.

Mrs. Casey sat down gingerly and listened intently as Mrs. Busby rattled off the different types of pies. After she settled on the peach pie that Mrs. Busby highly recommended, Lainey and Sarah walked back to the main counter.

Sarah glanced over at Mrs. Casey and smiled as the ladies all burst into laughter again. She was relieved to see Mrs. Casey smiling along with them. It almost made her forget about Cade.

"I think you need one of my special mugs, filled to the brim with coffee," Lainey said, "and a slice of that banana chocolate chip bread that…" Her voice trailed off, and her cheeks went pink. She no doubt had been about to say that it was the one Cade had brought to the picnic.

"Don't worry about it, Lainey. You can say his name. I'll survive. And yeah, coffee and that banana bread sounds amazing."

"Okay. Give me a minute to get pie over to that table, and I'll be right back," she said, quickly going about filling the order.

Sarah glanced at her phone while the chatter in the diner floated around her. Of course there were no missed calls or texts. It was silly to expect that there would be. It's not like Cade would text her saying, *Sorry I was such a jerk, want to spend the night with me at the Highwayman again?*

A few minutes later, Lainey was back and placing a mug with the words *Don't Stop Believing* on it, filled with a delicious-smelling coffee. She handed her a carton of dairy-free creamer and a plate with the banana bread on it. "Wow. If this isn't comfort food, I don't know what is. Thank you so much. This is exactly what I needed," she said, touched. This was what real friends did. Real friends who she'd met through Cade.

Lainey poured herself a cup and added some of the dairy-free creamer, then leaned against the counter.

"You use that creamer, too?" Sarah asked.

Lainey scrunched up her nose. "I have a bit of an issue with dairy. I usually try and avoid it, but sometimes my love for cheese gets the better of me. Hope usually keeps me in line."

Sarah broke off a piece of the banana bread. "I was thinking I might go and see Hope about my migraines."

Lainey nodded. "She really is great at what she

does. It's worth a try."

"That's what I was thinking. I haven't tried anything new in years."

Lainey leaned forward. "So how are you doing?"

Sarah stirred her coffee, not that it really needed it. She wanted to place her head on the counter and moan like a dramatic teenager, but that would alarm Mrs. Casey, so she remained upright. "I'm pretty crappy, to be honest. Still a little blindsided. Cade was not the guy I'd ever expect to lie to me. It's weird. The man I argued with on that last day and the man I fell in love with were two different people. I honestly don't know how we could be further apart in how we think. He wanted to be the big man and shield me from my father's problems. Ugh. I don't want to get into all this." She put her mug down and took a big bite of the banana bread. She could at least console herself with carbs.

"Okay, but what about hearing him out? Giving him another chance?"

Her stomach dropped, and she put the banana bread down. "He's not asking for another chance. He's not speaking to me. We've barely said five words to each other."

Lainey tapped her finger against her chin. "He's going to come around; I know he will. I've never seen Cade the way he is with you. He's like a different man. He's sweeter, softer. The way he looks at you. He made a mistake, and I'm sure he knows it."

"Well, I'm not waiting around," Sarah said, picking up her mug.

"Good for you. Just maybe wait a *bit*. How about getting your mind off things? Why don't I call Hope and the three of us meet at River's tomorrow night?"

River's…Cade. "I don't know if I can handle seeing Cade there."

"I don't think he's going to be there. Tyler would have told me."

Sarah took a deep breath and forced a smile. "Okay, then. What have I got to lose?"

Lainey glanced up as Martin Donnelly walked into the diner. Sarah waved at him as he slowly made his way to the counter.

"Good morning, ladies," he said with a sparkle in his eye.

"Good morning," they both said.

"I wasn't expecting to see you this morning," Lainey said, pouring him a mug of coffee and adding cream to it.

"Well, I needed to run an errand in town and thought I'd stop by and see my favorite daughter-in-law," he said with a charming wink.

Lainey rounded the counter, gave him a kiss on the cheek, and held his coffee out for him. "Mrs. Busby is over at the table if you'd like to sit there?"

Martin glanced in the direction of the table. "Too many women. They'll outnumber me," he said.

Sarah and Lainey laughed.

"Actually, now that I see Sarah here, I think I'd like to chat a bit."

Sarah was surprised but nodded. "Sure."

He gestured to one of the tables on the opposite end of the diner. Sarah slid off the seat and followed him. Lainey gave her shoulder a squeeze once she set Martin's coffee down and went back to the bar area.

Sarah sat opposite Martin and took a sip of her coffee, surprised that he wanted to talk to her.

"I hope you have a few minutes," he said.

"Of course. Is everything okay?"

"Yes, yes. It wasn't actually me I wanted to talk about. It's Cade," he said, lifting his cup slowly and taking a sip.

Sarah's stomach dropped, and she forced herself to keep her expression neutral. She really did have a good poker face. "Oh, Mr. Donnelly, I'm not sure that's a good idea."

He patted her hand. "Well, now, you don't have to agree with what I tell you, but I'd really appreciate it if you'd listen," he said, in such a kind voice that she didn't have the heart to shut him down. She knew there was nothing he could possibly say that could change what had happened between her and Cade. There was no going back after that. He'd had her groveling, in a weak and vulnerable position, and then she'd even been so stupid as to tell him she loved him only to have him coldly tell her it was over. Yeah, definitely not salvageable. "Fair enough," she said finally.

"When did you first meet Cade?"

"Not that long ago. Two months."

He folded a napkin and blotted his mouth. "I've known him since he was a boy. He was in pretty rough shape when he came to Wishing River. But in all the years I've known Cade Walker, I've never seen him like this."

She tore her eyes from his, not wanting to see the concern for Cade in them. She didn't want to hear what a good man he was or the reasons she had made a mistake.

"I'm not the kind of man who likes to pry into people's personal affairs," he began. She waited patiently for him to continue, even though dread was now pooling in her stomach.

"I first met Cade when he was sixteen. Seemed to come out of nowhere. Ty brought him home one day after school, and that boy was like a lost puppy. Sure, he was rough around the edges, tough as nails, but Ty's mother and I saw something in that boy right away. Maybe it was my wife who saw it first, because I'll admit I was a little worried about him hanging around Tyler. But, uh, Tyler hid him at our house for a couple of nights. It was Tyler's mother who figured it out and told me. We sat down with Cade and asked him about his family. He was defensive, not unlike so many boys that age. But beneath that tough-guy act, we saw the hurt in his eyes, the fear. I asked him if he wanted a job as a ranch hand. I'd give him room and board and a chance to finish school."

Sarah was trembling, and her throat was tight as she pictured the man she'd come to know and love as the young man Martin was describing. "He accepted?"

Martin shook his head, a slight smile appearing on one side of his mouth. "Nope. He politely thanked me for the job but told me he didn't accept charity and that he'd find his own way."

Sarah leaned forward, hanging on to his every word. "What happened?"

"Pride can ruin even the best of men, Sarah. But sometimes when a man has nothing, the only thing he can cling to is that pride."

Her stomach twisted painfully, and she squeezed her eyes shut, her mind going back to her conversations with him, about his family, how he grew up…how he felt he had nothing to offer her. She hadn't understood that. She had just accused him of being from another century, that kind of thinking irrelevant now. But to him, it wasn't. It was deeply relevant. It was part of who he was, the identity he'd grown up with.

She let out a shaky breath.

Martin placed his hands out in front of him, the stronger hand clasped over the one that hadn't fully regained all its strength. "He left our house. Of course, Tyler was mad at me and blamed me.

Tyler and Dean looked for him everywhere. I'll admit I was afraid I'd been too hard on him, and Tyler's mother was upset with me. Then, Saturday morning, we had a big storm raging, and I wanted to make sure everything was okay in the barn, so I walked over. Cade was standing there, looking like hell. He was all wet, thin, and holding a bag. He said, 'Mr. Donnelly, if you still have that job open, I'll take it. But no special treatment. Just consider me one of your employees.'"

Sarah covered her face for a moment, trying to get it together, uncomfortable with showing her feelings to someone she barely knew. She forced herself to draw a deep breath and drop her hands. "What happened?"

"I told him that yes, the job was still open, but that I had a condition, too. He'd start on Monday, but for the weekend, he was Tyler's guest. I said my wife would divorce me if I didn't bring him in, give him a bed in our home, and let her feed him like one of her own."

Sarah wiped the tears that finally fell from her eyes.

"I got to know that boy over that year, and he became like a son to me. I've never seen a man work harder than he did. He worked himself to the bone, year after year. When Tyler's mother died, we got into a really bad place, and old issues came to the surface. Tyler and I both made mistakes, and he left…for eight years."

She sat on the edge of her seat, already knowing part of this story because of what Cade had told her. Martin's eyes were teary, and she followed his gaze to the picture he pulled out of his wallet. It was of a younger version of himself, Tyler, and a woman.

Sarah swallowed hard, seeing the longing in his eyes, feeling the emotion in him. "I'm sorry."

He blinked and turned from the picture. "Cade stepped up when I needed him most. He stepped up on the ranch, I made him foreman, and he stepped up in my home. No one could ever replace my own son, but Cade would come around after a day's work just to sit on the front porch with me and have a beer. It was Cade and Lainey and my friends who kept me going when I couldn't go on. Cade became family. Sorry…I'm rambling, but the heart of what I want to tell you is that Cade doesn't truly understand that when you love someone, it doesn't matter what they can or can't do for you."

"What do you mean?"

"Like I said, he worked himself to the bone. After Tyler left, he distanced himself for a bit but worked even harder. At first I thought it was just because he was angry with Tyler, but after a while I confronted him. He was worried I'd fire him because Tyler was gone. He was proving his worth there on the ranch. I was shocked because he'd already earned everyone's respect and he deserved his promotion. I couldn't have run the place without him. But it wasn't what he said that bothered me; it was that he thought he meant so little to me.

"I would have kept that boy on even if he couldn't work anymore. I would have kept him on because he'd become family to me. I loved him, regardless of what he could offer me. He couldn't believe me. He couldn't believe that, because his entire damn life, he was only kept around while he could be useful to people, and then he was tossed out like yesterday's trash."

Sarah's stomach swirled painfully. She wiped her sweating palms down the front of her jeans, nausea making her clench her teeth. Remembering every time Cade had gone above and beyond…which included him trying to find a way for her to hold on to the ranch. She squeezed her eyes shut and bowed her head, hating herself and the things she'd said to him. He was trying to prove his worth to her. As if his worth could ever be measured by a land deal. She had never met anyone like him, anyone who had ever made her feel truly alive and truly loved. And she had discarded him…

She took in a gulp of air and stood abruptly. "Thank you," she managed to choke out.

"Don't misinterpret what I'm saying, Sarah. I just wanted you to see that there is a more vulnerable side to that proud man. Don't let pride on either side ruin what you have. I lost eight years with my son because of pride, and when I got my second chance, I almost blew it again. Life is too short to be afraid of taking chances, of not falling in love because of fear. When you find that special person, you hold on to them fierce."

Sarah nodded rapidly, finding it impossible to speak. She reached out to squeeze his hand briefly and managed a wobbly smile before he stood and walked out of the diner.

She sat at that table, replaying everything Martin had told her. She finally knew, she *understood*, where Cade was coming from.

CHAPTER NINETEEN

"Come on, Sarah, what have you got to lose?"

Sarah glanced up at Aiden and shook her head. "I really am not in the mood for the piano tonight. I'll end up playing depressing music and get booed off the stage," she said, finishing off what remained of her glass of wine. She had taken Lainey up on her offer to go to River's and was currently sitting across the table from her new best friends. After eating a River's burger on a gluten-free bun and a heaping portion of fries, she was at least feeling the calming effects from the comfort food and wine.

Aiden gave her an undeniably endearing, lopsided grin that had no effect on her. Only one guy's grin could make her heart accelerate and her toes curl. "Just a song. The crowd loved you last time. Do you know how many requests I get for you to come back here and play? Which, by the way, is an option anytime."

Sarah smiled. "That's really flattering. I'm honestly touched. I just can't do it tonight."

He held up his hands. "Okay, but if you change your mind, just give me a signal and that piano is all yours."

After he was out of earshot, Hope leaned forward. "Would you ever consider playing here on a regular basis? That sounds like it could be fun. You were amazing."

Sarah shook her head. "I don't like crowds. But who knows? Maybe in the future."

"I have to say I kind of miss singing, not that I ever performed…after Brian died. Now I just stick to rousing renditions of 'The Wheels on the Bus,'" Hope said with a laugh before she took a long sip of wine.

"I didn't know you could sing," Sarah said.

"Well, those days are long gone, I guess." Hope glanced over at Lainey, who was frantically typing on her phone. "What's with the emergency texts?"

Lainey looked up, her face red, her eyes slightly panicked. "There, um, might be an unexpected situation happening. I'm trying really hard to fix it."

Sarah's back stiffened. "Oh no, what kind of situation?"

"The Cade kind," Lainey said.

Sarah sucked in a breath. "He's coming here?"

Lainey sighed. "I'm sorry. They're all coming. I told Tyler it wasn't a good night and that you were here, but he's insisting. I think he's trying to help."

Sarah put her elbows on the table and her head in her hands. "I can't see him, you guys. Everything Martin told me about him made my heart break and I almost went to him, but…I can't humiliate myself again. I told him I loved him and not only did he not say it back, he told me he wasn't interested. I can't grovel. I just can't. There is not enough wine in your stash here to make seeing Cade okay."

Hope patted her on the back. "It's no problem. We can leave. You can come back to my place. Sadie is sleeping over at my parents' house."

"Too late. They're here," Lainey said, her voice heavy, grim, as though announcing that Aiden had stopped importing their wine.

Not a minute later, Cade, Tyler, and Dean walked into River's and headed their way.

"Your hair looks really great. And I love what you're wearing," Lainey said to Sarah with a hopeful smile.

Sarah sighed. "Thanks. I did the beachy waves thing and went to the effort of putting on mascara." Sarah frowned at her glass and empty plate of food. No. There was no way she was going to sit here with Cade and pretend like everything was normal. She stood abruptly. "I'm playing the piano. Hope, do you want to sing?"

Hope broke out into a gorgeous smile. "I don't think there's a better time to get reintroduced to the stage."

"I can't believe you guys are doing this! I'm so excited," Lainey squealed.

"Just make sure you clap even if we get booed," Hope said, finger-combing her hair frantically.

"Obviously. I'll force Ty to clap, too. Don't worry," Lainey said, giving them a shove.

"I think I have the perfect song for us," Hope

said, wrapping one arm around Sarah's shoulders.

They weaved their way through the crowd. Excitement raced through Sarah's body in a way that it hadn't in years. This version of herself was one she had never known as an adult—the last time she'd been fearless, she was a child. She hadn't revisited that girl in years, but she was back; she was going to reclaim her. She didn't need Cade to survive.

She watched as Hope spoke to Aiden, and then she glanced over at Lainey and knew that this was all the beginning of her new life, with real friends, daring to go in front of a crowd.

Hope came back over to her. "You ready to do this?" she asked, shoving Sarah her phone with the music to her selected song.

Sarah read the title, a smile slowly forming, before she looked back up at her friend. "Let's do it."

"Cade, it can't be that bad," Lainey said, leaning across the table to pat him on the shoulder like he was a lost puppy.

"Oh, it's actually way worse," Tyler said.

Lainey punched him, and show-off that he was, he grabbed his wife's hand and kissed it. Cade scowled because he remembered doing something similar to Sarah, and now that was so far from where he was. But Tyler was right; it was way worse than even Lainey was thinking. He'd wanted to talk to her and try to get her to at least hear him out so he could go through with his plan, but she'd walked away before he reached the table.

"What are they doing?" Cade asked, his eyes fixed on Sarah and Hope as they talked to Aiden near the piano. Sarah looked even more beautiful tonight if that was possible, or maybe he was just starved to see her. He'd missed her so damn much. Her hair fell in those soft waves like the night of Lainey's party, and he smiled remembering how she'd yelled at him for not noticing after her hair got all wet. But he'd noticed everything.

She was wearing a V-neck navy T-shirt and dark jeans that hugged her body and made him ache with his need for her. He was a fool.

Lainey gave him an excited smile. "Aiden was over here asking if Sarah would play tonight. She turned him down, but then Hope kind of encouraged her, and now Hope is going to sing along."

"Hope can sing?" Dean asked.

"Oh yeah. She has an amazing voice," Lainey said, turning in her chair to look at them.

"Why doesn't she ever perform?" Tyler asked.

Lainey turned back to them and slowly twirled the stem of her wineglass. "She stopped when Brian died," she said softly.

None of them said anything for a minute, just

sat there silently watching Hope and Sarah set up. Life was this crazy mix of highs and lows, and no matter where you came from, how much money you had, you couldn't escape them. But you had to keep going, like Hope just kept on going, for herself, for her little girl. Like how they all kept on going. He'd been alone in the past, and he knew for certain that he'd rather be drinking with friends at a bar any day than by himself.

He smiled slightly as he watched Sarah sit down on the piano bench. Her face wasn't pale like that first night she'd played. Her shoulders were back, and she was laughing at something Aiden and Hope said. She was the most beautiful woman he'd ever seen; she made him believe that he deserved more in life. But now he just had to make her believe in him again, that he could give her what she needed.

His stomach dropped when Sarah played the first notes of their song.

Lainey gasped.

Tyler shook his head, doing a poor job of hiding his smile.

Dean sank down a little farther in his chair and turned to him. "You're toast."

"I Will Survive" was not exactly the song choice he'd been hoping for and frankly, he didn't think he'd ever heard any kind of disco song in River's. Ever. But as soon as Hope's throaty, sultry voice filled the room, telling them all about how she'd felt sorry for herself but that she'd changed now, you couldn't hear a pin drop.

It took all Cade's self-control to keep his ass in the chair and his mouth shut, because he wanted to walk right out of there, as Hope kept belting out that he should just walk out the door while Sarah played like a pro.

Tyler and Lainey kept giving him pitiful glances while Dean's eyes were fixed on Hope. Clearly, Sarah had been right about that, too.

When the song ended, the entire place was silent for a long moment. Then Lainey stood from her chair and whistled, and River's Saloon, deep in rural Montana, went crazy for Sarah and Hope's performance. He forced himself to stand, to make his move before he lost his nerve, but then the two of them started up another song, and he sat his ass back down.

Except this time Lainey shook her head and covered her face for a second. Tyler put his arm around her and whispered something in her ear. She nodded and gave him a kiss.

"What's wrong?" Dean asked, his eyes still on Hope.

"That song she's singing? That was her and Brian's song," she said with a sad smile.

Dean froze for a second and then pulled a twenty out of his wallet and stood. "I, uh, I better get going. I just got called into the hospital."

Cade didn't want to rat his friend out because

there was clearly something going on, but he knew for a fact that he wasn't on call tonight. Normally he would have gone with him, but tonight he had a bigger problem to solve.

He had to convince Sarah that he'd been wrong. After Dean left, he slowly weaved his way through the tables, the feeling in his gut unlike one he'd ever had before. When the song ended, he almost smiled at the sound of the enthusiastic crowd, but he was anticipating Sarah shutting him down. Aiden appeared, and Cade overheard the man asking the two women to be regulars on Friday nights. Hope and Sarah looked at each other and then burst into smiles, hugged each other, and agreed.

Happiness for them flooded him, and he watched the woman who a little over a month ago, without a friend in the world, with the weight of the past keeping her silent and sad, turn into the woman she was meant to be.

He took a few steps forward, and Sarah made eye contact with him. His muscles tightened, and he rolled his shoulders as he closed the gap between them. "Hi."

Hope gave him a wink and walked away.

Sarah lifted her chin, and her gorgeous green eyes were void of the usual warmth. "Hello."

"You and Hope were great together," he said.

"Thank you. I'm going to get going. It was nice to see you," she said, lying politely.

"Sarah…will you give me two hours?"

She glanced away for a moment, and he shoved his hands in his pockets, trying not to panic because he had no idea what he'd do if she turned him down. "Two *hours*? For what?"

"To explain myself, to apologize, to just hear me out."

She sighed and looked deep into his eyes, reminding him of how she'd done that very early on, how he'd almost squirmed under her gaze because it made him think that she would see the man he used to be, the kid he once was. "Cade…"

"I'm sorry. I'm so damn sorry for everything. Just come with me. Two hours, that's all I'm asking for."

She nodded, and he let out a breath. He knew he couldn't just reach for her, grab her hand, but he wanted to hold her again so badly. Instead, he just motioned to the door, following her outside. He glanced over at their table of friends, and the three of them gave him a thumbs-up before he walked out the door.

The cool night air was exactly what he needed against his hot skin. Holding open the door for Sarah, he prayed he could pull this off. Once they were on the road, she turned to him, breaking the silence. "Any clues as to where you're taking me?"

He gave her a quick glance before returning his eyes to the road. He didn't want to miss the turnoff. "Nope. I have this all planned out. Telling you will ruin it."

She didn't reply, and they drove in silence for the next twenty minutes.

When the Highwayman sign came into view, he clenched the steering wheel, bracing himself for her reaction. Carl had better have come through for him. He wasn't even going to acknowledge just how low he'd sunk when his life plans involved *Carl*.

"Are you kidding me, Cade, *the Highwayman*?"

He kept his mouth shut. He pulled into the parking lot, in front of the room they'd had last time, and hoped like hell he could pull this off.

CHAPTER TWENTY

*C*ade quickly hopped out of the truck before Sarah could yell at him and went around to her side. She was already standing by the truck glaring at him. "I'm trying really hard to think you have the best of intentions here."

The door to the motel room swung open, and Carl stood there smiling. He was clean-shaven, his hair was combed and slicked back, and he was wearing a clean button-down shirt with a pair of skinny jeans that may not have been the best look but were still a vast improvement from the pleated polyester pants he'd been wearing last time.

"Carl?" Sarah gasped.

He spread his arms wide. "In the flesh. Nice to see you again, Sarah."

"Carl, you look fantastic! You look so happy!" she said, hurrying over to him. Cade didn't move. He really loved this part of Sarah. He hadn't known it the night she tried to give Carl marital advice, but he loved how nonjudgmental she was, how genuinely caring she was. He had missed so many things about her.

Carl actually blushed beneath Sarah's gaze, and if Cade weren't so nervous, he might have even had a chuckle about it. "Well, I can't take all the credit for it. You kids reminded me how important my marriage was. But it was all Cade who helped me get this new look."

Sarah turned slowly to him, her eyes wide. "You went shopping with Carl?"

Cade shrugged but took it as a good sign that she seemed impressed by that. "Technically, no. I just guided him to some online shopping items. He went rogue with the skinny jeans, though," Cade said, shooting Carl a look.

Carl smiled sheepishly. "Sorry, but Mary Beth really likes them."

Sarah laughed and patted him on the shoulder. "I'm so happy for you both."

Carl rubbed the back of his neck, his face still red. "Well, thank you. Now I'm going to repay the favor to my new friends." He gave him a wink—again, nothing Cade had approved of—and opened the door wider. Cade hoped like hell that he'd followed instructions and hadn't gone rogue on anything else.

Sarah stepped in and gasped.

Following her in, Cade surveyed the room. Carl gave Cade a thumbs-up before he quietly left, shutting the door behind him. Sarah hadn't said anything yet, but he could see she was taking in the arrangements of roses—the flowers she'd told Carl were a safe bet if you didn't know a person's favorite—the picnic basket on the middle of the bed that he'd had filled with gluten-free versions of her favorites, and also the new white cotton bedding that he'd given Carl strict instructions for, and maybe she even noticed the lack of decorative pillows. On one of the nightstands was the same brand of organic wine that Lainey and Hope drank from River's, with real wineglasses, and a bottle of her favorite strawberry hand sanitizer.

"Cade," she said softly before turning around.

He took the sheen in her eyes as a good sign and walked closer, stopping a couple of feet away. "I'm sorry, Sarah. I'm sorry I didn't tell you right away about your dad and the financials. I'm sorry for the reason I didn't tell you sooner. I..." He struggled for the words to express his feelings, the stuff he'd been holding inside for so long. "There are people you meet and immediately know they're bad, like they're rotten from the inside. You see it in the hardness in their eyes; you hear it in the bitterness in their voice. Then there's those people you know, deep in your core, that they're your people, the kind who always assume the best about you. They can hurt you, but you know they'll find a way to make it right.

"I learned early on not to trust anyone, and then I learned to trust myself, my instincts. The moment I met you, I knew you were my people. Then I spent time with you, and I knew you had guts like I've never seen before. I will never be that man who holds you back, who dampens your spirit. I thought that meant you could trust me with your weaknesses and I wouldn't use them against you, but I did. I love you. So much. I couldn't stand to see you hurt and in pain and I justified lying to you. I'm sorry."

"Cade, I stood there and told you I loved you, and you rejected me," she whispered, her eyes filling with tears.

Self-loathing washed over him. "I know. I will never be able to take that moment back. I'm sorry. I…I just…" He took a deep breath and broke her stare, finding it within himself to be brutally honest because that's what you had to do when you loved someone. "No one has ever said that to me before. No one has ever loved me, and for it to be you…a thousand thoughts ran through me, and I couldn't handle what that meant. I still don't think I'm worthy of it. But I'm here, and I love you more than I knew was possible," he said, his voice raspy and thick.

He didn't move, even though he wanted nothing more than to close the gap between them. She did take a step toward him and he thought that was pretty promising.

"I know why you did it," she said. "I know it wasn't because you wanted to control me, but the result was the same."

He took a deep breath and spoke the rest, the stuff he was embarrassed to say out loud, to be so vulnerable, but he knew he would lay it all out there if it meant a chance with her. "It wasn't just about wanting to protect you; it was about me and my self-worth. I've always had to prove myself to everyone, to be useful in order to be accepted. If I couldn't fix things for you, then what did I have left?

"It's not something I think about day-to-day. It's not something I've ever talked about with anyone except you. But when you're told every day that you're nothing, you begin to believe it. It doesn't mean I think I'm worthless or that I wallow in self-pity. I've never been the type. But when no one wants you, after a while you think there's a reason, that there's something wrong with you. No one has ever wanted me to belong to them. And that was fine. For my entire life, that was fine. Until you. I *want* to belong to you. I want you. I want you with my mind, my heart, my body. I want to love you."

He stopped speaking when she rushed into his arms. "I love you, too," she whispered. She raised one hand to his face and gave him a look that was almost his undoing. "You never had to prove anything to me, and you never have to be more than the man I know you are. That is already enough. You are enough, just the way you are. You're perfect."

That almost broke him, but he had to lay the rest out there. "What about your ranch? The fact that I bring nothing to the table?"

"My ranch? It's yours, too. You build it with me." She put her hands on either side of his waist, and it took all his self-control not to move.

"It's not mine," he said roughly.

"It is. It's your ideas that will save the ranch. Your work. You're the one who figured out what had happened to the money. You're the one out there every day before dawn and after sunset. You're the one who leads that team. How did you get it into your head that it isn't yours? It's as much yours as it is mine."

"I can't change where I came from, but I can change where I'm going," he said. "I just want to be clear before we go any further. I don't want to hide who I am. You need to know I have nothing to offer you."

"Nothing to offer me?"

He managed a nod while also managing not to lean down and kiss her and tell her how sorry he was, because he loved her more than anything or anyone in his entire life. He stood motionless as she slowly unbuttoned the top three buttons of his shirt. He sucked in a breath as her soft hand slipped inside and stopped...covering his heart. She stared up at him, her eyes glistening with tears. "This. Your heart. You. This is all I ever wanted."

She pressed her hand over his heart, and he felt it throughout his body. His gut tightened, his eyes were wet, and his chest constricted painfully. She was offering him everything, telling him that all she needed was him. There had never been a day in his life where anyone had told him that he was enough, just the man he was, yet here was this woman, a stranger a few months ago, now the most important person in his world. He loved her for that. For that fierce loyalty and sheer confidence in him.

Knowing he'd never be able to say no to her, to let her walk away from him again, but not knowing what that said about him, he leaned down to kiss her. He wanted to pull her into him, to feel the woman he never really ever thought himself worthy of. He kissed her like he'd never have another tomorrow, and he kissed her like she was the only woman he'd kissed before.

Forcing himself to pull back before they couldn't, because he needed to finish what he'd started, he spoke the words that she'd said to him, that he'd rejected that night, that he couldn't really believe. "I love you, Sarah. I love you so much, and if I could take it all back—the decisions I made and how I treated you that night—I would in a second."

"I can handle life, Cade. I can handle the bad stuff, the good stuff. I need to know that you'll let me handle it. I know that you'll have my back if I need you, but that has to be my decision."

He nodded. "I know that now. I will be there for you when you want me to. But from now on, we make the decisions together."

"Deal," she said, still holding on to him.

This time when they kissed, there were no secrets left between them. He kissed her with a liberation and an honesty he'd never felt before. When she undid the rest of the buttons on his shirt, it wasn't in anger, and when they fell onto the bed, he reminded himself he had one thing left to do. "Wait a second," he said, giving her one more kiss before standing and grabbing the bag of Peach Rings.

Her gaze went from him to the candy. "You have got to be kidding me. Please tell me this isn't some kind of fetish you haven't told me about?"

He laughed, some of his nerves dissipating slightly. He ripped open the bag and pulled one ring out, dropping the bag on the dresser. "I…I wanted to do this properly, but there was no time to get out to the city to buy what I wanted to buy," he said, slowly getting down on one knee.

Her eyes widened, and she scrambled into a seated position. "Cade, what are you doing?"

"I know I never got to meet your parents. I know your last years with them after Josh were rough. But I also heard the love in your voice when you spoke about those earlier years. I know how much you loved them, how much their approval meant to you. I think your parents would have wanted you to have a real marriage proposal, and I think it's what you would want, deep down. It's what I want to give you, too." He grabbed a Peach Ring and gently took her hand in his.

"I've never had a real family until I met you. You are family. You are everything to me, Sarah. I love you more than I knew was possible, and I want to spend the rest of my life loving you, if you'll have me."

She threw her arms around him, and he almost toppled backward, but the idea of being sprawled out on the carpet at the Highwayman made him steady them. He pulled back slightly to look into her eyes. "Yes. I love you, yes!"

She held out her hand, and he tried to put the Peach Ring on her finger, but it wouldn't slide past the tip. She threw her head back and laughed at the absurdity of it all. He took the opportunity to kiss the exposed part of her neck, and when she gasped and tugged at his hair, he trailed his mouth along the smooth, fragrant skin exposed in the V of her shirt. "I swear, tomorrow we go into the city and get a real ring."

"Our overdue road trip," she said, kissing him.

He lifted her onto the bed. "We need to get off this carpet," he said, kissing her again as she tugged him onto her. He covered her body with his and knew it didn't get better than Sarah, that he was finally home. "And I promise you, our honeymoon won't be at the Highwayman."

EPILOGUE

*I*t was almost sunset. Cade put down the pliers and found himself admiring the way the sun caught the lighter shades of blond in his wife's hair. Just like he'd admired not that long ago and yet it seemed like a lifetime ago. He'd been a different man. His gaze roamed her body, his eyes settling on the buttons of her shirt, straining against her breasts. Okay, so he was *almost* a different man. Thankfully, some things didn't change. In fact, over the last few months, he'd noticed how desire could change, how it could deepen, with love.

Sarah glanced over at him and smiled, and that familiar surge of happiness hit him. He leaned over and kissed her, his hand at the nape of her neck, her silky hair against his hands. "Have you ever wondered why I always volunteer the two of us to the farthest stretch of fencing?" he asked against her soft lips.

She shook her head, her hands going to the top button of his shirt.

"So that we could do this and not have anyone around," he said, kissing her again.

She pulled her hands from his shirt and glanced at her watch. "Actually, while that's very sweet, I forgot that we need to get back."

"For what?"

"Our friends are coming over for a late dinner," she said, smiling.

It hit him then, how casually she said that. *Our* friends. This was the woman who hadn't had friends. She had thought herself awkward and referred to them as *his* friends. But Sarah had found best friends in Lainey and Hope and, for some reason, even adored Tyler and Dean. This getting together with their friends had become a weekly tradition. Sometimes at Ty and Lainey's, sometimes at River's…and sometimes at *their* house.

If he had asked that little boy he once was to dream the wildest dream, he would never have pictured himself here. He never could have imagined loving a woman as incredible as Sarah, let alone being married to her. She had given him everything; her trust, her love, her faith, and she had made him a better, stronger man. She'd shown him that his worth wasn't measured by how hard he could work or how valuable he was on the ranch. That it was his soul and his ability to love.

"Come on," she said, mounting her horse, the brilliant sun behind her, casting her in the most gorgeous flood of light. The mountains spread wide in the distance, the sky painted pink and blue, and "awe" was the only word that came close to describing what he experienced out here with Sarah.

He swallowed, forcing himself to get back to

reality as they rode back to Joshua Ranch. These were the best days of his life, and he wasn't taking even one of them for granted. "So everyone's coming over?"

"Yup. Even Martin and Mrs. Busby are coming to hang out with Mrs. Casey."

He laughed. Somehow he'd even managed to win Mrs. Casey over these last few months and was a regular recipient of homemade pies. He returned the favor with a glass of her favorite whiskey every time. It was a mutually beneficial arrangement. "That's nice," he said.

Sarah gave him a wide, gorgeous smile. "And Dean is picking up Hope."

He let out a choked laugh. "Are you sure that's wise?"

She shrugged, her eyes twinkling mischievously. "It's for a good cause. Their feud has gone on long enough, Lainey tells me."

"As long as I'm not in that car, then that's fine with me," he said, slowing as they approached their home pasture.

Wishing River glittered like diamonds in the distance and he glanced over at his wife, knowing she must often think about that night with her brother, those years of grief. But they had found each other. Their worst days were behind them, their future solidified by the bond they shared. He could never reclaim his old life, his old ways, because his new life surpassed all his wildest dreams.

Once the horses were tended to, Sarah leaned up on her tiptoes and whispered in his ear. "If you hurry, you might be able to help me wash off all this dust," she said with a wink and ran out of the barn.

He chuckled and chased her, knowing he'd never miss an opportunity to love Sarah, happy to chase her for the rest of his days.

ACKNOWLEDGMENTS

To Liz Pelletier… Thank you for believing in my writing and for your incredible insight. I always await your edits with a mix of trepidation and excitement…and always finish them with gratitude, knowing what an impact you've had on my book. If only I had you on my shoulder while writing—it would save us so much work!

To Heather Howland… It was such a pleasure and privilege to work with you! Thank you for your meticulous and tireless editing. I owe you a bag of Ringolos!

To Louise Fury…for having my back and making me feel like no dream is unachievable.

To Jessica Turner…for making the most stressful part of my writing career manageable and fun. Thank you for the countless hours of brainstorming and marketing that you put in. It is always wonderful to work with you!

To Stacy Abrams…Thank you for your thoughtful edits and for always keeping an eye out on the weather in Wishing River, Montana :)

To Hang Le…for creating another heartfelt and rich cover that manages to capture the mood and emotion in my book.

To Curtis Svehlak… Thank you SO much for always being a ray of sunshine in my inbox! Trust me, you make me laugh just as much.

To everyone at Macmillan for believing in my books and giving me the opportunity to write books true to my heart. Thank you!

To the countless other talented people who have had a hand in making this book possible and I haven't mentioned by name—thank you for everything you do and all your hard work.

Finally, to my readers and book bloggers: your support, your reviews, your emails, and your loyalty are what make it possible for me to keep writing. I treasure and value all that you do. Knowing you're reading always makes me want to give you the best story I can deliver. I hope this book leaves you with a blissful sigh and believing that a happy ending is possible for all of us.

Victoria

xo

Want to read another Victoria James book without leaving your chair?

Simply visit **bit.ly/VJnewsletter** and sign up for her newsletter!

❖ ❖ ❖ ❖

By signing up for Victoria's newsletter, you'll receive her *New York Times & USA Today* bestselling novella *Sweet Surrender* absolutely **FREE** as a thank you gift!

❖ ❖ ❖ ❖

As a newsletter subscriber, look to your inbox for exciting insider news on upcoming book releases, member-only contests, promotions, exclusive perks, and more!

Discover the gripping and heart-wrenching new release from critically acclaimed author Rebecca Yarros that explores issues of family, betrayal, and ultimately how far we're willing to go on behalf of those who need us most.

GREAT AND PRECIOUS THINGS

How do you define yourself when others have already decided who you are?

Six years ago, when Camden Daniels came back from war without his younger brother, no one in the small town of Alba, Colorado, would forgive him—especially his father. He left, swearing never to return.

But a desperate message from his father brings it all back. The betrayal. The pain. And the need to go home again.

But home is where the one person he still loves is waiting. Willow. The one woman he can never have. Because there are secrets buried in Alba that are best left in the dark.

If only he could tell his heart to stay locked away when she whispers she's always loved him, and always will…

Don't miss USA Today *bestselling author*
Tawna Fenske's latest romantic comedy!

the two-date rule

Willa Frank has one simple rule: never go on a date with anyone more than twice. Now that her business is providing the stability she's always needed, she can't afford distractions. Her two-date rule will protect her just fine...until she meets smokejumper Grady Billman.

After one date—one amazing, unforgettable date—Grady isn't ready to call it quits, despite his own no-attachments policy, and he's found a sneaky way around both their rules.

Throwing gutter balls with pitchers of beer? Not a real date. Everyone knows bowling doesn't count.

Watching a band play at a local show? They just happen to have the same great taste in music. Definitely not a date.

Hiking? Nope. How can exercise be considered a date?

With every "non-date" Grady suggests, his reasoning gets more ridiculous, and Willa must admit she's having fun playing along. But when their time together costs Willa two critical clients, it's clear she needs to focus on the only thing that matters—her future. And really, he should do the same.

But what is she supposed to do with a future that looks gray without Grady in it?

How to Lose a Guy in 10 Days *meets*
Accidentally on Purpose *by Jill Shalvis in this*
head-over-heels romantic comedy.

the aussie next door

by *USA Today* bestselling author
Stefanie London

American Angie Donovan has never wanted much.
When you grow up getting bounced from foster
home to foster home, you learn not to become
attached to anything, anyone, or any place. But it
only took her two days to fall in love with Australia.
With her visa clock ticking, surely she can fall in
love with an Australian—and get hitched—in two
months. Especially if he's as hot and funny as her
next-door neighbor…

Jace Walters has never wanted much—except a
bathroom he didn't have to share. The last cookie
all to himself. And solitude. But when you grow
up in a family of seven, you can kiss those things
goodbye. He's finally living alone and working
on his syndicated comic strip in privacy. Sure, his
American neighbor is distractingly sexy and annoy-
ingly nosy, but she'll be gone in a few months...

Except now she's determined to find her perfect
match by checking out every eligible male in the
town, and her choices are even more distracting. He
doesn't want to, but he's going to have to intervene
and help her if he ever hopes to get back to his
quiet life.

Find out where it all began with
Tyler and Lainey's story!

The Trouble
with Cowboys

by *New York Times* bestselling author
Victoria James

Eight years ago, Tyler Donnelly left Wishing River, Montana, after a terrible fight with his father and swore he'd never return. But when his father has a stroke, guilt and duty drive him home, and nothing is as he remembers—from the run-down ranch to Lainey Sullivan, who is all grown up now. And darn if he can't seem to stay away.

Lainey's late grandma left her two things: the family diner and a deep-seated mistrust of cowboys. So when Tyler quietly rides back into town looking better than hot apple pie, she knows she's in trouble. But she owes his dad everything, and she's determined to show Ty what it means to be part of a small town...and part of a family.

Lainey's courage pushes Ty to want to make Wishing River into a home again—together. But one of them is harboring a secret that could change everything.

AMARA
an imprint of Entangled Publishing LLC